WHITE
SANDS,
RED
MENACE

WHITE SANDS, RED MENACE

ELLEN
KLAGES

VIKING

VIKING
Published by Penguin Group
Penguin Young Readers Group, 345 Hudson Street, New York, New York 10014, U.S.A.
Penguin Group (Canada), 90 Eglinton Avenue East, Suite 700, Toronto, Ontario,
Canada M4P 2Y3 (a division of Pearson Penguin Canada Inc.)
Penguin Books Ltd, 80 Strand, London WC2R 0RL, England
Penguin Ireland, 25 St Stephen's Green, Dublin 2, Ireland (a division of Penguin Books Ltd)
Penguin Group (Australia), 250 Camberwell Road, Camberwell, Victoria 3124, Australia
(a division of Pearson Australia Group Pty Ltd)
Penguin Books India Pvt Ltd, 11 Community Centre, Panchsheel Park, New Delhi – 110 017, India
Penguin Group (NZ), 67 Apollo Drive, Rosedale, North Shore 0632, New Zealand
(a division of Pearson New Zealand Ltd.)
Penguin Books (South Africa) (Pty) Ltd, 24 Sturdee Avenue, Rosebank, Johannesburg 2196, South Africa

Penguin Books Ltd, Registered Offices: 80 Strand, London WC2R 0RL, England

First published in the United States of America by Viking,
a division of Penguin Young Readers Group, 2008

1 3 5 7 9 10 8 6 4 2

Copyright © Ellen Klages, 2008
All rights reserved

LIBRARY OF CONGRESS CATALOGING-IN-PUBLICATION DATA IS AVAILABLE
ISBN 978-0-670-06235-5

Printed in U.S.A. • Set in Granjon • Book design by Sam Kim

The publisher does not have any control over and does not assume
any responsibility for author or third-party Web sites or their content.

Although this is a work of fiction, the historical events surrounding the V-2 rocket program
and the postwar politics of the atomic bomb are quite real, as are White Sands and the town
of Alamogordo, New Mexico. The author has used these as a setting for fictitious characters,
and any resemblance of those characters to actual people is unintentional.

To Spencer Klages,
Grayson Klages,
and Rebecca Caccavo,
my hopes for the future.

"One faces the future with one's past."
—Pearl S. Buck

WELCOME
TO
THE
FUTURE

ONE WORLD OR NONE

MAY 12, 1946

"Girls? In the car. Fifteen minutes," Philip Gordon called up from the bottom of the attic stairs. "You can unpack tomorrow."

"Okay," his daughter, Suze, yelled back. "Be right down." She turned to her friend—and roommate, for the last year—Dewey Kerrigan, who was arranging jars of nuts and bolts on the bookcase near the window. "We gotta go."

Dewey nodded. They'd only been in the house in Alamogordo for three days, and she itched to have all her things out of boxes and organized. But that could wait, and the trip this afternoon couldn't. She aligned one more jar with the others, then took off her glasses and wiped her face with her bandanna. "What time's the launch?"

"Two o'clock, I think. Dad says if we get out there early enough, he'll show us the rocket close up, before they put the gas in it and it gets too dangerous."

"It's ten thirty now. What about lunch?"

"Dad made sandwiches." Suze looked down at the box of magazines she'd been unpacking. "I *know* I saw pictures of V-2s in one of these, from when the Nazis were bombing London. I guess I'll find them later." She pushed the box aside with one foot. "Let's go."

Dewey followed her down two flights of stairs to the kitchen, the only room in the house, so far, that looked like people *lived* here: dishes in the sink, the coffeepot on the stove, and Rutherford, their ginger-striped cat, basking in a patch of sunlight by the back door.

Terry Gordon sat at the kitchen table in her bathrobe, a cigarette in one hand and a coffee cup in front of her. She looked like she'd just woken up. She had her reading glasses on and was staring at a pamphlet, one of a large stack.

"You're not dressed," Suze said.

"Your powers of observation continue to amaze me." Her mother stubbed out the cigarette.

"But Dad says we're leaving in a few minutes."

"*You* are. I've told him—I'm staying here."

Dewey frowned. "You're not coming with us?"

"I don't need to see the army blow anything else up, kiddo. We've killed too many people as it is." She held up the pamphlet. "I've got to get fifty of these to the post office before it closes this afternoon."

"What is it?" Dewey asked.

"Essays by Einstein and some of the fellows from Los Alamos, to help educate the public about the Bomb." She took a sip of coffee. "We built it. We're the only ones who can stop it. These are going to schools and libraries all over the country. Take one. It's an eye-opener."

Dewey picked up a booklet. "*One World or None?* Weird title."

"Not if you think about it. It's either the United Nations and international control—or World War Three." She lit another cigarette. "Nobody's going to win that one."

"Do you need some help?" Suze asked.

"Nah. You've barely seen your dad in two months. Scoot."

Dewey climbed into the car and started reading. Suze looked back at the house once, then sank onto the seat and opened the lunch sack. "Bologna and cheese," she said. "And root beers. Thanks, Dad."

"Can't have you starving. Not on my watch." Dr. Gordon sat up front like a chauffeur in a pith helmet, a pile of notebooks on the seat next to him. Dewey took a deep breath. There hadn't been any new cars since before the war. The upholstery of the 1946 Plymouth still smelled like fresh carpet. Faint grease pencil marks remained on the back window, and the wood-grain interior gleamed.

Alamogordo, New Mexico, was a small, dusty place an hour from the Mexican border, tucked between the steep wall of the Sacramento Mountains on the east and the railroad on the west.

They drove through town, past the depot and the gas stations and the lumberyard on Pennsylvania Avenue, until the street became a highway again. U.S. 70 was a straight line running southwest across the arid desert of the Tularosa Basin—fifty miles of flat sand with spikes of yucca and twists of cholla cactus. Most of it was the White Sands Proving Grounds, owned by the United States government, where the army was going to test a rocket today, and where they'd tested the first atomic bomb ten months ago.

Sixty miles north, at Trinity, the heat of the blast had melted the desert sand into a sea of green glass. Dewey figured that was why, on the radio, newsmen seemed to say the name *Alamogordo* as if the town itself were evil, the place where the fear had begun.

When the war ended, life in America was supposed to go back to normal. It hadn't. After Hiroshima, everyone in the world knew about the atom bomb, the secret "gadget" that the Gordons and her papa had worked on at Los Alamos. Now it was *the* Bomb, with a capital *B*, as if it were the only one, ever. People were afraid that they might all die in an instant, without any warning.

That had always been true, Dewey thought. Nothing was certain. Nothing was forever. Papa had died with no warning either, just crossing the street.

Dewey felt like she had almost fallen, almost walked off the end of a plank like in a Laurel and Hardy movie. But she had survived, because another plank, the Gordons, had swung by just in the nick of time, and become her family. She looked over at Suze and smiled, but Suze didn't notice.

"What exactly are we going to see?" Suze asked her father.

"The first American rocket launched into outer space."

"Isn't it a German rocket—a V-2?"

"Not anymore."

"How many did the army get?" asked Dewey.

"Functional units? None. But we captured three hundred boxcars full of parts. The sand's playing hell with the electronics, and there was a lot of damage in transit, but we hope to get twenty or thirty put together in the next year."

"Did they come with instructions?"

Dr. Gordon chuckled. "Fourteen tons' worth, all in German. That's why we brought von Braun and his boys over. We'll be building missiles of our own—bigger and better—before you know it." He turned his attention back to the road and began tapping his fingers on the steering wheel to the jazzy rhythm of "Atomic Cocktail," playing on the radio. Dewey rolled her eyes. Stupid song.

Forty-five minutes later, the car slowed as they approached a line of vehicles waiting at the gate to the base. When they reached the head of the line, the guard wrote down their license-plate number in his logbook.

"Big crowd today," said Dr. Gordon.

"Better believe it. Navy brass, army brass, press, you name

it. There'd better be a show this time." The guard shook his head. "The guys from the War Department aren't here to watch another dud."

"Crossing our fingers." Dr. Gordon nodded.

The base was small, a cluster of green wood-framed buildings, a few warehouses, and a large curved-roof hangar. It looked a lot like the Hill—Los Alamos. Dr. Gordon turned and headed out into the desert.

"Isn't this it?" Dewey asked.

"Nope. The launch site is ten klicks—about six miles—farther out."

"Is there a bathroom?"

"More or less. Portable latrines."

"For girls?"

"Hmm. Probably not." He sighed and slowed the car. "No female personnel on this project." He turned, a wide U, and drove back to a small building with a red cross on it. "First-aid station," he said as he turned off the ignition. "You can use the one in there."

FIRST ROCKET

Low gray-green scrub bushes spotted the pale red desert on either side of the road. They drove into a large area where the sand had been rolled smooth and flat.

"There she is," Dr. Gordon said. He sounded as if the rocket were his own possession, the way he had yesterday when he'd driven home in the new car. He parked in front of a low fence, thin wire strung between posts.

Suze stared. It *had* to be a joke. It was shaped like a rocket all right—a tall cylinder with a pointed nose, resting on four broad triangular fins, just like the ones in comic books. But those were silver, gleaming metal, shiny and space-looking.

This one wasn't.

It was painted like a checkerboard, huge black and taxicab-yellow squares. Two fins were black, two were yellow, like Halloween from a cartoon planet.

"Why is it painted like *that*?" she asked.

"High visibility. A few are black and white. The pattern's so we can tell if it's spinning or rolling in flight. Come take a look."

The fence surrounded a slab of concrete the size of a school playground. After the still emptiness of the desert, the launch site was a startling contrast. Jeeps and army-green trucks with big white stars rumbled across the sand. Suze figured there must be a hundred people—all men, about half in uniform, the rest in shirtsleeves and khaki pants, some of them stripped to the waist and sweating in the hot sun—yelling back and forth:

"Toss me the wrench."

"Tighten that sucker up."

"Where the hell is Ed?"

Everywhere she looked was a bustle of activity, with the sounds of metal clanking and motors running. The air smelled like gas and oil and the ozone of hot wiring. Men with short-billed mechanic's caps swarmed around the base of the rocket, carrying cables and wires, attaching hoses, looking at clipboards, talking into bulky black headsets. The V-2 dwarfed them all.

It was the biggest thing Suze had ever seen close up, higher than any building in New Mexico. "How tall is it?"

"Forty-six feet, give or take an inch. And five feet in diameter." Dr. Gordon held his arms out wide. "She weighs five tons, empty."

"It must take a *lot* of gasoline," Dewey said, watching a

shirtless man in army pants and cap screw a nozzle into the side of a fuel truck.

Dr. Gordon chuckled. "Nope, not a drop. Germany didn't have much gas during the war, so she runs on moonshine. They made it from potatoes. Eight tons of grain alcohol and liquid oxygen for about a minute of flight."

A minute? That wasn't so exciting. "That's not very long," Suze said out loud.

"Maybe not. But it's a start. At the end of that minute, she'll be sixty miles into space. Three thousand miles an hour, once she gets going."

Suze watched Dewey's face wrinkle up. It did that when she was thinking hard.

"So with enough fuel, it could go from here to *New York* in—what, forty-five minutes?" Dewey said slowly.

"Someday. For now we just want her to go straight up. First man-made object to ever penetrate the upper atmosphere."

"Not counting all the Nazi ones," Suze said.

"First *ever*." Dr. Gordon sounded proud again. "The wartime missiles had a horizontal trajectory. They went up, crossed the water, came down." He made a shallow arc with his arm. "This one's going into *space*."

"Oh, okay." Suze scuffed her sneaker in the sand and stared up. New Mexico was mostly sky. The land was a flat brown plain, edged with mountains in all directions. Everything else was a vast blue bowl. She wondered what was up there that was so important that they weren't back home in Berkeley right now. Dad and Mom had argued about that for the last six months. All she saw were huge, motionless white clouds.

"If it's going that fast," Dewey said, "it's going to get tiny pretty quick, and we won't be able to see it. So how do you measure how high it goes?"

"Good question." Dr. Gordon patted her shoulder.

"Telescopes?" Suze said. She moved a step closer to him but only got a smile, no pat.

"You're partly right," he said. "The Germans didn't need that kind of tracking, so we're using good old American ingenuity—a kind of combination telescope and movie camera called a cinetheodolite. It's a work in progress—hell, this is all a work in progress—but we've got a guy coming out from Harvard this summer who'll get it up to snuff. Clyde Tombaugh. He's the best there is."

Dewey nodded. "I'll say. He's the man who discovered Pluto. The planet, not the dog," she added, looking at Suze.

"I knew *that*." Suze stuck out her tongue. Sometimes Dewey was a pain.

"Stay here," said Dr. Gordon, then waved to a man in a white shirt who was gesturing at the base of the rocket. "I gotta go find out what Jim wants."

Suze pushed her blunt-cut, blonde hair out of her face. "Ouch." She pulled her hand away. Her forehead was starting to burn, and they'd be out here for hours with no shade. "Dad? Do you have hats for us?"

He turned and snapped his fingers. "Damn. I knew I forgot something. I'll see if I can borrow a couple from the guys in the blockhouse. They'll be inside all afternoon." He jerked his thumb at a windowless concrete structure on the far side of the paved area. Its roof looked like a pyramid with a tower on top.

Suze nodded, watching as half a dozen men scurried up the narrow metal ladders that canted into the side of the rocket. Two stood on a platform midway, opened a panel that was half yellow, half black, and began making adjustments to the tangled nest of wiring inside. A pipe down by the base hissed and vented steam. It looked very complicated.

"Here you go," Dr. Gordon said five minutes later. He handed Suze a floppy khaki GI hat and gave Dewey a pith helmet. When she put it on, it came down over her ears, covering her face all the way to her nose.

Suze snorted a laugh. "I think we better swap." She was tall for her age, five-eight, and not yet thirteen; wiry little Dewey barely came up past her shoulder. She put the helmet on. The brim perched just above her eyebrows. She handed Dewey the hat. "Better?"

"Yeah. It's still too big, but it beats a sunburned nose, that's for sure." Dewey tucked her dark curly hair under the cap. "That'll work."

Men detached hoses and turned wheels and valves, then the

tanker truck rumbled slowly away from the rocket. Now Suze could see that the fins were marked with Roman numerals, II and IV visible from where she stood.

Dr. Gordon looked at his watch. "Right on time. X minus one hour, and they're done with the oxygen fueling. We've got thirty minutes before they clear the launch site. Let me show you around, introduce you to some of the guys."

The first man frowned at Dr. Gordon. "You brought your *girls* out here?" He sounded surprised, and like he didn't approve at all.

"Why not? It'll be their world soon enough," Dr. Gordon replied.

More Dewey's world than mine, Suze thought. Dewey asked everyone a lot of science questions and seemed to think that even hoses and spools of wire were the most interesting stuff in the world.

Suze was wondering if anything exciting would ever happen, when a loudspeaker blared: "All personnel proceed to safety areas. Repeat, all personnel clear the launch site."

"See you after, Phil," said the man. "I'm on impact watch for this one."

"Where does the rocket come down?" Dewey asked.

"That's not my department," said Dr. Gordon.

WHAT GOES UP

The viewing stand was a section of desert marked off with rows of white flags. A curve of jagged mountains rose steeply behind them, close enough that Suze could see individual slabs of rock jutting up. To the east and south, the land was flat and wide and spread out forever, like a dust-filled ocean fading to blue near the horizons. Close up, low pale-green plants with small yellow flowers were scattered underfoot.

Dr. Gordon handed Suze the lunch sack. "Go ahead and stand anywhere—or sit, if you want. Just stay inside the white flags."

"Something's wrong!" Dewey tugged on Dr. Gordon's arm, pointing back toward the launch site. A plume of red smoke rose from the top of the blockhouse.

He looked down at his watch. "Nope. That's just the stand-by signal. We're at X minus 20—twenty minutes to the launch.

I'll be back after they fire the all-clear—that'll be green smoke. Enjoy the show, kids."

"It's hot," said Suze as he drove away. She looked around at the small crowd, a dozen groups of men—and one lady in a dress and a red hat—then sat by some of the yellow flowers. The glass bottles clinked inside the sack.

"Yeah." Dewey sat next to her. "I'm glad it's only May and not July. Gimme one of those root beers."

Suze pulled the sweating brown bottle out by its neck. "Crap," she said. "Dad forgot hats *and* the opener." She stared at the bottle top for a long minute. "Did you bring your pocket-knife?"

Dewey shook her head.

"I used to be a Boy Scout," said a man standing to their left. He pulled a folded knife out of his pocket and tossed it underhand to Suze. "Be prepared."

"Thanks." She popped the tops of the two bottles of root beer and looked at the sack. "Trade you back," she said, handing him his knife and the third bottle.

"Deal." He took a long, slow swallow. "Boy, does that hit the spot." He sat down, a few feet away, legs crossed Indian style. "I'm Frank. I'm with *Popular Science*. You two look a little young to be press."

"I'm Suze. This is Dewey. My dad's a consultant for General Electric," Suze said. "On the—whad'ya call 'em?" She turned to Dewey.

"The graphite vanes for the tail fins," Dewey supplied. "They stick out into the hot part and either steer or keep something stable. I'm not quite sure which." She shrugged. "I'm better with mechanics than aeronautics."

"You are, are you?" Frank smiled. "So you're an engineer?"

"Not yet. But I'm working on it." She took a drink and burped softly. Suze giggled. "Sorry," Dewey said. "Bubbles. Is this going to be in your magazine?"

"Yep. July issue." He fished in the pocket of his pants, found a small white card, and wrote something on the back. "Here. Mail this to the magazine office with your address, and they'll send you one." He paused. "What the heck. You can have a whole year." He scribbled more words and handed the card to Dewey.

"Really?" Dewey stared. "You mean it?"

"Sure. My contribution to science."

"It looks tiny from back here," Suze said. She held her arm out and squinted, pinching the yellow rocket between her thumb and forefinger. "Like a toy."

"Don't let the Brits hear you say that." Frank tipped his head to the right, indicating four men in shirts and ties, jackets draped over their arms. "They lost three thousand people—and a big chunk of London—to those things. Back when Herr von Braun worked for the other side." He said the name as if it tasted bad.

A loud murmur began, like wind rustling through a

cornfield, and people pointed to the sky. Suze looked up and saw a bright red flare explode a hundred feet above them. Fireworks in the daytime.

"Two-minute warning," Frank said. "So if you'll excuse me, I need to get to work." He tipped his hat, a battered gray fedora, and stood up.

Suze leaned back on her hands and stared at the faraway rocket, its base shimmering in the desert heat like a mirage. None of this felt real—more like a Buck Rogers serial at the movies.

A loudspeaker mounted on a tall pole broadcast a man's tinny voice, excited but controlled. "Ten . . . nine . . . eight . . ." Suze waited. "Two . . . one . . . zero. Rocket away!"

For a fraction of a second, nothing seemed to happen. Then she heard a crackling sound, like logs in a fireplace, and saw yellow flame appear at the base of the rocket, followed by a huge *poof* of horizontal fire, and billowing clouds of dust. The rocket rose slowly into the air, like a balloon floating gently upward.

The crackling noise became a roar that grew and grew until it filled the world with sound, and the rocket gained speed and height. A bright white plume, straight as an arrow and as wide as the rocket, formed an immense tail. It flew up and up, impossibly fast, and within seconds there was no rocket, just a brilliant white streak in the sky, like a smear of pure sunlight.

Everything was silent, so quiet Suze could hear the leather soles of people's shoes scraping on the sand as they shifted to lean back and follow the light.

A minute later, a corkscrew of white clouds appeared high in the sky, roiling and curling in on itself to form a loop that looked to Suze like the head of a dragon, its tail trailing away behind it.

"It's not flying straight. Is something wrong?" Dewey whispered to Frank.

"I don't think so," he whispered back. "At the press briefing, they said the winds in the upper atmosphere might play havoc with the vapor trail."

"Oh."

Suze watched, openmouthed, as the curling dragon wisped and began to unform. Then nothing. Nothing at all for a minute. Two. No one spoke. Every head was tilted back toward the sky, waiting.

Frank had stopped writing. "Where does the rocket land?" Suze asked.

"It doesn't," he said. "It crashes. That's what it was designed for—to make a big hole, as much destruction as possible when it hits."

Dewey frowned. "But there's no explosives in this one, right? Just cameras and stuff?"

"Doesn't matter. There'll still be a little fuel left, and five tons of metal hitting the ground at three thousand miles an hour is going to make one hell of—excuse me, ladies—one *heck* of a bang."

As if to prove his point, a few seconds later the mountains reverberated with the sound and shock of a distant explosion. Off to the east, a narrow cloud of grayish-pink smoke rose from an invisible crater.

A cheer went up and sped through the crowd. All around her Suze saw men flinging their hats into the air, shouting as if they'd just won a football game.

"Go ahead, Uncle Joe, bring on the next war," a man in a white T-shirt yelled. "We put A-Bombs on a couple hundred of those babies, the commies'll never know what hit 'em."

"Got that right," another man laughed. "We got everything we need, now."

Frank shook his head and looked over at Dewey and Suze.

"Welcome to the future," he said.

ROCKET
SUMMER

I'M A STRANGER
HERE MYSELF

May 31, 1946

Dewey walked down New York Avenue, on her way "downtown," a block of one- and two-story brick and stone buildings with awnings, plate-glass and tile fronts, a few neon signs. Some had stores on the street level—Rolland's Drugs, Stevenson's Hardware, Dale's Piggly Wiggly grocery—and offices on the floor above, black lettering painted on the windows.

She swung a book under one arm, humming to herself as she stood in front of Alamo Drugs, waiting to cross Tenth Street. To her left, it was lined by huge shady cottonwood trees for a few blocks, then ran straight east to the base of the mountains. At the far end, a hundred yards up, was a huge block capital *A*, whitewashed onto the rocks every year by the "Alamo" High School boys. From where she stood, it didn't look much bigger than the *A* on the Alamo Drugs sign.

A block to her right, cars sped down Pennsylvania Avenue,

past the railroad depot and the tall black water tower. It and the giant *A* marked the edges of town, the limits of civilization. Beyond them were only rocks and sand and sky.

Corner Drugs was on the ground floor of a redbrick building with a tall stucco turret, topped by an onion dome with copper scales, green with age. Dewey thought it looked more like India or Constantinople than New Mexico. She opened the glass door, a bell tinkling overhead, and stepped inside. It was cool and dark after the bright sunshine and was filled with a heady mix of smells: old wood, the pungent tang of medicines, the sweet aromas of hot fudge and lilac perfume.

The pharmacist stood behind a high counter, flanked by tall glass jars labeled in Latin and filled with colored water, and shelves of pills and salves and syrups. The soda fountain had a wooden back bar with gleaming chromed spigots and cardboard pictures of ice-cream sundaes and sodas.

Dewey sat on the wire-legged stool, put her book on the marble counter, and ordered a chocolate malt. Frank Sinatra crooned from a radio. The soda jerk, a boy in a white jacket and paper hat, set a tall tapered glass in front of her. She pulled the wrapper off the straw and sank it into the thick shake.

Life was pretty swell. She was thirteen—and a half—just an ordinary teenage girl sitting in an ordinary American drugstore. She smiled as she sipped her chocolate malt, then opened *Fundamentals of Mechanical Physics* and began to read.

She was halfway through a chapter on gravity and inclined

planes when Suze plopped onto the stool next to her.

"We need more junk," Suze said, after she'd ordered a cherry Coke.

"For what?"

"I don't know yet. But we've got the whole summer before school starts, and there's enough room in the attic to make *any-thing*."

Dewey nodded. The house on Michigan Avenue was the best place she'd ever lived. The attic had two big windows and had come with some furniture—shelves and tables, a thread-bare rug, and a battered couch with stuffing coming out of the pillows. Suze had unpacked her art box and magazines, Dewey her Erector set and Mason jars of parts, and they'd painted a pegboard to hang Dewey's tools on. But most of the room was still empty. The house was a rental, just for a year—until Dr. Gordon's rocket team had done twenty-five launches and he went back to the university. But Suze was right. It was a perfect place for trying out new ideas.

"I wonder if there's a dump," Dewey said.

"Probably." Suze took a drink, then snapped her fingers. "I know where we can find out. In the alley, on the way over, I saw some high-school guys working on an old car. Boxes of parts all over the garage. They had to get 'em somewhere."

"Let's go ask." Dewey closed her book and slurped the last of her malt.

Alleys ran through the center of each block of houses,

narrow gravel thoroughfares with mohawks of grass between ruts and puddles, bounded by adobe walls and wooden fences with fringes of wildflowers. The neighbors' backyards were mostly dirt, cactus, and yapping dogs. Halfway between Tenth and Eleventh Streets, Suze put her finger to her lips. "Shh. Next house down. The garage door's open."

They ducked behind a telephone pole, like spies. Dewey saw the backs of two boys, one in jeans and a T-shirt, one in chinos, his shirt off, bent over an engine up on concrete blocks. A third boy slouched against a wall, hands in his pockets.

"Half-inch socket?" the shirtless boy asked. When the other boy came back, wrench in hand, Dewey stepped forward. "Hey," she said.

The boy turned. He was a couple of years older than she was, almost a man. "What'cha want, kid?"

"We just moved here," Dewey said, jerking a thumb back at Suze, "and we need to find the dump."

"What? Your dollies got thrown out with the trash?"

"Nope," Suze said, moving up beside Dewey. "We make stuff."

"Like charm bracelets?" the boy in chinos asked. He stepped out into the sunshine. "My sister messes with some of that. Sewing, too."

"Nah," said Dewey. "Machines and gizmos." She pointed into the garage. "Like that rack-and-pinion slide over there. Where'd you get that?"

"You know what that *is*?" the boy said, startled.

Dewey nodded. "I know what it does, too."

"Jeez. Where *you* girls from?"

"Los Alamos," Suze said. "Our folks built the Bomb."

"*The* Bomb?" He looked up at the sky, his eyes wide, like one might be falling, right then.

"Yep."

The boy whistled through his teeth and took two steps back.

Blue-jean boy wiped his hands on a rag and stepped out into the alley. "The dump's way out on the edge of town. Past First Street, the other side of the tracks. Not worth the trip. It's just garbage. Rotten lettuce and broken glass garbage."

"So where'd you get the car parts?" Dewey asked.

"Tim Pratt's salvage yard, on the highway, between Seventh and Eighth. If you want little junk, not worth the price for scrap, you might get a sackful for a quarter."

"Sounds good to me," Dewey said.

The boy nodded. "Tell him Bobby Callaway sent you." He turned back to the engine.

Dewey took her book home, then they cut back to New York Avenue at Eleventh Street and walked past the White Sands Theatre, with a poster for a dopey love story framed by colorful glazed tiles. At the corner they heard giggles inside Alamo Drugs. Dewey looked in and saw four girls in pleated skirts and saddle shoes with bobby sox, perched on stools at the soda fountain, drinking Cokes. They'd been too busy unpacking to meet any other kids yet. Dewey wasn't sure if she wanted to. They might make fun of her, like the girls on the Hill, and she'd had enough of that.

Suze must have thought the same thing. "They could be in our class," she said. "I hope they're not like Joyce and her crowd, all lipstick and movie-star crazy."

"Me, too. Hard to tell, just by looking." *At least this time I'm not alone,* Dewey thought, but said nothing.

THE LUCKY ONES

The highway was like another world, asphalt and low buildings—adobe, brick, and cement. Parked cars, a tourist court, and cafés with neon signs lined both sides between Tenth and Ninth. A freight train whizzed by on the far side of the depot, its whistle so loud they had to cover their ears.

They stopped by the bottling company, a narrow storefront with a big window, and watched crates of grape soda slide down a clanking conveyor belt. After that the buildings were farther apart—open-bayed garages, welding and repair shops—and the sidewalks disappeared, just dirt and sun-bleached weeds against chain-link fences. Lots of the signs were in Spanish.

The salvage yard was huge, compared to the dump on the Hill, stretching nearly a full block. Mountains of tires, rows of sinks and bathtubs, and piles of old bricks lined the narrow path that snaked through the county's discards. Oil drums, washing machines, ribbed metal culverts, a tractor with its seat miss-ing—a jumble of rust and pitted chrome.

Tim Pratt, a thick man in bib overalls, walked over, looking puzzled. "You little ladies lost?"

"No, sir," Dewey said. "Bobby Callaway sent us."

"He's sending *girls* to pick up his parts now?"

Suze shook her head. "No, he just gave us directions."

It took a few minutes to convince him that they really did want to look at junk, and no, they didn't have a truck, or a daddy coming to fetch them. He finally pointed to a covered area in the far corner and said that was where he tossed the little stuff. He left them alone when a man came in and asked for some eight-inch pipe.

Most of the yard was just construction material, but Dewey found some really big, long springs and the motor from a mixer, and Suze discovered a shoe box full of old keys. Not useful, but interesting shapes. Tim Pratt waved off their money. "Take 'em. No one else wants 'em." Dewey asked if he had any busted radios or intercom sets.

"Not now. But something comes in, I'll set it aside." He wrote her name on a lined yellow pad, its pages so greasy they were translucent. "Don't got a phone," he said. "You just stop by every couple of weeks, you and your sister."

Suze shook her head. "She's not my—"

"We're not—" Dewey said at the same time.

They looked at each other and shrugged.

"I'll check back," Dewey said, and they headed home.

"We don't even look alike," Suze said after a block. She sounded annoyed or confused, Dewey couldn't tell which.

Except for the jingle of the bag of keys, the rest of the walk was silent.

When they reached the back door, Suze shouted, "Mom! We're home!"

No reply. Terry Gordon stood in the front hall, one hand on the receiver of the phone. She'd hung up, but she wasn't moving, and her face was pinched like she might cry.

Dewey felt sweat prickle under her arms, felt her heart beat a little faster.

"Mom?" Suze said in a voice just above a whisper.

Terry Gordon looked up, but Dewey had the feeling that she was staring *through* them, seeing something very far away.

"Mom?" Suze said again, louder, sounding scared. "What's wrong?"

Her mother blinked, slowly took her hand off the phone. "Jean Bacher just called from the Hill. Lou Slotin died."

"Lou—?" Dewey asked.

"Another chemist. We used to eat lunch together in the lab, talk about books we liked. He was at that last cocktail party we had. Dark curly hair?" She sat down on the stairs and stared out the open front door.

Dewey walked over to the banister and put a hand on her shoulder, rubbing it a couple of times. "I'm sorry, Terry."

She saw Suze flinch at the name.

Damn, Dewey thought. *Not in front of Suze.* She wanted to say something, but this wasn't the time. She stood back and let Suze sit down next to her mother, kiss her on the cheek.

"I'm sorry, too, Mom." An emphasis on *Mom* as Suze looked at Dewey, just for a second.

"I'm going to head upstairs," Dewey said, even though she wanted to stay. She stopped on the second step. "How did he die?"

"Tickling the dragon's tail," Terry Gordon said after a minute. She looked up. "That's what Dick Feynman calls it. A week ago, some plutonium went critical. Lou saved everyone else in the room, but he died this morning of radiation sickness, like the people we killed in Hiroshima."

"I thought they died from the explosion," Suze said.

"Only the first hundred thousand," her mother said in a whisper. "And they were the lucky ones." She put her head in her hands.

Dewey longed to comfort her, but she wasn't really family. She watched Suze hesitate, then put her arms around her mother. When Terry leaned her head on Suze's shoulder, Dewey went up to the attic, one slow step at a time.

THE THING IN THE ATTIC

JUNE 1946

By summer, Suze's side of the attic was colorful and not very organized. The four built-in shelves were stacked with paint cans, bottles of rubber cement, and dozens of tattering magazines, their cut pages sticking out at odd angles. Piles of cigar boxes—some of them even labeled with black crayon: BOTTLE CAPS, CUT-OUT FOOD, GREEN GLASS (TRINITY), BLUE GLASS (BROKEN)—covered an old kitchen table, its metal top stained and chipped. She'd built a little cupboard that held a caramel-colored stone with σηαζαμ painted on it in black ink. *Shazam*, in Greek letters. She'd made it back on the Hill, one of the secret talismans of the Shazam Club. She and Dewey were the only members.

Dewey's work space was more precisely cluttered. A book-shelf held jars full of nails and screws, each with a neatly lettered paper label. *Her* Shazam rock, dark gray with shiny silver ink, lay on top of a square of red felt. Tools hung from hooks on a three-foot square of white-painted pegboard, each screw-driver or wrench outlined in red paint, marking *exactly* where it went.

A hammer and pieces of track from a busted train set lay on her workbench, a long wooden table. Suze had cut out pictures from some already wrecked comics and glued a line of flying men in capes to a narrow piece of wood. While she waited for the glue to dry, she watched Dewey move the pieces around, then stare up at the Wall, trying to figure out where they could go.

Dewey had started the Wall by accident, the week after they'd been to the salvage yard. She'd held the top of a long coiled spring with one hand and rolled ball bearings into it with the other, playing with the curves and the speed. The bearings made a sort of thrumming noise that got higher the faster they went, and if she sent a lot of them down at once, or twirled the spring, the "music" changed.

A sandwich plate, left from lunch and padded with a paper napkin, was supposed to catch them at the end of their ride, but a lot of them overshot or bounced off the china with a muffled *tunk* and clattered to the bare wooden floor. They rolled off into dusty corners and fell into splintery cracks too narrow for her fingers to rescue them.

After she'd lost her sixth or seventh bearing, Dewey'd got-ten frustrated, nailed the top end of the coil to a wall stud, and hung a tin sand pail from another nail two feet below. The pail was rusting, with faded painted children and beach balls, but the bearings dropped in with resonant *bong*s, every time.

The Wall grew bit by bit. Alleys were great for picking through trash without anyone seeing, and they got to know the garbagemen pretty well. The dump on the Hill had been mostly science junk; trash in Alamogordo was full of busted toys. They added slides and gates, a little tin Ferris wheel, a loop-the-loop, and a conveyor with Dixie-cup buckets made with Dewey's Erector set.

Dewey figured out most of the engineering. Suze painted backgrounds and laminated them with magazine pictures— circus monkeys and ringmasters in tall black hats, words from headlines for signs. Playing cards riffled through the spokes of a wheel, paper clowns pirouetted on spindles, and a pair of celluloid penguins shuffled along a canted raceway.

It got even better after the Fourth of July. That was a big event in a town this small. Everyone lined the streets of the business section, two or three deep, to watch the parade, led off by the patriotic flags of the American Legion color guard. The high-school band played Sousa marches and "America the Beautiful." Cowboys twirled lariats, and *vaqueros* on silver saddles shot pistols into the air. Men and women dressed like pioneers waved from farm wagons and carriages from the turn of the century.

The last entry had not been from the past. A huge truck and trailer carried a V-2 rocket, lying on its side, half a city block long. Most people cheered, but Suze noticed that some faces looked worried.

When the parade ended, everyone went out to the ballpark, where there were booths with blue-ribbon jellies and prize-winning sheep, and a small carnival with rides and popcorn and cotton candy.

Suze took pictures of the bright colors and decorations with her Brownie camera, getting ideas for the Wall. While they waited in line for the rides, Dewey talked about Archimedes and simple machines, identifying the physics underneath the fun. *On* the rides, Dewey squealed like everyone else, but once she was back on the ground, she took notes and drew diagrams. Twice she got back in line to ride again and double-check her theories.

Levers, wheels, screws, gravity, centrifugal force—Suze had rolled her eyes at first, but Dewey was right. Even the most scary-looking ride was based on something pretty simple, something they could use for the Wall.

After that, the Wall started to look like a wild carnival itself, a flat, vertical amusement park, eight feet wide and more than four feet tall, with at least a dozen different paths, depending on how Dewey set the openings and obstacles.

Suze scoured her magazines for airplanes and rockets—real photos of V-2s cheek-to-jowl with red-and-blue comic-book spaceships. Dewey made them shoot up a track with the plunger from a discarded pinball game.

It was the most fun Suze had ever had. Downstairs, Dewey sometimes got on her last nerve, especially when Mom was around, but that disappeared when they worked on the Wall. They'd created most of it together, each of them adding an occasional surprise for the other to discover. Suze made a slender tightrope that hung a few inches from the ceiling, and when Dewey pulled a string, it released a teetering cardboard elephant, cut from a cereal box. He wiggled and tipped across the room to a platform on the bookshelf above her table.

Two days later, Suze came upstairs and found a whole series of noisemakers—typewriter bells, a doorbell run by a battery, some New Year's Eve junk—arranged so that when she rolled a few marbles out of the box at the top, the whole Wall popped and clanged, rang and whizzed and crackled for more than a minute.

On an afternoon in mid-July, Dewey stood staring at the Wall, humming to herself. Suze wasn't sure if she knew she was humming. When Dewey was working, she didn't pay much attention to anything else.

She had a little wheel in one hand and *The Boy Mechanic* open flat on her workbench, reading for a minute, looking at the wheel, then back at the book. Suze sat down at her table and opened a cigar box full of cut-out comic-book people. "Let's put up Billy Batson and Captain Marvel. You can make them fly with wires and stuff, right?"

Dewey looked up from the composition book where she

tried out her ideas with math and little drawings before nailing anything up. "Piece of cake. Put Mary Marvel up, too." Dewey'd only read one of those comics, but liked the idea of a girl with superpowers.

"No way. Her Shazam is wrong."

"How? Shazam's Shazam. Solomon, Hercules, Atlas—"

"—Zeus, Achilles, Mercury," Suze finished. "That's the problem. The wizard says she gets—" Suze flipped the pages. "Selena, Hippolyta, Ariadne," she said in a girly-girl voice. "Zephyrus, Aurora, Minerva. Take a look." She tossed the comic across.

"What a crappy deal," Dewey said. "They both get strength and wisdom and speed, but instead of power and courage, she gets grace and beauty?" She made a face. "Like that's gonna stop bad guys." She put her hand on her hip. "Don't rob the bank. I'm *so* pretty."

"See," said Suze. "That's why I don't want her on the Wall. It's part of the Shazam Club, right?"

"Sure. That's the rule. No *girls* allowed."

Suze nodded and glued Captain Marvel to a piece of cardboard. "Have you thought about what's going to happen to the Wall when we move next June?" she asked. "After school's over, and Dad's done with his rocket job?"

"Yep," Dewey answered without looking up.

Suze waited a minute for more of an answer. Two minutes. "Dewey!"

"What?"

"*What* have you thought? Can we take some of it with us?"

Dewey closed the book, leaving her pencil in it to mark her place. "Are you kidding? All of it. Except for some nails and screws. We can get those in Berkeley."

"We're going to need a hell of a big box." Suze looked around. The Wall covered half the attic.

"No, it comes apart in sections. The biggest one's about three feet by two."

"Sections?"

"C'mere." Dewey motioned Suze over and pointed to a spot about shoulder height. "See that red board? I bolted the Ferris wheel onto it, along with the top of the slide and these two ramps. The *board's* the only part screwed into the attic wall. So we can just unscrew it and pack that section by itself." She swung her arm around. "Same with everything else."

Suze stared. Dewey was in charge of the actual construction, so she didn't pay much attention unless she had to hold a board up while Dewey nailed, or drill a hole Dewey couldn't reach.

"You thought that up from the beginning?" *That's a pretty nifty solution,* Suze thought. *Pretty damn nifty.*

"I got the idea from an article in *Popular Mechanics.* A guy built his whole *house* this way, so when he moved, he could take it apart and reassemble it."

"So we can just put it back together in the attic in Berkeley?"

"Pretty much. We might have to dismantle *some* stuff, to make it fit the other space, but not much."

"Wow. Good thinking, Kerrigan," Suze said with a little salute.

"It's a rented house. Doesn't make sense to build anything permanent." Dewey shrugged. "I've moved a lot. I never like it, but it's not as bad if I can plan ahead." She took the pencil out of her book and started drawing another diagram of a series of pulleys.

ADAPTATION

JULY 1946

When they'd first moved in, Suze had found some old books on one of the attic shelves—no pictures, most of them about cattle diseases. Useless, until Dewey had used one to drill on, so the bit wouldn't dig into the table.

Suze set a painted and paper-covered cigar box down onto *Hoof and Fetlock Care* and set the point of the drill bit on the **X** she'd made, so they could bolt the box to the Wall. It was hard, at first, to keep the bit in the right place *and* press down hard enough for it to bite into the wood *and* turn the handle fast enough for it to do anything, but she was starting to get the hang of it.

Dewey had said that Suze could borrow tools as long as she didn't get paint or glue on them and she put them back where they belonged. That was easy—when she remembered. Yesterday she'd been in the kitchen making a snack when Dewey came in the front door, and she had to race to the attic to hang up the hammer before Dewey noticed.

Suze could kind of see the point of it. This morning she'd hunted for her scissors for fifteen minutes, which was annoying. She wasn't going to paint scissors pictures on her shelves or anything, but when she'd finished cutting up a pile of comics into little squares, she *had* tossed them into a shoe box with the jumble of pencils and rulers and rubber bands, random things not worth labeling or sorting.

The drill chewed through the wood, and under the sound of the mechanical whirring she heard the attic door open, footsteps on the stairs. She didn't look up, kept her eyes on the disappearing black **X**. A minute later, she felt the bit dig into the buckram cover of the book, and stopped. The attic was quiet.

That was odd. Suze realized she hadn't heard Dewey come *into* the room, no footstep on the squeaky board, no thump and rattle of new junk onto her workbench, or hollow clink of a tool lifted off the pegboard.

Suze turned around, the drill in her hand, bits of sawdust trickling off.

Dewey stood at the top of the stairs, a comic book dangling from one hand and a big smile on her face.

"What?" Suze said.

No answer. Dewey grinned like she'd won some sort of prize. Acting goofy.

"What?" Suze asked again.

"Notice anything?" Dewey said after another minute.

Suze looked Dewey up and down, back up again, even looked behind her.

"Um, you've got the new *Wonder Woman*?"

"Anything else?" Dewey's grin faltered.

Suze squinted and looked closer. She was good at seeing colors and details and the way shadows made shapes no one else noticed. *Hmm.* Dewey's hair didn't look any different, so she hadn't gotten it cut. She was wearing the same shirt and shorts she'd had on at lunch, the same saddle shoes, the same—

Suze shook her head, looked again. Dewey was wearing *two* saddle shoes, one on each foot. Which would have been ordinary for anyone except Dewey. As long as Suze had known her, Dewey had worn one regular shoe and one ugly brown shoe that laced up the side. She'd had an accident when she was a baby, and one leg was a little shorter than the other.

"Nice shoes," Suze said.

Dewey's smile seemed to fill her entire face. "Aren't they great?"

"They're aces. What happened to your"—Suze stopped, groping for a word that wasn't too insulting to Dewey's weird shoe—"your brown one?"

"It got too small, 'cause my feet had grown since Nana bought it in St. Louis three years ago. It was *way* too big then, and I had to wear lots of extra socks, but she said she wasn't made of money, and I couldn't have a new one every year." She moved over to her workbench, put the comic down, and leaned against the table's edge. "It started pinching really bad, but I didn't know where to get another one. You can't just find them on the shelves. So I went to the shoe store last week to see if Mr. Staley'd have a catalog or something."

Suze nodded. Dewey was grinning *and* chatty, which didn't happen every day. She stared at the shoes, a puzzled look on her face. "So what did he do, paint the new one to match your regular shoe?"

"No, that's the really swell part. I've got *two* regular old shoes."

"Won't you walk goofy?"

"Uh-uh. Take a look." Dewey lifted up her left foot.

"It's a shoe."

"Yep. Now look at the other one."

Suze looked, then smiled. "That cooks with gas! It's just got a thicker sole."

"Yep." Dewey put her foot back down. "Mr. Staley measured my feet—he's got this great machine that does real X-rays so you can see the bones and *every*thing—and said that there was only about half an inch difference."

"Nobody'll even notice. How does it feel?"

"A little strange, but okay. I used some of Papa's insurance money and got a pair of sneakers, too. Mr. Staley said to try them for a month—to give me some time to get used to them and break 'em in, like you do with any new shoes, right?"

"Sure. They always feel stiff and weird at first."

Dewey nodded. "And if my feet hurt, or my legs, or I get a backache from walking weird, then he'll either adjust the soles again, or find out where to get another *orthopedic* one." She made a face.

"If it hurts, will you say?"

"Only if it hurts a whole lot. I don't want to snafu my leg forever. But if it's just a little achy now and then . . ." She shrugged. "I can live with that. Better than having everyone stare at me." She looked down at her feet. "This'll be the first time—ever—that I've started in a new school not looking like a drip."

"Wow." Suze had gotten so used to Dewey—her shoe, her gizmos, her math books—she'd almost forgotten Dewey was weird. "That'll be good."

"Yeah," Dewey said with a contented sigh. "And no one here knows I was 'Screwy Dewey.'"

"Or I was 'Truck.'"

"We can be anyone we want, at this school," Dewey said in a fake British accent. "Perhaps I shall be called Clarissa." She chuckled.

Suze snorted. "Right. And I'm Marie of Romania."

"Dibs on Marie. It's *my* middle name."

"Oh!" Suze snapped her fingers. "Your real name. Mom

went to the post office, and there was a whole bunch of stuff that got forwarded from the Hill. There's a letter and a big box for you. They look official."

"From who?"

"I dunno. Mom just said to tell you. They're in the kitchen."

"Okay." Dewey looked down at her new shoes again. "Lemme take these off and put 'em in the closet. It's hot and my feet are sweaty. I'll wear the sneakers this summer, so these won't be all smelly when school starts."

"I'll wait." Suze walked over to the pegboard and carefully hung Dewey's drill in its drill-shaped spot.

THE LETTER OF
THE LAW

The mail was piled on a large cardboard carton on the kitchen counter—a postcard, some bills, the latest issue of *The New Yorker*. On top was a cream-colored envelope covered with official stamps in vivid red and purple inks—NOT AT THIS ADDRESS. FORWARD. POSTAGE DUE—that had made its way across postal clerks' desks and a U.S. Army installation.

Dewey looked at the envelope without touching it. It was addressed to (Miss) Duodecima Marie Kerrigan and was from St. Louis. She bit her lip and felt sweat trickle under her arms. It couldn't be good news. She picked it up, turning it over front to back. The gummed flap was still sealed. She sat down at the table.

"Neat," Suze said. She opened a bottle of grape soda. "Can I have it when you're done? Just the envelope?"

"I guess. How come?" Dewey laid it flat in front of her.

"It looks so messy and official at the same time. All the

colors. I might cut it up and paste it on something." She took a drink of soda. "Where's it from?"

"St. Louis, but it's not Nana's address." She couldn't read the date on the postmark, too smeared and obscured. "It was mailed to the Hill—P.O. Box 1663—but I can't tell when." She touched the envelope gingerly, as if it might give her an electric shock, like the doorknob in the carpeted living room on a hot, dry day. "Hand me a knife?"

Suze got a butter knife from the silverware drawer, and Dewey slit the heavy cream envelope open with one swift motion. She pulled out a single sheet of matching stationery. A pale green rectangle slid out and sailed across the table, fluttering to the floor by Suze's chair.

"Whoa!" Suze's eyes opened wide in surprise. "It's a check for three *thousand* dollars." She handed it back to Dewey. "What's that for?"

"Nana Gallucci died," she said after a minute. She took off her glasses and wiped a tear from her cheek. "The letter's from the lawyer who made her will. She told him to sell her house and send me the money. For college." She folded the check and put it in the pocket of her shorts. "I'll ask your mom to put it in the bank with Papa's money."

Robert Oppenheimer had made the army pay, as if Papa had been a soldier and died in battle rather than in traffic. "In service to his country," the letter said. She'd read it once, then folded it and put it in the cedar box with the rest of Papa's things, and had not looked at it again.

Papa was a war hero the same way she was a displaced person, a refugee in her own country—not false, not exactly true. "With thanks from a grateful nation," the letter had also said. Dewey wondered if *that* was true. The Bomb had ended the war, but a lot of people weren't so thankful. She felt the same way about the check.

She sighed. "I want to go to college, but it's creepy to only get money when someone dies. Nana would probably say it was a blessing. She was old and in the Home, and I knew she wasn't going to ever get better, but still—"

"She was your gramma."

"Yeah." She sniffled once, wiped her eyes again, and replaced her glasses.

Suze went to the fridge and came back with a bottle of root beer.

"Thanks." Dewey drank half the soda in one long swallow.

"Does it say what's in the box?" Suze asked.

She looked at the letter again. "'Personal mementos and objects of a sentimental nature.'" She shook her head. "Nana died in *March*. She's been gone for four months and I didn't even know."

"I guess it took a while to sell her house and mail everything. Kind of amazing that it got to you, way out here."

"That's what lawyers do. They find people. Like Perry Mason on the radio."

"Are you gonna open the box?"

Dewey nodded. "I don't know *what's* in there. I took everything of mine when I went to the Hill, and I when I lived with Nana, I wasn't allowed to look at her private things." She shrugged. "I did, sometimes, when she played pinochle Thursday afternoons. Hankies and pictures of my grandpapa. He died before I was born." She stood up. "Gimme a hand?"

They wrestled the carton from the counter down onto a kitchen chair. It was big, two feet square, covered with more stamps and seals and labels. One corner was a little bashed in.

Dewey slit the brown paper tape and peeled back the cardboard flaps. An odor of mothballs and talcum powder, sweet and dusty, wafted up from yellowing layers of the St. Louis *Post-Dispatch*. She pulled out a heavy bundle, wrapped in more newspaper, tied with yellow twine. It held six china plates with tiny pink roses. The plate on the bottom had cracked in half.

"You want that one for art junk?" she asked.

"Okay. Can I bust it up more?"

"Sure. It was Nana's Sunday china. I guess it's mine now. I never really liked it. Sundays we ate in the dining room. I had to sit up straight and cut my chicken with a knife. In the kitchen I ate it with my fingers, but not on these plates."

She set the five intact plates off to one side and lifted out an oblong bundle, wrapped in blue felt. "The carving knife and fork," she said without opening it. "They're silver, and only for Thanksgiving."

"Is it all going to be kitchen stuff?"

"Probably. Nana didn't have much fancy in the rest of the house." Dewey removed another thick layer of newspaper, revealing a red leather jewelry box. When she opened the lid, music tinkled for a few notes, then stopped. "'The Blue Danube,'" she said, and picked up a pair of earrings.

"They're garnets. She wore them to Mass, but only Sunday Mass. Weekdays she just wore a hat." Dewey laid them on the top plate. "Her rosary." She coiled the chain of beads around the earrings in a loose spiral.

"Was she real religious?" Suze asked.

"Pretty much. That's why I had to go to Catholic school." She removed a filigreed brooch, shaped like a butterfly, dotted with chips of colored glass; a small gold lapel watch; and a strand of pearls, pale rosy pink with a gold clasp. Dewey looked at the array of jewelry for a minute, then replaced each piece in the velvet tray and closed the lid of the box. "I loved Nana, and she took care of me, but I don't know what I'm supposed to do with all this."

"Save it until you're old?"

"Nana old? That's a long time." She began to unwrap a

round, lumpy shape, swaddled in newspaper and cello tape, then smiled. "When I stayed home from school sick, she'd make me cocoa in this." She held up a ceramic teapot, white with pink roses and a gold handle. The lid was a web of chips and cracks. "Nana always said, 'My best teapot is the one with the mended lid.'"

"How come?"

"Got me. Something about Jesus, I think. You love it enough to fix it, even though it's busted." Dewey ran her finger over the spout of the teapot. "I only saw this when I was sick. Those shouldn't be *good* memories. But Nana'd sit in the chair in my room and read me a story, or we'd listen to music on the radio while she knitted. She was big on knitting. All my socks itched."

Dewey shook her head, but she was still smiling. She petted the teapot as if it were a small animal, then set it down on the counter and reached into the carton.

A shiny slate-blue box with THE MAY COMPANY in white script filled the bottom, wedged tight. Dewey had to use the butter knife to pry up one side. The lid of the box came off with a soft whoosh of air. She rapped a knuckle on the folds of tissue paper. "Good. It's hard, so it's not her clothes. That would be too creepy."

"Ick. Old-lady clothes." Suze grimaced. "So what *is* it?"

Dewey unfolded the paper. A dark oval frame with curved

glass held a hand-tinted photograph. An unsmiling man and woman, their cheeks an unnatural pink, stood next to a potted plant. She wore a hat with feathers and an ivory shirtwaist dress, her arm resting on the elbow of his dark suit. He had a round bowler hat, a huge, drooping mustache, and fierce dark eyes.

"Who are they?"

"Nana and Grandpapa. When they got married." She turned the frame over. "Marie and Alberto Gallucci. August 11, 1912." She turned it back. "Nana had this over her dresser. Jesus on the cross was over her bed."

"I'm not sure I could sleep with either of those guys staring at me."

"Me neither. We can hang it in the hall." Dewey patted the tissue paper. "Something flat." A thin cardboard folder the size of a notebook, muddy brown with soft deckled edges, lay at the bottom of the department-store box. She opened it and made a small sound in her throat, half surprise, half pain.

A very young Jimmy Kerrigan stood smiling out at her, his arm around the waist of a woman a few inches taller. His hair was cut very short, and he had rimless glasses that Dewey had never seen before. He wore a pinstriped suit and a wide, short tie. She couldn't tell what color, because the photo was black and white. The woman had on a short, pale dress, a white corsage pinned to one shoulder. Her hair was dark and curly, to her shoulders, and she was smiling, too.

"Wowza." Suze whistled. "She's *really* pretty. Who is she?"

Dewey sat down, heavy, in the kitchen chair and stared at the picture.

"Rita Gallucci Kerrigan," she said slowly. "That's my mother."

SHADOW, SHADOW ON THE WALL

Late that night, the house was quiet. Dewey lay next to the open bedroom window, listening to the distant swish of cars out on the highway, thinking about Papa.

She thought about him every night as she was falling asleep. Sometimes she talked to him in a silent whisper, moving her lips but not making a sound. She wondered if that was what it felt like when religious people prayed, talking to someone important who wasn't really there.

He had been gone—dead—for more than a year. Some nights she couldn't remember him as much as she wanted. She could recall bits and pieces, little details like the shape of his face, or his bare feet under his bathrobe, or the sound of him whistling while he shaved. But more and more the pieces wouldn't come together to make a whole memory, and that bothered her.

Tonight she had a new piece, the Papa from the picture

in the box, and that bothered her, too. She hadn't known that man, when he was only Jimmy. He was too young. But tonight *his* face was more vivid than her real memories, because it was a photograph, the only one she had.

She wondered if she'd said any of that out loud when Suze asked, from the other twin bed, "Have you ever seen that picture before? The one in the box?"

"Uh-huh. When I first went to St. Louis, when I was seven. Nana had it on her dresser. Then she put it away in a drawer."

"How come?"

"She never said. Maybe she thought it'd be easier if I didn't see Papa's face every day. I missed him a lot, the first couple of months, and I cried." A pause. "If she wasn't home, sometimes I snuck into her room to look at him."

"Just him? Not your mother?"

"No. I didn't miss her. I don't really remember her."

"Do you ever wonder what happened to her?"

"Not very often. But I am, tonight."

Her, Dewey thought. *Not Mom or Mama or Mommy. She was only "my mother." A noun, not a name.*

When people—teachers and shop clerks—asked about her mother, Dewey had always said that she left when she was a baby. She didn't feel bad when she said those words. They were simply true, and had been her whole life.

But now, when people asked about Papa—just as often—it hurt, every time. At least when she said he died in the war, no one asked more questions. It would never become an ordinary fact: he had brown hair, he liked Bach, he died. But each time she said the words, they became more true.

"What do you think she's like?" Suze asked.

"I don't know. Nana wouldn't talk about her. Her face got all tight and she'd just shake her head. I asked Papa, too." She paused. "It was the only question he wouldn't answer. But I know he met her at Columbia, so she's probably smart."

"And she's pretty."

"Yeah. I look more like Papa." A longer pause. "Until I went to the Hill, the only grown-up women I knew were nuns, except for Nana and her friends—the Church Ladies. They pinched my cheeks and didn't like my experiments." Dewey hesitated, because what she wanted to say next might piss Suze off. It was hard to tell sometimes. "The first time I met a lady I *hoped* she'd be like, it was your mom. Except—" She stopped and waited for a clue from Suze.

"Except what?" Suze's voice sounded normal. Sleepy, but not mad.

"Except if she really was like your mom, she wouldn't have left." Dewey's throat tightened. Not at the memory, but at the thought of losing Terry Gordon.

Silence for a minute. Two. Dewey was about to turn over and go to sleep when Suze said, "That must feel so weird, not knowing if your mother's out there somewhere, or dead, or—" She stopped and Dewey heard her slap her hand over her mouth. "Sorry. That was a rotten thing to say."

"It's okay. I've wondered, too. She might be. It wouldn't change anything."

"I guess not." Suze yawned. "I'm falling asleep. G'night."

"Night." Dewey turned over and stared at the shadows on the wall as if they might have answers.

Because it *would* change things. If her mother was dead, the Gordons could adopt her. She bit her lip, because that was a terrible thing to want. She silently added that she wasn't *asking* for Rita Kerrigan to die, in case there was a God and he was listening. She'd just like to know if it had already happened, so she could start making other plans.

THE POWER AND THE GLORY

AUGUST 1946

The air in the kitchen was hot and still, even with the back door open. No breeze at all. No clouds, no rain. No relief. The night before it had been too hot to sleep, even with just a sheet, and the radio said it would be hotter today. It might hit 105 degrees, which would be a record. Everyone said, "Well, it's a dry heat"—but then, so was an oven, Dewey thought.

Sweat ran down her back, under the sleeveless cotton undershirt, an old one of Papa's, thin and threadbare, the closest she could come to wearing no clothes. She wiped her face with a cotton bandanna, then took a long swig of orange soda. Yuck. Warm. She got another out of the fridge and held the cool bottle to her forehead for a minute before popping the cap with the opener.

She rolled a gummed paper label into Terry Gordon's typewriter and looked at the list by her elbow. Almost through page three. She should be able to finish them all before Suze came back from the pool.

Dewey had just pecked out the word PHOENIX when she heard a spray of gravel hit the side of the house. Moments later Suze banged in the back door and threw her towel and some comics onto the counter. She wore her bathing suit under her shorts. They were dry, and she was red faced and even sweatier than Dewey.

"I thought you were going to stay at the pool until dinnertime," Dewey said, half turning. Suze had left an hour ago, and it was only a little after three now.

"I was," she said, so angry that Dewey could see spit in the air when she spoke. "I even rode my bike to the drugstore and bought some comics to read during rest periods. But the pool's closed."

"In the middle of the afternoon?"

"For the whole summer. It's only open on Saturdays and Sundays—and you have to be eighteen to get in." Suze jerked the refrigerator door open so hard she knocked the saltines tin off the counter. She put it back and glared at the bottles of soda as if it were their fault.

"*Kids* can't use the pool at all? That's stupid. How come?"

"Polio," Suze said, a Coke in one hand. She slammed the door. "Jumping into cold water on a hot day can give you polio. Hanging out in public places can give you polio. Getting too tired can give you polio," she said in a fakey Church

Lady voice. "There's signs all over the pool fence."

"Polio's pretty bad," Dewey said. She glanced down at her leg, then typed ARIZ. and rolled the label out of the typewriter, laying it next to the last one. If she stacked them, the gummed parts stuck together. "Roosevelt never walked again."

"If I can't swim for the rest of the summer, I might as well be paralyzed. It's hotter than hell outside." Suze sat down with a thump. "What're you doing?"

"Typing labels for your mom. She forgot she had a dentist appointment, and these need to get done today, so she's paying me two cents each."

"Why didn't she ask *me*?" Suze said.

Her voice sounded like she wouldn't mind getting into a fight. It wouldn't be the first time. She was already pissed off, and it was that kind of hot. "You'd just left." Dewey chose her words carefully. "But she's sending letters to all the Kiwanis Clubs in Texas, next week. You can have dibs on those." She made a neat pencil mark by the next name on the list.

"Okay, then." Suze picked up one of the labels, ASSOCIATION OF LOS ALAMOS SCIENTISTS printed across the top. "How many do you have?"

"Forty-two. I've done about fifteen."

"What're they for?"

"They're sending pieces of trinitite to the mayors of cities all over the country, so they can see what would happen if an atomic bomb fell on them."

ELLEN KLAGES

"Only if their cities are made of sand," Suze said, scorn in her voice.

"I know. But it's supposed to be educational."

"Mom better not be giving them any of *my* green glass."

"She's not. They sent some down from the Hill, already packed up. These are just the labels for the boxes."

"Eighty-four cents, huh? That's *sweet*." Suze still sounded mad.

"Yeah, but I'm spending it on somebody else."

"Who?" Now she sounded suspicious.

Dewey smiled, just a little. She didn't get to set Suze up very often. "You."

"Me?" A surprised squeak.

"Yeah. I thought I'd take you to the movies tomorrow. It's a year since we saw all the green glass, and it's almost your birthday. I'll buy popcorn *and* Cokes."

"It's probably just a Western."

O-kay. Suze was ready to blow over just about anything. "Nope. For once it's pretty good. A double feature with *Tarzan and the Leopard Woman* and *Spider Woman Strikes Back.* And cartoons and newsreels and junk." Dewey finished the BOSTON label and added it to the array. "Plus, the Alamento's air-conditioned."

"All right then," Suze said, finally smiling. "You better get back to work."

62

"Aye, aye, Captain Bligh," said Dewey, and picked up another label.

The Alamento Theater looked like a cross between an Indian pueblo and a movie palace—a plaster palace from a very small kingdom. The marquee below the arched front spelled out the name in garish neon. It was more impressive at night than on a hot August afternoon. The sun seemed to bleach the color out of everything—the sky, the buildings, even the dirt. Thunderclouds loomed to the south, promising rain by nightfall, and the air was hot and muggy.

Dewey and Suze stood out on the sidewalk, the cement burning their feet, even with shoes on, waiting in the ticketbooth line with what seemed like every other kid in town. Might have been, since the pool was closed and the White Sands, the only other theater, was playing Lassie and some Disney thing.

At the window, Dewey bought two tickets. She'd raided her piggy bank, and with the label money, they could splurge on popcorn and drinks *and* candy. A real birthday treat. Suze was thirteen. Her grandmother had given her a subscription to a magazine called *Seventeen*, which was mostly ads for clothes. Dewey was glad *she* got *Popular Science*.

They stood in another line at the concession stand, boys bumping and jostling each other. One kid's popcorn had spilled all over the carpet before Dewey got to the counter. "One large popcorn with butter. And two Cokes." She handed the red-and-white-striped box to Suze, carrying the paper cups herself.

Suze stopped inside the doorway and groaned with pleasure. The air was cool and dry, like standing in front of an open refrigerator. "Oh, jeez. I *love* air conditioning." She lifted her shirt away from her skin and flapped it as if she were airing out laundry.

"Where do you want to sit?" Dewey asked.

"Near the back? If I sit up front, little kids can't see over me."

"Okay." Most of the really little kids were probably at the White Sands, watching Lassie, but it was nice for Suze to think of it. "If some tall guy sits in front of me, I'll just flip my seat up. I've done it before."

The noisy theater was filled with swarms of kids running and shouting for their friends, but they found two seats on the aisle, six rows from the back. Dewey sat on the outside, so she could stretch her leg. Sometimes it ached if she sat for too long.

The red plush seats looked kind of elegant, but were scratchy. Not the best fabric for a desert town. She didn't notice, much, once the room got dark and the screen filled with pictures.

First came the newsreel, with marching parade music that lurched on in midnote, black-and-white pictures of the week's important events. Today it was just one—the atomic bomb tests in the Pacific Ocean near a real place with a cartoon-sounding name: Bikini.

The explosion was huge, a tower of water that spread up and out, filling the screen as the announcer's voice, both ponderous and excited, filled her ears.

Up goes a geyser like a thousand Niagaras in reverse, half a million tons of water, up, up, seven miles into the sky. The awe-inspiring cloud billows and surges, blotting out the destruction below.

It was beautiful, Dewey thought. Better than the best clouds she'd ever seen. That felt wrong to think, that a bomb could be beautiful, because she knew there was radiation and fish being poisoned, all kinds of terrible things. But it really *was* awe-inspiring, a plume of water so big it didn't belong on earth.

She thought about Bikini all through the previews until one, *Song of the South,* had a song called "Zip-a-Dee-Doo-Dah" that her brain wouldn't stop singing, not even after five cartoons and Chapter Nine of *Captain Midnight*. When the real movies started, the theater got quiet. Spider Woman was supposed to be scary, and parts were a little creepy, but only the younger kids actually squealed.

Life was good. She wasn't sweaty, she had popcorn, and she was at the movies with her best friend. She had a best friend. How had *that* happened?

So many afternoons in St. Louis, she'd watched other girls go off together, arm in arm, laughing, and had wondered what it felt like. Dewey wasn't a dreamy girl who wished on stars, or pennies in fountains. But this afternoon? This was exactly what she would have wished for.

Except the New Mexico part. That wouldn't have occurred to her in a million years.

At the intermission she bought another Coke, to split, and a box of Milk Duds, which lasted longer than other candies. *Tarzan* was swell, with menacing crocodiles, villains dressed up in animal skins, and Cheetah the chimp, who was funny and ended up rescuing everyone. Pretty good, for a monkey.

When they left the theater, just before six, the air outside was a shock. Still hot, and even muggier. The thunderclouds had moved closer, and the breeze was starting to rustle the edges of the cottonwood leaves. They walked down the alley for a block, but after the third ambush of little boys—leaping from behind garbage cans, growling like leopards and making fierce claws with their hands, or giving the Tarzan yell as they jumped out of garage doors—they cut over to the street again.

"*Kids,*" Suze said. At the corner of Twelfth Street, she stopped for a minute to tie her sneaker. "Thanks. That was great. And the newsreel—zowie. I'd like to see that again. Except without the sound."

"They play that cheesy parade music no matter what the news is."

"It sounds patriotic, I guess."

"It's still cheesy."

Mrs. Gordon lay on the porch glider, reading a book, her bare feet propped up on one armrest. A full ashtray and an amber beer bottle sat on the floor within easy reach. She looked up when she heard them on the steps and smiled, more relaxed than Dewey had seen her since they'd moved.

"Oh good, you're back," she said, looking over the top of her glasses. She picked up her beer bottle and took a drink. "Daddy's out at the site this weekend, so *we're* going to have a hen party. A celebration." She raised the bottle in a salute.

"My birthday," Suze said, nodding.

"Nope. August fifth's not until Monday. I made Phil swear he'll come home for that." She pushed her glasses up into her honey-brown hair. "But it's too hot to cook, and I got some good news today. So I'm going to blow us to dinner down at the Lariat."

Suze whistled in appreciation and hoisted herself onto the railing, like a cowboy on a corral fence. "Musta been pretty swell news."

"You can say that again. All those letters and packets I've been mailing out?"

Dewey nodded. Terry had been busy all summer with Bomb stuff—doing mailings, lecturing to women's clubs, going to the Hill for meetings.

"Well, it's paid off. Congress—finally—passed the McMahon

Act. Truman signed it Thursday. I got a wire from Hans Bethe when you were at the show."

"That's nice," Dewey said, to be polite. She'd read most of what Terry had sent out, but she didn't remember all the details.

"*Nice?* The future of the free world, and that's all you can say? Nice?" Mrs. Gordon finished her beer and thunked it down on the wood as punctuation.

Dewey suspected it wasn't the first one of the afternoon. She looked over at Suze, who shrugged, and mouthed, "*You ask.*"

"Okay," Dewey whispered back. She cleared her throat. "Um, I should know this, but Congress has been kinda busy this year, so remind me—which one's the McMahon Act?"

"Oh, come on. It's the Atomic Energy Act. It means that from now on, all atomic research will be controlled by civilians—by *scientists*—not the military."

"That makes sense," Suze said. "You're the ones who understand that stuff."

"Exactly what the fellas have been testifying about on the Hill—*Capitol* Hill, Washington—for the last year. This guarantees the freedom of scientific research. It's a major, major victory."

"But—" Dewey started to ask about Bikini, then stopped herself. Terry was home and in a good mood, and she didn't want to wreck it.

"But what, kiddo?" She closed her book and swung her feet down.

"At the movies?" Dewey said. "The newsreel was about the new bomb at that Bikini place, and it was *all* army."

"And navy," Suze added.

"I know," Terry Gordon sighed. "Generals just have to blow *some*thing up. The Association did everything we could to stop those tests, but the brass needed bread and circuses— 'See how mighty we are, Mr. and Mrs. Public? Why, there's nothing to be afraid of. The *liberal crowd* and their talk of radiation? Lies. It's perfectly safe.'" She stood up and stretched. "Give me a break."

Dewey thought about the giant column of water. "So, now that the scientists are in control, there won't be any more atomic bombs?"

"That's the best part. The Commission will have time to get up and running, and put some safeguards in place. For the first time in a year, the world is safe from idiots with itchy trigger fingers."

"Huh?" Suze said.

"According to the guys on the Hill, the army has components, but no functional bombs. The second Bikini blast was the last one." Terry smiled. "Production'll take at least two years. They've shot their wad."

"But in the papers, General Groves said they're making more every week," Dewey said.

"I know. They want the press to keep the public scared. But it's not true." She put her hand over her mouth and, for a moment, looked just like Suze. "Oh, Christ. I just breached national security six ways from Sunday."

She pointed to Suze, then Dewey, and said in her sternest, I-mean-this-young-lady voice, "Not a word leaves this porch. *Not. One. Word.* You tell no one." She frowned and looked at Suze. "Especially not your father. He's so wrapped up in missiles and rockets, he's starting to think anyone working for peace is one step from joining the Communist Party."

"Promise," Suze said after a moment. She crossed her heart. "The secret's safe with me."

Dewey nodded. "Me, too. After two years on the Hill, I'm used to them."

ALL ON A SUMMER'S NIGHT

Suze wasn't looking forward to starting in a new school, but she was ready for summer to be over. It had been *hot*—close to 100 degrees—every day for the two weeks since her birthday. She sat out on the front porch after dinner, kicking her heels on the wooden planks as she rocked the glider back and forth. The sun was still visible over the mountains, casting long shadows across the pale bleached grass. An hour before dark, the perfect time to play some gin rummy—if Mom wasn't busy or in a bad mood again.

She and Dad had argued again late last night, loud enough that Suze could hear them from upstairs, even with the bedroom door shut. After the atomic act got passed, Suze had thought things would calm down, but they hadn't.

She got the deck of cards and the score pad from the drawer of the coffee table. "Want to play some gin?" she said softly, but out loud. She tried to make it sound casual, like she was thinking of it right on the spot. All she wanted was a chance to sit and chat with Mom. Not a serious *talk* or anything, just *So, Suze, how do you like this new town? What'cha been up to?*

"Hey, Mom," she said, walking toward the kitchen. "I thought maybe—" She stopped in the doorway. Her mother and Dewey sat at the kitchen table, their heads bent together over the composition book filled with numbers and diagrams. Dewey pointed at something and they both started to laugh.

"What, sweetie?" Her mother glanced up, smiling.

Suze looked from her mother to Dewey and was mad at them both. Dewey, because coming up with ideas for new parts of the Wall was something *they* did together. And Mom, because if she finally had some free time, why wasn't she laughing with Suze? Science wasn't *that* much fun. *Not as much fun as gin rummy!* she wanted to yell. But she didn't. She held the cards behind her back. "Nothing," she said. "I thought I'd go outside, watch the sunset."

"All right. Enjoy," her mother said, and looked back down at the drawings.

That's all? Enjoy? Suze stood there for a moment before returning to the living room. The deck of cards felt like lead. She threw them into the drawer and banged it shut, toppling a stack of magazines.

"Watch it there," her father said. He stood outside his den, a book under his arm, his pipe in his mouth.

"Sorry." Suze restacked the pile of *Time* and *National Geographic.*

"You want to take a little drive with me?" he asked, nodding in the direction of the kitchen. "Just the two of us?" He checked his wristwatch. "If we leave right now, we can stop for ice cream and still make it."

"Make what?" Suze asked, but she was already putting on her sneakers. Dad *had* come home for her birthday, but since then he'd only been around a few nights. He'd gone to New York—Schenectady—on General Electric business, and before that he'd been at the proving grounds, preparing for another rocket launch.

"The greatest show on earth," he said, smiling.

"The circus?" She knew it wasn't. There'd be posters all over town.

"Even better. Hop in the car. I parked out front."

They stopped at Walker's Walk-In and got ice-cream cones—strawberry for Dad and mint chip for Suze. She had to lick quickly to keep it from melting. Even after dinner, it was almost ninety degrees outside.

Her father turned left on the highway, one hand on the wheel, one hand holding his cone. After they passed the city limits, they were the only car on the road. The sky was a hundred shades of blue, studded with clouds that hung miles above the desert floor, their tops glowing a warm, luminous peach, like whipped cream lit from within.

Dr. Gordon put on his sunglasses, and Suze squinted as they drove straight into the setting sun an inch or two above the mountains to the west. She watched her father, without turning her head or staring, not wanting him to know. He had lines around his eyes and mouth that she'd never noticed before, and his hair was going gray on the sides. He was very tan, brick red from being out in the desert all day, and when he shifted his arm, his short shirt sleeve rode up a bit, exposing pale white freckled flesh, the division between light and dark as straight as a ruler.

He drummed his fingers on the steering wheel once his ice cream was gone, keeping time to some music only he could hear. Off to the south, massive thunderheads purpled the sky, and Suze saw a faraway sheet of rain spread from cloud to ground, thin gray tendrils like pencil shadings smeared by a finger.

"You'd think I'd be used to this drive," her father said after a few miles. "But it's never the same. It's my favorite part of the day, an hour of quiet after the chaos of the site," he said, as if he commuted daily, instead of sleeping out at the base half the time. "The sun's behind me, coming home. Easier to see what's out there."

"How 'bout the mornings? You're gone before breakfast."

"Sleepyhead," he teased. "It's still dark when I leave the house. The desert's different at night. I've shared this road with tarantulas and owls, coyotes, rattlesnakes the size of your arm. When the sun comes up, the whole world changes."

He turned toward her. "Everything with any sense sleeps during the heat of the day," he said. "Except us. 'Mad dogs and Englishmen go out in the noonday sun,'" he sang in a robust voice.

Her no-nonsense father was *singing*? Suze stared at him, her mouth open. He was so familiar, but tonight he felt like a stranger, someone she was meeting for the first time.

He saw her surprise and smiled. "Noel Coward. He wrote it about Borneo, or Singapore, someplace tropical, but it's just as true about New Mexico. Ah, here we are." He turned in through the wood-and-stone gates of the White Sands National Monument, fifteen miles from town. "On my way home from the base, I like to stop off here in the evening, just to—well, you'll see."

Outside the car windows, white dunes rose on either side of the narrow road. Swirls of powder eddied like mist across the pavement, and it seemed as if they'd driven from August into winter. A hot, dry winter. In the west, the Organ Mountains were dark jagged shapes silhouetted against the vivid sky. The sun was just barely above the tallest peak. Suze watched the mountain seem to slice into the blood-orange ball like a black dagger.

"This'll do," her father said. He pulled into a turnout. "We don't have time to go much farther." He got out of the car.

Suze followed him across the road and up the face of a steep dune, fifteen feet high, more vertical than horizontal. Climbing was easier than she'd thought—her feet sank into the sand, up to her ankles, and small avalanches cascaded down behind her, but she made steady progress, the dense white powder under her feet firm and squeaking a little with each step. Not like beach sand at all.

At the top, she reached down and pinched some between her fingers. She put it on her tongue, expecting salt and grit. It dissolved a bit, her teeth pulverizing it to a finer and finer powder, like peppermint or chalk, but it had no taste.

"What kind of sand *is* this?" she asked.

"Sand's just a measurement—particles larger than dust, smaller than pebbles—to us metallurgists, anyway. Most of the sand in the world is ground-up quartz. This is gypsum."

"It feels like chalk."

"Running an experiment?" he chuckled. "You're pretty close. Chalk's calcium carbonate, and gypsum's calcium sulfate. They make plaster of Paris out of it. Useful, for an artist type like you."

Suze smiled, pleased that he had any idea what she liked to do.

They crested another dune, and she gasped. As far as she could see, in every direction, the land was a vast, rolling, pale-pink bowl, the edges blade-sharp against the sky, like the peaks of roofs, flattening as they approached. The windward sides were corrugated with endless, symmetric ripples.

"It's beautiful," she whispered. She could see no sign of human civilization. Far-distant mountains cupped the dunes in hazy crescents to the north and east. She felt like they were walking on another planet.

Her father stopped at a flat space sheltered between two dunes and sat down. To their right, miles and miles away, a huge bank of clouds filled the horizon, rounded towers and crevasses golden with sunset, a Maxfield Parrish painting come to life. A forbidden city. Shangri-la. Suze ached to go there. Behind and to her left, forks of jagged lightning lit up the darkening sky. She counted, *one-one-thousand, two-one-thousand*—even at twenty, no sound of thunder reached them. The light show continued; the world was silent.

"Close your eyes," Dad said. "Just sit here and listen."

At first, she heard nothing at all. Then she noticed the soft whisper of the warm breeze in her ears, like listening to the inside of a seashell. She heard the sound of her own breath, and small crunches as her father shifted his body, a few feet away. A puff of wind whisked sand against the fabric of her shorts, as much texture as sound, and not too far off a bird called, its tones round and low.

"Now look," her father said a few minutes later.

Suze opened her eyes, and gasped again, startled by a feeling of weightlessness, of falling up—or down. No way to tell.

No distance, no detail, just the pale pink bowl of the dunes. Above her, on all sides, another inverted bowl tinted a deep, delicate blue, shaded from pastels to ink.

"Amazing, isn't it?" he said softly.

Suze couldn't speak. She nodded.

Her father lit his pipe, the smoke sweet and sharp for a moment, then carried away into the desert air. "When I was a kid, back in Pennsylvania," he said, "I used to go out to the edge of the farm after supper and lie down in the grass and watch the sky, like this. I'd imagine what it would be like to *go* there. I'd stare at the moon and think that someday in the future, a guy like me might visit that silver world. I'd shiver, even on a hot summer night."

He spread his arms wide. "See, *this* is where we are, where we always have been. But *that*?" One arm swung up and pointed to the sky. "That's where we could be. We know as much about that world as a fish knows about dry land. But soon—oh, Suzie, I can't wait to see what's up there."

Suze turned to see his face, and, as if years and layers had suddenly been peeled away, she could imagine what Phil Gordon must have looked like when he was a boy. When he was her age.

"Why didn't you become an astronomer?"

"That was my plan, when I started college." Pause. "But back then it was all observing, and I'm too much of a hands-on guy. I like experiments, making something happen, seeing a change. I stumbled into a Metals class my sophomore year, and it was a better fit."

"You've never told me that before."

"You were just a little kid when the war started, and then I got too busy, I guess. Everything on the Hill was so important, and . . ." His voice trailed off. After a moment he relit his pipe and blew a stream of smoke up into the air. "I came home from my trip last week and saw you in the kitchen, talking to your mom. You're taller than she is, and I don't know when that happened."

He reached out and found her hand, squeezed it. "How're you doing, new town and all? Are you settled in? Made any new friends?"

The question surprised her. It was what she'd wanted her mother to ask. "Not so far," Suze said. "Just Dewey. You've got to see what we've built, up in the attic. I'll give you a tour tomorrow, soon as you get home."

"I'd like that," he said slowly. "But—I'll have to take a rain check. Ten days or so. The last two launches didn't go well, and I'll be out at the base for a while."

"Again?"

"I'm sorry, hon. It's important. Essential, really."

"Just like the Hill." Suze could hear the disappointment in her voice as the magic of the sands and the sunset and her dad's company faded into the reality of his day-to-day life.

"It is, in a lot of ways. We're in a race again. You wouldn't want the first man in space to be a Russian, would you?"

"I guess not," Suze said, although she didn't know what difference it'd make. "But Mom says we have to be one world now, or there'll be another war."

"Your mother," he started, his voice tense. He paused, took a breath. "Your mother and I disagree. Look back at history—three, four, five thousand years. Exploration and war have always gone hand in hand. It's human nature. It's inevitable. So we *have* to have the best weapons, to defend ourselves. You're old enough to understand that, aren't you?"

Suze nodded and hugged her arms to her chest, not sure if she was cold on the outside. They sat in silence for a long time as the last wisps of color faded from the sky and the stars began to appear, one by one. When they stood up to walk back to the car, all she could see was gray—pale gray sand and blue-gray sky, like walking through a faded newspaper photo whose edges flickered with lightning.

TOMORROW'S
CHILDREN

MINORITY REPORT

Suze hoped the end of August really would be the last of monsoon season. It sounded more like jungle than desert to her, but that was what people called the summer months in Alamogordo. Hard rain, most afternoons, thunderclouds massing behind the mountains for hours before drenching the town for fifteen minutes, then moving out over the desert. Two months, and she was tired of it.

The air in the attic was hot and still, even with the windows open. Her bra chafed under her arms. She had started wearing one a year ago, when she got her period and—wham!—her whole body had changed. When she put it on in the morning, she felt trapped by all the straps and hooks. It was worse in the heat, but *Seventeen* said that girls—even eighth-graders— should also wear foundation garments, girdles, every day, because they'd look and feel *so* much better. Hah. There was no way Suze was ever going to wear that much underwear.

She reached around to rub at the sore place and knocked over the bottle of model cement. The fumes made her dizzy. She turned on the big fan over the window, but hadn't anchored one pile of cut-out paper and lost a nice Coke ad to the blades, rough-shredded confetti drifting out onto the driveway.

Suze tucked a can of paint and a brush into the wooden box she was working on, and moved out onto the drawbridge over the moat. That was what she and Dewey called the four wide, rough planks that crossed the irrigation ditch in front of the house, a walkway from the dirt street to the cement sidewalk. Nobody cared if she spilled a little paint there.

The ditch was about two feet across and two feet deep, a narrow channel that surrounded the entire block. During a thunderstorm, it filled within minutes, becoming a small, roaring river that disappeared back into the porous sand and the roots of the thirsty cottonwood trees when the rain stopped. Every block on their side of Tenth Street was lined with ditches and the huge trees, taller than the houses. Spreading canopies offered cooling shade and gave the town its name—*álamo gordo*, fat cottonwood. Suze wondered how many Alamo places she was going to live.

Dewey'd come back from the library and was at the end of their block, down in the ditch, looking for black sand. After each rain, the bottom always had a few long, dark streaks. Dewey thought they might be iron, washed down from the mountains, and wanted to collect enough to test with a magnet.

She walked with her head down, an empty jar in one hand, the curved glass winking in the sun.

Suze looked up at the clouds. It'd be an hour before the rain drove them back inside. She sat on the planks, her bare feet dangling, and dipped her brush in the can of midnight-blue paint. It went on smoothly, because this was the third coat. The cheap cigar-box wood had absorbed the first two as greedily as cottonwood roots. The newsstand had a really nice varnished box, but she had to wait for it to be empty. That could take a while. Men in Alamogordo only smoked fifty-cent cigars for weddings, or when babies were born.

Dewey had found a box of quarter-sized brass gears and given Suze the busted ones. She'd snapped off more teeth with the pliers, and now they looked like the Indian sun on the New Mexico flag. She held one near the blue box, squinting at it, imagining what it would look like painted bright yellow. To her left, she heard the clicks of a bicycle wheel, regular, but very slow.

She looked up to see three Mexican kids wheeling an old girl's bike down the street. Patches of rust covered the red paint and the faded word ROLLFAST slanted across the frame. The girl, about Suze's age, wore her thick dark hair in a long braid, like Carmelita Martinez, the woman from San Ildefonso Pueblo who'd cleaned their apartment on the Hill. She pushed the handlebars, and a little boy, about six, held on to the wire bike basket. His other hand gripped the striped T-shirt of the toddler beside him. The basket was full of small brown paper bags.

The girl stopped at the end of the bridge. She was almost as short as Dewey, with a round face and dark eyes, her blue jeans rolled up to midcalf. The tails of her sleeveless white shirt were tied at her waist. "Tamales?" she asked.

Suze was suddenly hungry. Whatever was in the bags smelled wonderful. Her mother was giving a lecture and wouldn't be back until late, so it was her turn to make dinner. If she bought food, she wouldn't have to use the stove. She tried to remember how to say "How much?" in Spanish. "Um— *¿Cuándo es, por favor?*"

"Three-thirty, quarter of four?" the girl said, chuckling. "But nice try."

"Huh?"

"*Cuándo* is 'when.' You meant *cuánto*. They're ten cents. A buck a dozen."

"You speak English."

"Well, yeah. I'm American. *¿Tú comprendes? Norteamericana?*"

"Sorry," Suze said. "I mean, I just thought . . ." She let her sentence trail off and could feel her face turning red. Not just from the sun.

"Yeah. I know. You want some?" She gestured at the bags of tamales. "They're cheese and green chile, 'cause it's Friday."

"Huh?" Suze said again.

"Friday. No meat. You're not from around here, are you?"

Suze shook her head. "We moved the beginning of May, from—" She hesitated. Too many times this summer, when she'd said Los Alamos, people looked at her weird, because of the Bomb, like *she* might blow them up without warning. The checkout guy at the grocery made jokes and asked if she glowed in the dark. "From up north," she finished.

"What, like Canada?"

"Not that far. My folks worked near Santa Fe during the war. You?"

"I was born here. My dad's family's been here four hundred years. *Los Conquistadores.*" She gave the *r* a rolling, dramatic trill. "But that's nothing. My mom's half Apache, and *they've* been here forever."

"You're part Indian?"

"Geronimo was my grandfather's cousin."

"The parachute guy?" Suze asked. She spread out her arms and mimed jumping into the ditch. "Geronimo-ohhhh!"

The girl rolled her eyes. "Yeah, him. And no, I don't know why they say it."

Suze guessed Geronimo jokes were about as funny as Bomb jokes. "Sorry."

"S'okay." She rebalanced the bike. "So. Tamales?"

"I've never had any."

"Try one." She handed Suze a thick, pale-orange bundle.

"Jeez, that smells great." She bit into the end, but it was covered in something stiff and crinkly that tasted a little spicy, and didn't tear under her teeth.

The girl smiled, trying not to laugh. "O-kay. *My* people only eat what's *inside* the corn husk. But if you—"

The older boy giggled.

"Now, now, Tony," the girl said. "It is important to educate people from other cultures." She said it in a teacher voice, then winked, so Suze would know she was kidding. "That's just the wrapper. Peel it and eat it like a Snickers bar."

Suze nodded. Inside the husk was a dense, moist oblong of cornmeal. When she took a bite, melted cheese and piquant, vinegary chiles oozed from the end. "Wow," she said, finishing it in four quick bites. "I'll take a dozen. Hold on."

When she came back with a dollar bill, the older boy held the handlebars of the bike. The girl stood over the painted box, a curious expression on her face. "How come a *gringa* like you is making a *nicho*?" She handed Suze the sack of tamales, the brown paper speckled with translucent spots of grease.

"A *what*?"

"The box. We've got 'em all over our house. My grandma takes them to El Paso to sell to tourists. Hers are mostly full of saints and Jesus. I like your clowns."

"There's a *name* for them?" Suze stared at the box and the brass gears and the cut-out pictures of circus acts she'd shellacked. She'd never thought about what to call the pieces she made, or known anyone else who did.

The girl nodded. "*Los nichos.* Little cupboards. Doña Luisa's have doors and everything. Come over sometime, I'll show you."

"Okay. Uh— *¿Dónde está su casa?*"

"*En Chihuahuita*—Little Chihuahua, where else?" She made a face. "Only palefaces like you can live north of Tenth."

"You're kidding."

"Wow. You're *not* from around here. It's a law. My people aren't allowed to buy on this side." She shook her head. "I live at Sixth and Maryland. Red roof, big porch. If you help roll tamales, we'll work on your accent."

Paper rattled behind her and she turned. "Raymundo! No!" The toddler stood on tiptoe, trying to pull one of the sacks out of the basket. She swooped him up and planted him on her hip in one practiced motion. "My brother Frank's got football practice, so my turn to babysit."

"How many kids in your family?"

"I got three brothers and a sister. This little guy's really my cousin. His mom's only sixteen, and his dad's in jail, so we adopted him." She pulled the end of her braid out of his mouth. "How 'bout you?"

"I'm an only—" Suze stopped when she heard Dewey yell, "I got some! Hey, Suze—I got some!" She reappeared at the corner of the ditch, mayonnaise jar tucked under her arm, and clambered up into a neighbor's yard.

"You're Suze?" the girl asked.

"Suze Gordon."

"Ynez Esquero. The kid with the glasses, she your little sister?"

Suze sighed. She was sick and tired of trying to explain Dewey. It would only get worse when school started. "Not exactly. She lives with us, but we aren't related. She's kind of a war orphan."

"Is she foreign?"

"Nah," Suze said, watching Dewey approach. "Just a little strange."

THE SQUARE PEGS

Three days later, Dewey sat at the kitchen table, her chin resting in her hands. Some purple mimeographed papers lay off to one side; a physics book, a slide rule, and a pile of scrap paper were in front of her. The top sheet was covered with numbers and symbols, many of them crossed out or scribbled over, and a row of crumpled paper balls lay on the seat of the chair to her left.

One very tightly wadded ball lay on the linoleum below the sink, where she had thrown it in frustration a minute before.

She wanted to talk to Papa. She missed him at odd moments, like yesterday in the drugstore, when she saw a display of Brylcreem and was surprised by the stinging at the back of her eyes. She'd been missing him half her life. But this time he was really gone, and there were never going to be any more letters with codes to break, or surprise packages on her birthday.

And, hardest of all, right now, he would never be able to

answer her questions, like he had most nights after dinner on the Hill. He'd sit down with a glass of whiskey and unwind a problem into smaller steps, drawing pictures and explaining, in his soft, calm voice, until he was sure she understood.

She stared at the textbook in front of her, at the Greek letters and the diagrams, the blocks of text that were supposed to explain what they meant, but didn't. She had hoped that when school started next week, there'd be teachers to talk to, the kind who didn't mind girls who asked a lot of questions.

It wasn't looking good.

She heard a crunch of gravel in the alley at the back of the house, then the metallic thunk of the car door. Dewey got up to take a break from the equations that were making her head hurt.

"Hey, kiddo," Terry Gordon said. "Just in time." She opened the trunk of the old black Chevy. "Grab the beer and the Orange Crush. I'll get the grocery sacks."

Dewey slid her fingers through the handles of the six-packs of brown bottles, one in each hand. She opened the screen door with the side of her foot, and put the beer down on the counter to open the heavy refrigerator door.

"Anything else go in here?" She put the drinks onto the bottom shelf. The sunny kitchen was familiar, after four months, and everything had a place—bread in the breadbox, cans in the cupboard, silverware in the drawer by the sink. It felt like home.

"Just about everything except the soup. It's too hot to even think about serving, but it was on sale. Twelve cans for a dollar." She handed Dewey a jar of mayonnaise and a carton of eggs. "There's fried chicken left over from last night, so if I make a batch of potato salad, we can eat out on the porch."

"The thermometer at the hardware store said it's a hundred and one."

"Jesus. What a place." Mrs. Gordon handed her a bunch of celery, a melon, and a bundle wrapped in white butcher paper, then opened the cupboard below the sink to put away the cleanser.

"What's this?" she asked, picking up the ball of paper.

"Sorry," Dewey said. "I didn't mean to throw it, but I got kinda fed up."

"With what?"

"Friction and surface tension and inclined planes. I'm building three different ramps, and I want the marbles to end up at the bottom at the same time."

Terry Gordon looked over at the book on the table. "I can see why you were frustrated. That's my college textbook." She turned to the flyleaf, where *T. Weiss, 414 Schafer Hall* was written in blue ink.

"It was in the bookcase. I didn't think you'd mind if I borrowed it."

"I don't mind at all. But it's an advanced text, not easy reading, even with a professor and lectures. *I'd* never have been able to figure it out on my own." She lit a cigarette. "Help me skin the spuds, and I'll see what I can do. I may be a little rusty, but we can get a handle on the basics."

"Thanks." Dewey opened a drawer and got the peeler.

They sat at the corner of the table, the kitchen trash can between their knees, rough brown skins curling onto the wilting lettuce from lunch. "Is Dr. Gordon coming home for dinner?" Dewey asked. They'd had another launch Thursday, and he might not have much to do at the proving grounds for a week or two.

"I think so. He's just out at the airfield today, running calculations, but I never know. At least chicken and salad will keep."

"It's just like the Hill." Dewey reached for another potato. "Working late and not even coming home some nights. Most nights."

"At least *he's* got a lab to go to."

"I thought you didn't want to be part of the rocket program."

"I don't. And it's a stag party anyway. But I want to be doing my own work. The field's changing so fast. I'd like to get my hands on some of the radioisotope studies they've started using with cancer patients."

"Can't you get a job here?"

"Doing *what*, kiddo? Waitressing in the café? Bagging groceries?" She smacked her knife down on the table with a force that startled Dewey. "I've got a doctorate in nuclear chemistry, and all I'm doing is typing letters nobody reads and lecturing to bored housewives about horrors they really don't want to hear. Christ on a crutch." She lit another cigarette with an angry snap of her Zippo.

Dewey looked down at the potato in her hands. "I'm sorry."

"Don't be. It was my choice. Phil badgered me for months, even before the war ended. 'The V-2s are the beginning of a brand-new era, Terry. Just one more sabbatical year, Terry?' I gave in. That's what marriage is all about, compromise."

"I guess."

Terry sighed. "Look, I didn't expect the Welcome Wagon to show up at the door with flowers, but we've been here since May, and I don't have a single friend. There are women who avoid me in the goddamn supermarket line because of what I helped create—or destroy."

"How do they know?"

"News travels fast in a small town. I just had no idea *how* small."

"The Hill wasn't much bigger."

"No, but that's not the point. Phil's got a whole crew of guys just like him, and I'm starving for someone who has a clue what I do. When the war ended and the whole gang split up to go back to 'real life'"—she made quote marks with her fingers—"I hardly managed to say good-bye. I was still reeling from what we'd done. Ironic, if those turn out to be the best years of our lives."

Dewey thought of Papa. "I sure hope not," she said.

SURFACE TENSION

They peeled the rest of the potatoes in silence. When the pot was simmering on the stove, Terry Gordon opened the refrigerator and pulled out two bottles of Orange Crush. She held one to the side of her face. "Not very cold yet, I'm afraid. They say the new postwar fridges are going to have built-in freezing compartments. How handy would that be? Ice cubes, anytime I want, right in my own kitchen." She popped the caps off the bottles. "Let's take a look at friction."

Dewey positioned the thick textbook between them. "Okay," she said. "I got as far as this paragraph on the angle of repose—"

Half an hour later, she had two pages of neatly printed equations, interspersed with notes and a few diagrams. She felt good, the way she always did when the lightbulb came on, and she could move ahead with what she was building. She could hardly wait to go upstairs to the Wall and try it out.

"You're a very good teacher." *Almost as good as Papa,* she started to say, but decided that was rude. She tucked the papers into the book and stood up. "What time do you want to eat? If you don't need any more help, I'll go do some *applied* science." She grinned.

"About seven." Terry looked at her watch. "It's just five now. Where's Suze?"

"It's Tuesday, so after we left the school, she was going to Rolland's to see if the new *Superman* was in. Then to Safeway to check for empty fruit crates. They've got good labels."

"Oh, school. Right. How did registration go?"

In the pleasure of figuring out the physics, Dewey had almost forgotten. "Fine," she said. But even she could hear the lie in her voice.

"Dewey?" Mrs. Gordon raised an eyebrow.

Dewey looked at the mimeographed pages on the kitchen table, wishing that her glance could light them on fire, like Superman's heat vision. It wouldn't solve anything, but it would feel good. She sat down again.

"It sucked eggs, Terry."

"How come?"

"Well, the register lady looked at me and tried to give me directions to the elementary school. She said it slow, like it was a spelling word—*el-eh-men-ter-ee*—'cause if I'd been standing in the wrong line for half an hour, I was probably too stupid to know a five-syllable word, right?"

"I know the type."

"So I told her I'd be fourteen on December twelfth, and that I was going to be in eighth grade, thank you very much, Mrs. Birdbrain." She paused. "I was a little more polite than that."

"I'm sure you were. Admirable, under the circumstances. I might not have had such restraint."

"I thought about it." Dewey nodded. "Then it went a little better. I got English and Social Science and Biology. That may be interesting. I haven't done much with organic materials."

"Sounds reasonable so far."

"It was, until I signed up for Trigonometry. The lady said no. *Eighth*-graders have to take Algebra." She took a long pull on her soda. "I told her I'd already done that, and she wiggled her finger at me like one of Nana's Church Ladies." Dewey pitched her voice into a singsong. "'Now, now. Don't get ahead of yourself, dear.'"

"Maybe the math teacher will have more sense, once class starts."

"I hope so," Dewey said, although she doubted it. "Then I signed up for Mechanical Drawing in the morning, and Shop in the afternoon. It's mostly wood shop, but I figured they'd have machines and tools. I really need to learn to solder."

"Sounds great." Terry Gordon lit a Chesterfield.

"Yeah. Those were the classes I was most looking forward to." She sighed, a sigh so deep it felt like it might go all the way to tears.

"But?"

"But *I* don't get to choose. The lady took a pencil and drew a big red **X** through both classes." Dewey pitched her voice again. "'Oh, *no*. Those are *boys'* classes. We'll put you in the afternoon section of Home Economics. The eighth-grade girls are going to learn to sew. Won't *that* be fun?'" Dewey shook her head.

"Oh, dear," Mrs. Gordon said. Her eyes were sympathetic, but Dewey could also see that she was trying not to laugh.

"It's not funny."

"I know. Really. I had those conversations every semester, even in grad school. What amuses me is—Did Suze have to sign up for Home Ec, too?"

"Yeah. That's the only good thing about it."

"And you think my darling daughter will be thrilled by the domestic arts?"

"Even less than me." Dewey smiled. "At least I can cook. And if something goes haywire, I may get to take one of the sewing machines apart." She drank more soda. "But it still pisses me off. How'm I going to get into MIT—any engineering school—if I can't even take Shop?"

"Want me to talk to the principal? We could fight it."

Dewey thought for a long time before she answered. "I'd like to," she said finally. "But I'm not sure it's worth it."

"Don't be afraid to make waves, kiddo. It's the only way those things will ever change."

"I know. But . . ." She paused. "But I really don't want anybody paying extra attention to me."

"How come?"

"What if some Church Lady type found out I'm not related to you? And thought it was her job to let the authorities know? They might take me away," she said in a small voice.

"That's a lot of ifs, kiddo." Mrs. Gordon shook her head. "Truth is, lots of families were shaken up by the war. You're not the only girl who lost her father."

"True."

"So no one's going to think twice. You live with responsible adults. You're clothed and fed, you're smart as a whip, and you're not a truant or a vandal or any other kind of troublemaker."

"Unless I put up a fight about Shop class."

"Damn." Terry Gordon let out an exasperated sigh and lit another cigarette. "I see your point. Less chance of busybodies sticking their noses in if you lay low." She nodded slowly. "You're right. That does suck eggs."

"Yeah, and that's not all." Dewey pointed to the mimeographed sheets. "The lady said my *parents* have to sign these forms."

"Not a problem." She patted Dewey's hand. "I can do that."

"Our last names aren't the same."

"God, you *are* detail-oriented, aren't you?" She chuckled. "Don't worry, I'll do my in-a-hurry scrawl. No one can read it, and Gordon has an *n* on the end, same as Kerrigan."

"I guess so." She drained the last of her Orange Crush. "Oh. I also said Dewey was my real legal name. If teachers call me Duodecima the first day of school, no one ever forgets."

"Gotcha. Give me the papers."

Dewey hesitated, then pushed them across the table.

Mrs. Gordon uncapped her pen. "I hate to admit it, but you may be right about making waves. Best to get the lay of the land first. But if you do want to fight, count me in. I won't let *any*one take you away, Dewey Kerrigan. That's a promise."

Dewey took a deep breath. She'd wanted to ask this question for a long time, but had always stopped herself. Maybe now was . . . ? "Would you and Dr. Gordon adopt me, for real, if you could?" she asked in a whisper.

"In a New York minute, kiddo." She scribbled something that might have been a name at each **X**. "There," she said. "Signed, sealed, and delivered. It may not be strictly legit, but from now on, in the eyes of the state of New Mexico, consider me your mother."

"Really?"

"Really." Terry Gordon put an arm around her and kissed her on the cheek.

Dewey smiled, then froze. Out of the corner of her eye, she saw Suze standing just inside the front door, her body stiff, her mouth tight and narrow.

HELPING HAND

Dewey sat on the top step of the front porch Thursday afternoon, keeping out of Suze's way and pouring sand onto a pane of glass laid across two bricks. She moved a magnet beneath it, and some black particles followed its path. They *were* iron! She was so intent that she didn't hear steps on the walk, didn't look up until a shadow darkened the sand pile.

"What're you doing?" the tamale girl asked. "School hasn't even started."

"Separating out the ferrous particles." Dewey moved the tiny black pile to the edge of the glass.

"Right. Is—uh—is the girl who makes the boxes around?"

"Upstairs, gluing mountains to the Wall. Hold on." Dewey pushed the black sand into a baby-food jar and screwed the lid on. "C'mon in."

"Wow. Big house. You've got an upstairs and everything."

"Two. There's an attic."

"Snazzy."

Dewey climbed up to the landing. "Hey!" she yelled. "That tamale girl's here." She shrugged in apology. "Sorry. I want to rig up an intercom. Yelling drives Ter—Suze's mom—crazy. But the salvage guy hasn't found one yet."

"What!?" Suze rounded the corner of the landing, taking the stairs two at a time. Then she saw them. "Hey—Ynez. What's up?"

"It's time to make more tamales. But my mom's working an extra shift at the bottling plant. It's soda weather," she explained. "Come help, and my grandma'll tell you about building *nichos*."

"Sounds good. What kind? Mom's in Las Cruces—some ladies club—so I've got dinner again."

"Chicken."

"Wow. How'd you get *that*? Yesterday, the Piggly Wiggly's butcher only had hot dogs and bologna, 'cause of the meat shortage."

"We killed one from our yard."

"Ugh."

"Yeah, but *we've* got chicken. You have a bike?"

"Out back."

"Good. You're too big for us to ride double."

Dewey watched Suze's face change. She hated being teased about how tall she was. But Ynez just stood there, and after a moment, Suze smiled.

"True. My legs are *way* too long for your shrimpy bike, *camarón*."

"Your vocabulary is improving," Ynez said. "Let's ride."

Dewey had just piled more sand on the glass when Suze and Ynez came around the corner of the house, rattled over the wooden bridge, and took off down the street, each girl standing on her pedals, legs pumping.

She picked up the magnet and smiled. The house would be quiet and peaceful all afternoon.

Michigan Avenue didn't cross Tenth Street. On the other side, and a little catty-corner, it turned into Delaware, and the sidewalks vanished. The houses in "Little Chihuahua" were smaller, all one story, and there weren't as many trees. Most front yards were dirt with patchy grass and some cactuses.

Ynez lived in an adobe house the color of cinnamon toast. The grass grew right up to a cement porch as wide as the house. Two pine poles at the corners supported the overhanging roof, the red tile half-rounds overlapping like fish scales.

The roofline of the house echoed the shapes of the mountains a mile to the east. It reminded Suze of the pueblo buildings up north. Arched windows were set deep into the walls. The two girls propped their bikes against the porch supports, and Ynez opened the front door into a small living room.

"Just me," she called.

Inside, the house was dim and cool. It smelled like furniture polish and something sweet and spicy. A couch and two armchairs circled a cabinet radio, and a long table ran along the outside wall. Framed photos and candles covered its surface; a crucifix and a painting of the Virgin Mary hung between two windows.

"This way," Ynez said. A narrow hallway led to the back of the house. "The boys sleep there," she said, pointing to a door on the left. "My oldest brother's working construction in El Paso with my dad until winter. My folks' room is next to the bathroom. And this is mine," she said, pushing on a half-open door. "My sister Gloria got married last month, so it's just me and my grandma."

The room was about the size of Suze's bedroom on the Hill. That had seemed crowded, just sharing with Dewey. She looked at the two twin beds, a nightstand on either side, and wondered where Ynez's sister had slept.

"It got pretty tight," she said, as if reading Suze's mind. "Gloria's a slob."

The stand nearest the window held a framed photograph of a dark-haired man, and a painted box with pictures of women with haloes. Its two hinged doors were studded with tiny flat metal objects—sunbursts and tools and animals. A candle in a red glass holder flickered in front of it.

The wall beside the door was covered with magazine pictures of movie stars. Suze didn't recognize most of them. Damn. Was Ynez going to be like the girls on the Hill, all gaga over movies? She didn't seem that way, but . . .

Suze was surprised how disappointed she felt. She'd never been very good at making friends with other girls. Dewey had just happened. She sighed, soft, so it'd sound like she was only breathing. *Oh, well.* If Ynez got squealy and girly, she'd take some tamales and go home.

"Suze Gordon, meet Dolores del Rio, Cesar Romero, Maria Montez, Ramón Navarro, and Margarita Carmen Cansino." Ynez swept her arm at a picture that Suze *did* recognize.

"Yeah, right. You can't fool me. That's Rita Hayworth."

"It is now. The studio changed her name."

"Oh. So who's *that?*" Suze pointed at Ynez's nightstand. A black ribbon looped around a photograph in a cardboard frame, and a candle cast flickering shadows across the face of a pretty, dark-eyed woman.

"Lupe Vélez," Ynez said in the quietest voice Suze had heard her use so far. "She was married to the man who plays Tarzan. She's my hero."

"Oh. Okay." Suze stopped herself from rolling her eyes, because it was rude to make fun of someone's hero, no matter who it was.

Ynez looked at her. "Don't get the wrong idea. I'm not one of those goony girls who thinks movie stars are *dreamy.*"

Jeez. Maybe she can *read minds.* "Then why—?"

"I'm going to Hollywood someday."

"You want to be an actress?"

"Nah. I don't have that kind of looks. I just want to get out of *here*. I figure I can get a job doing hair or makeup—whatever they'll hire a Mexican girl for."

"Oh. Okay."

"That's just to start. One day—*Screenplay by Ynez Esquero*." She spread her hands out dramatically. "And *I* won't change my name."

"You want to *write* for the movies?" Suze was relieved. "What kind of stories?"

Ynez shrugged. "Ordinary life. Like my family. We're not outlaws or drunks or the Mexican Spitfire Lupe had to play." She straightened the ribbon around the picture. "C'mon. Time to meet my grandmother."

"Does she speak English?" Suze asked as they left the bedroom.

"When she wants to."

"What should I call her?"

"Señora Trujillo, for starters. If she likes you, you can call her Doña Luisa. Play it by ear."

The kitchen was the biggest room in the house. Two windows, white curtains with bright red cherries, flanked a screen door. The backyard was mostly dirt, surrounded by a low wooden fence, with a chicken coop in the far corner. Half a dozen hens and a rooster clucked and scraped at a scatter of dried corn.

Here, the spice smells were much stronger and a pot of

chicken broth bubbled on the stove, steaming up the window. A short, plump woman in an apron, her bun of dark hair shot with silver, sat at a big round table covered with corn husks and a bowl of shredded chicken. She sliced a scorched chile pepper in half with a paring knife, pulled the seeds out with her fingers, and chopped it into a mound of tiny green squares.

She added them to the bowl of chicken, then looked up and said something to Ynez in Spanish so fast and run together that the only words Suze caught were *amiga* and *nichos.*

"Abuela, this is Suze," Ynez said. She kissed her grandmother on the cheek. "Be nice to her." It almost sounded like a threat, but the older woman smiled.

Ynez looked at Suze. "You're on."

"Um—*Buenos días, Señora Trujillo*," Suze said. "Oops. *Buenos* tardes."

"*Sí.* You make tamales before?"

"Nope. I mean, no ma'am," Suze said quickly. "But the ones last week tasted great."

"*Gracias.* Sit." She turned to her granddaughter. "Ynez, make one for your friend. Show her." She smiled at Suze. "We'll see if she is as good with her fingers as she is with her tongue."

Ynez picked up a corn husk, laid it on her palm, then used a spatula to smear two thirds of it with what looked like very pale peanut butter, covering all but one edge and the bottom. "This is masa," she said. "Corn meal and spiced-up chicken broth. The meat goes on top, then we roll 'em and steam 'em." She laid that one down on the table and picked up another husk, repeating the process. "You wanna try?"

"Sure," Suze said. It looked simple enough. But the first corn husk was slippery, and softer than it looked. It ripped when she picked it up. "Sorry."

"S'okay. It takes practice. Here." Ynez laid another across Suze's open palm. It felt like a damp, scratchy washcloth.

Suze stuck the spatula into the bowl of masa. It was thicker than it looked, and not easy to spread. When she pushed harder, the second corn husk ripped.

"Crap," she said. *Oh, no. I said a bad word in front of her grandmother?!* Suze slapped her hand to her mouth, automatically.

The hand with a sticky, not-yet tamale on it.

Señora Trujillo looked at her for a long moment, long enough that Suze wanted to sink through the floor and disappear.

"I make tamales for forty years," the old woman said. "And a *gringa* teaches me a new trick?" She shook her head, then picked up a corn husk that Ynez had prepared, laid it on her palm, and slapped it onto her own mouth, like a clown with a cream pie.

She sat very still for a moment, straight and dignified, then she started to chuckle. A moment later she was laughing so hard that bits of masa flew onto the table. Ynez stared, and Suze felt her shoulders relax.

She and the old woman peeled the corn husks from their

faces, pale yellow clumps clinging to their chins like bad monster masks, which made them all laugh harder. It was ten minutes before they got back to work.

For the rest of the afternoon, the three of them talked and drank Crystal sodas from the bottling plant as they made tamales. Ynez spread the masa, Suze added a stripe of chicken and chiles, and the old woman rolled the husks with deft fingers, standing them in the steamer until it was full.

"Now, while they are cooking, you would like to see my *nichos*?"

"Yes—uh, *sí. Sí, Señora Trujillo.*"

"So formal?" she said. "We have an old saying: *Ella que nace para tamal, del cielo le caen las hojas.* Leaves fall from the sky on the girl who is born to the tamale." She patted Suze's hand. "If that's going to happen, you might as well call me Doña Luisa."

EX MACHINA

SEPTEMBER 1946

School started the week after Labor Day. Alamogordo High was a two-story redbrick building that filled an entire block of Tenth Street. Classes were larger and more organized than they had been on the Hill, and about half the students were white, half Mexican. Some Negro families lived south of Tenth, but those kids went to the "colored school," Miss Dudley's, and it only went as far the eighth grade. They weren't allowed at Alamo High.

Dewey didn't think that was fair, but she was new here, and it had always been that way. Being only one of a hundred kids in the eighth grade suited her just fine, though, because no one paid a whole lot of attention to her. It was harder for Suze, because she was so big—the tallest kid in their grade, and one of the tallest girls in the whole school. For once, *she* was the new kid everyone noticed, and Dewey didn't mind that at all.

ELLEN KLAGES

They shared three classes—English, Social Science, and Home Economics, the last class of the afternoon. The Home Ec room was at the back of the second floor. One side had a stove, a refrigerator, and three sewing machines. On the other, five tables of four girls faced the teacher's desk.

"Girls!" Mrs. Winfield clapped her hands and raised her voice to be heard over the small chattering group by the window. "Settle down. Take your seats."

Dewey was already at her table, a copy of *Popular Science* in her lap, half hidden by the folds of her pleated skirt. Most of the girls wore sweaters and skirts, but the ones who lived on ranches outside of town had chores before school and were allowed to wear pants, so Suze did, too. It wasn't against the rules, but the town girls looked at her funny. When it got colder, Dewey figured *she* might trade her skirt for pants, but for now, she liked feeling invisible.

Three weeks into the school year, Home Ec was her least favorite class. From the window, she could see the roof of their house, four blocks away. She thought about the project on her workbench. If she could attach the wires to the bell, then it would—

Mrs. Winfield clapped her hands again. "Girls! I have a surprise."

Dewey's three tablemates sat down, Linda Benitez huffing as if she'd been asked to do Mrs. Winfield a really huge favor. Dewey turned the page of her magazine while the other girls were still rustling their clothes and papers, before the room got so quiet someone might hear.

"Now, as you're all aware," Mrs. Winfield said, "there's a dance Friday night, after the football game." A small murmur of conversation began, and she held up her hand. "I know you're excited, and that everyone's going to have a wonderful time." She smiled, as if the dance had been her own doing.

Dewey rolled her eyes and looked over to the next table, to see if Suze was rolling hers, too. But Suze was doodling, as usual. Dewey looked back at her lap and read about a new kind of spring-operated toy called a Slinky. The teacher continued.

"But in order to have the best time possible, you all need to be on your *best* behavior. Remember, good manners make good citizens." This was greeted by one table's soft but audible groan, which the teacher ignored.

"Now, in the old days, I'd have to write our dos and don'ts on the chalkboard. But some of you wouldn't pay attention." She looked at Suze. "So today I'm going to try something brand-new—using modern technology. We're going to see a *movie*, right here in the classroom."

That made everyone, even Suze, sit up. A movie—in school? The buzz of conversation grew louder as Mrs. Winfield opened the classroom door.

"Owen, you may come in now," she said into the hallway.

Dewey saw the projector first, a big machine with two large reels mounted on top. It sat on a wheeled metal cart, pushed across the squeaking wooden floor by a very tall boy in a checked shirt and blue jeans.

A ripple of giggles swept the room. A boy. In Home Ec.

The boy heard, and his freckled face reddened. He ducked his head, his sandy hair flopping over his forehead to the tops of his eyebrows.

He wheeled the cart to the back of the room, stopped a few feet from Dewey's chair, and fumbled with a coil of thick rubber cord. He stared at the projector, not looking at anyone, and fitted the cord into a socket on the machine, then crouched down to insert the plug into a wall outlet.

As soon as the prongs touched the outlet, the light on the projector came on, blindingly bright, and one of the reels began spinning, the wide tail of brown film flapping with each rotation.

The boy jumped to his feet and grabbed the reel with one hand, flipping the OFF switch with the other. "Sorry," he said, his voice so soft Dewey doubted anyone heard it except her. "Last guy musta left it on."

Mrs. Winfield made a *tsk*ing sound and taped a sheet of butcher paper to the center panel of the blackboard. She reached for the map hook, then stopped and turned. "Susan, you can reach. Pull the shades down, please."

Suze sat for a moment, then got up with a sigh. While the boy threaded the film through the sprockets, she lowered the three canvas shades and slunk back to her seat. Dewey could still see the other girls, see Mrs. Winfield at her desk with her hands folded, waiting. But there wasn't enough light to read, so she bookmarked *Popular Science* and slid it under the cover of her notebook.

A few minutes passed. Mrs. Winfield looked at the clock. The boy was still fiddling with the film, muttering under his breath a few feet from Dewey. She heard him whisper a curse word, but not one of the really bad ones.

"Owen?" Mrs. Winfield called. "Is everything all right back there?"

"Yeah, just a sec." His voice was louder, so she'd know he'd answered.

Another minute. Girls began to giggle and shuffle in their seats.

Dewey looked over at the big projector to her right.

The boy had threaded the film through the front gate, but for some reason its holes weren't engaging in the sprockets that would feed it onto the take-up reel. He cursed again, bent over the machine, his voice frustrated and annoyed. She leaned over a little, squinting in the dim light.

Then Dewey saw it. A screw that held the sprocket gate had come loose and was lying on top of the cart, pale metal shiny against the black rubber surface. She sat still for a moment. She didn't talk much in class, didn't raise her hand to answer questions about seam bindings and selvage, kept a low profile. But when the boy sighed again, she picked up the screw, nudging his arm with her hand.

"Sprocket screw came off," she whispered as low as she could. "Here."

The boy looked startled—surprised that anyone was talking to him, or that a girl in Home Ec knew the word *sprocket*? Dewey wasn't sure. But he took the screw and shook his head, blew out a little puff of air. "Ah, shoot," he said. He pulled a screwdriver out of his pocket and replaced the part with a few deft motions.

The film began to wind onto the take-up reel.

"Got it," said the boy, loud enough for everyone to hear. He flipped the ON switch and a beam of bright light, bits of dust visible in its path, bisected the dark room. A series of gray numbers in circles flashed on the white paper, followed by a title, *Junior Prom*, as orchestra music swelled from the projector's speaker.

The boy leaned against the wall. Dewey turned toward the screen.

It was a boring movie. Two boys and two girls on their way to a dance. They didn't talk like real people, Dewey thought. What kind of kids had conversations about the "proper" way to shake hands?

When THE END appeared, the projector boy rewound the film with a noisy whirr while Mrs. Winfield pulled the shades up one by one. The last one got away from her and snapped up with a loud crack against the wooden roller. *Good thing that wasn't Suze,* Dewey thought. She pulled *Popular Science* back into her lap.

"Now, what have we learned?" Mrs. Winfield asked.

Not much, Dewey thought. The boy wheeled the cart out of the room, and for the next ten minutes, girls chattered about dates and dances and walking someone home. Dewey read about a man who had built a radio cabinet right into the side of his couch. The other girls had a lot to say, and Mrs. Winfield didn't call on her before the bell rang and the school day was over.

Everyone picked up their books and binders and headed for the door. Suze came over to Dewey's table. "That was lame," she said, plopping her books down. "But better than hemming. Or ripping out more seams."

"Lame," Dewey agreed. "You heading straight home?"

"Nope. Tuesday. New comics at Rolland's."

"Okay. I think I figured out why the intercom isn't working, and I kind of want to mess with it. And listen to KPSA. Whad'ya think'll happen to the guy who hid the gold from the Lone Ranger?"

"He'll get caught, but prob'ly not till Friday. I'll be home by four." Suze slung her books under her left arm. "See ya."

Dewey took her own books to her locker. She'd finished most of her homework in study hall, and just had a few algebra problems left. Mr. Ridenour had given her an extra set, to see if she really *was* ready to take Trigonometry. Dewey hoped so. She'd already worked her way through the whole eighth-grade math book.

She tucked the purple-inked problem sheets into her binder and put *Popular Science* on top, then turned—and ran smack into the projector boy. The magazine went flying.

"Ooof. Sorry," the boy said. "I didn't—I mean—" He stopped, his face turning red. He squatted down for the magazine. "Just wanted to say thanks," he said to the floor. "You saved my bacon in there." He stood up and smiled, just the corner of his mouth tilting up a fraction.

"S'okay," Dewey said. He was so tall, she was talking to the middle of his shirt. "I guess the last guy didn't check before he put it away."

"Nope. Gilbert, the log said. He's kinda sloppy." He shook his head.

"That's not good."

"Nope."

Silence. An awkward silence. The boy looked down at his hands, and realized he was still holding the magazine.

"This *yours?*" he asked, giving it back. "What class is that?"

"It isn't," Dewey said. "I got a couple of busted intercom boxes from Pratt's last week. Just wires missing. The diagram's inside, but I can't get the leads to stay on. This had an article on two-way radios. It wasn't very useful."

"What kind of solder you using?" asked the boy. "Maybe you need a different flux?"

"I don't have a soldering iron."

"Use the school's."

"I'm a girl. I can't even go *into* that part."

"Oh." He blushed even harder and looked down at the book in his hand. "My dad has a couple in the shop," he mumbled to *Introductory Chemistry.* "You could maybe use one."

"What shop?"

"Oh. Right. I'm Owen Parker. Parker's Fix-It?"

"The one over on Fifteenth with the big Motorola sign?"

"Yeah." He looked up and smiled, a real smile this time, showing a mouthful of metal braces that glinted in the fluorescent lights. He glanced at his watch. "Shoot. I gotta go fix the switch on Mrs. Garber's toaster by dinner. But if you wanna come down . . ." He stopped, looked away, looked back at her. "Soldering iron. I owe you. For the sprocket."

Dewey looked up at his face for the first time. She smiled back.

"Thanks," she said. "Maybe I will."

REPAIR JOB

Each day the next week, Mrs. McDonald, the Social Science teacher, wrote one of Roosevelt's Four Freedoms on the board. One freedom a day. Dewey figured there'd be a quiz on Friday. But since she'd memorized all that in third grade, she only pretended to listen, doing other homework and making notes for new parts of the Wall.

On Thursday, Mrs. McDonald wrote FREEDOM OF SPEECH and turned to the class. "We are very lucky to be living in America," she said. "If we lived in a country with a dictator, our newspapers could only publish what the government wanted us to know. We couldn't—Yes, Susan? What is it *this* time?"

Dewey winced. Suze and Mrs. McDonald had been at it since the first week of class, but Suze just couldn't keep quiet.

"What about the radiation sickness that's killing people in Japan?" Suze asked. "My mom says *our* government won't let the papers print anything because it might scare people and turn them against 'our new friend, the atom.'"

"That is simply not true. The explosion was devastating, but—"

"People throw up and burn from the inside out. Their skin comes off like—"

"That is disgusting!" Mrs. McDonald slammed her hand down on her desk so hard a pile of papers spilled onto the floor. "Mr. Wolfe's office. *Now!*"

"But it is—" Dewey said.

Mrs. McDonald glared at her. "You want to keep your friend company?"

After a few seconds, Dewey shook her head. It *was* true. There'd been a whole issue of *The New Yorker* about Hiroshima, and how awful radiation sickness was. But would it help anything if she got in trouble, too? She looked at her lap as Suze left.

Suze wasn't in Home Ec, and on her way out the front door after the bell rang, Dewey saw Mrs. Gordon walk into the principal's office, wearing a dress and a hat, not the shirt and jeans she'd had on when they'd gone home for lunch. *Uh-oh.*

At home, Dewey paced around the attic, waiting for Suze to come home, so she could apologize. She should have stood up, too. Forty-five minutes later, she couldn't stand it. She had to do *some*thing. She put the intercom boxes into a grocery bag and left a note on the kitchen table. *Out. Back around 5:30—D.*

She turned right down the alley, away from downtown. It felt better to be outside. The cottonwoods arched overhead, beginning to turn yellow. The crunch of gravel under her shoes changed when she stepped over the culverts at each cross street, her footsteps hollow over the metal pipes.

Parker's Fix-It Shop was a one-story, tin-roofed concrete building behind a house at the corner of Fifteenth and Indiana, the edge of town. Only the blind school and the golf course lay beyond Sixteenth. A painted red sign ran across the top of the whitewashed wall, and the wide wooden door stood open.

She stopped just beyond the corner of the building, feeling awkward, as if she were walking, uninvited, into someone's house. It wasn't like the Hill. There, she'd asked anyone for help, army or civilian. They were all in it together, to win the war. But now . . . ?

Dewey hoped the tall boy—Owen, his name was Owen—would remember that he'd said she could come by. A long metal sign hung above the door, like an old friend, familiar yellow script on a black background: MOTOROLA RADIOS. She took a deep breath and walked into the shop.

A wooden counter with a cash register and a display of vacuum tubes divided customer from repairman. Half the counter came up to Dewey's shoulders, and half was only waist high. Probably so people with really heavy things—cabinet radios and record players—wouldn't have to lift them up.

Behind the counter was a shelf of household machines—

fans, radios, kitchen clocks, an electric mixer—each with a stiff paper tag, customers' names in bold black ink. Beyond that, workbenches and tables held parts and repairs in progress. Hundreds of drawers, some a few inches square, others as big as a breadbox, covered one wall.

It was Dewey's kind of place.

Owen sat in front of a high workbench, hunched over a complicated array of tubes and wires, a printed diagram propped in front of him. She saw his lips move, as if he were reading not quite out loud. Dewey smiled, because she did that too, when she was trying to match a picture in a book with an object in real life, walking herself through, step-by-step.

"Hey," she said.

He jerked his head up, his finger still in place on the diagram. He looked confused, then nodded. "Amazing Sprocket Girl," he said, then closed his eyes, tight, as if that had been *such* a wrong thing to say.

"Shazam," Dewey replied. It just popped out.

They looked at each other for a long second, then smiled.

"I've never had a superhero name before," Dewey said.

"How many people have you rescued?"

"Just you, so far."

"See." He marked a tiny, precise X on the diagram and stood up. Unfolded, it seemed to Dewey. "What'cha got?"

Dewey set the two oak boxes on the counter. "Intercom."

"Samson Pair Phones," he said. "They're old, but they

oughta work." He turned one so the open back faced him, tubes and wires exposed. "Speaker wire's not connected, that's all."

"Yeah. I *know* that." Dewey tapped the speaker cone in the second box. "I need to solder the contact, and you said you had an iron I could use?"

"Right. Right." He tapped his head with his knuckles. "Get a brain, Parker," he muttered, and lifted the hinged edge of the low counter. "C'mon back." He opened a flat drawer and held up an iron with a dangling cord. "Done this before?"

Dewey shook her head. "I've read about it, but never had a chance to try."

"Today's the day." He plugged the cord into a wall outlet above the table. "Couple minutes to heat up."

"Nice setup," Dewey said as she climbed onto a metal stool. Her feet dangled an inch or two above the crossbar. Owen pulled another over; the tip of his sneaker grazed the floor when he sat down.

"It's coming along. We'll have to add a bench when we start servicing televisions. New components."

"There aren't any televisions, yet."

"Are you kidding? In New York you can buy one right now!"

"Seriously?"

"Yeah. Broadcasting in Los Angeles, too. El Paso can't be far behind. Parkers'll be *the* fix-it shop soon."

"You know how?" Dewey's eyes widened.

"Not yet. But there's this course—hold on." He jumped off the stool and sprinted to a pile of repair manuals and magazines, opening one to a dog-eared page. "See." He held out an issue of *Popular Mechanics*.

Dewey read the headline: BUILD A TELEVISION SET IN YOUR OWN HOME. "I've seen that," she said.

"Well, Pop lets me keep the receipts for anything I fix myself, minus parts. I'll have enough saved by summer." He touched a finger to the tip of the soldering iron. "Just about ready. I'll grab something you can practice on."

Dewey looked around. Half the workbenches and tables were low, but the rest were chest high, like the lab tables at school. She could see pale rectangles farther up on two walls, as if everything had been moved down a few feet. Even *she* could reach most of the shelves without standing on a step stool. She liked that idea.

At the back of the room, she recognized a lathe and a drill press from her visits to the Hill's machine shop. "Do you make your own parts?"

"Not yet. That's Pop's department. Custom jobs, and things that still aren't back in production." He laid a postcard-sized sheet of copper and a dozen snippets of wire on the table. "I'll do one, talk you through it, then you try a few." He patted the intercom box. "Don't want to wreck this baby."

Owen's movements were skilled and precise. He showed her how to wipe the tip of the iron on a damp sponge for a clean

ELLEN KLAGES

contact, how to heat the wires first, then gently touch the solder to them. He told her what to watch for—the silver gleam as the lead-and-tin mix melted, the wisp of smoke when the contact was made—then handed her the iron.

On her first try, the wire didn't get hot enough and pulled away. He gave her more advice and the second held—with a huge blob of solder.

"You got it!" he said after her third attempt. "One more like that and you can do the real McCoy. Wow. Took me half a spool of wire to get one that nice."

"Thanks." Dewey felt good. She was finally getting to solder, and she was pleased by the compliment. She attached one more wire to the copper plate, the electric iron starting to feel familiar in her hand. "Okay," she said, turning the first oak box over. "Let's do this."

The second speaker connection was cooling when a man's voice called through a door at the back of the shop. "Owen? Time to start supper."

"Be right in," Owen shouted back. He turned to Dewey. "I gotta go."

"Okay. You can cook, huh?"

"Yep. Learned during the war. Pop was gone and Mom worked all day. Now I just do Thursdays. It's her late night. She's Mr. Mobley's secretary. The lawyer?" Owen unplugged the soldering iron and put it into a wire stand.

Dewey nodded. "What're you making?"

"Mac and cheese with wieners. It's easy, and Betsy'll eat it. My little sister," he explained. "She's five, and kinda picky." He pointed to the two intercoms, long wires trailing from their backs. "You want a carton?"

"The sack's easier for me to carry," Dewey said. "Got a rubber band? I'll coil the wire and tuck it inside the chassis."

"Copacetic."

Dewey packed up the oak boxes while Owen turned off the shop lights. He flipped the OPEN sign to CLOSED and shut the door behind them.

The sun was setting on the other side of the desert, an orange sliver barely visible between the trees and houses. The whitewashed walls of the shop glowed a warm, pale gold.

"Thanks—Owen," said Dewey. "That was fun."

He nodded. "Come back. Bring some other junk."

"Okay, I've got a—"

"Owen!" The man's voice came from the house, sharper and more insistent than the first time.

"*Gotta* go," Owen said. "Pop only fires one warning shot." He turned toward the house, stopped, looked back.

"Amazing Sprocket Girl—you got a real name?"

"I'm Dewey," she said, and turned down the alley toward home.

BREAKING POINT

Suze was setting the table for dinner when Dewey walked in the back door.

"You okay? What happened when—?" she asked.

"Later." Suze put a finger to her lips. "Dad doesn't know."

The meal was quiet. Dr. Gordon talked about firing mechanisms and azimuths and didn't notice that no one else said much. The girls headed upstairs as soon as the dishes were done.

"Why didn't you say something?" Suze dropped onto the couch. "You read that *New Yorker* piece, too."

"I know. I'm sorry." Dewey sat next to her. "I chickened out. But what if they'd looked in my file and tried to call *my* mom?"

"They'd get mine." Suze was quiet for a minute. "That would've been tough to explain."

"A whole 'nother can of worms." Dewey nodded. "So what *did* happen?"

"I'm not sure. I sat by the secretary's desk forever. Then, all of a sudden, there was Mom, dressed up in her talk-to-the-ladies lecture clothes. I figured I was done for." Suze shook her head. "But when Mr. Wolfe came out and said, 'Come in, Mrs. Gordon,' Mom stood up and said, 'It's *Doctor* Gordon.' You know that voice. Like she was going to lecture *him*. Then they shut the door."

"Could you hear anything?"

"Just sounds. Not words. I've got two days' detention with McDonald, but Mom bought me a cherry Coke on the way home."

"What?"

"Yeah. For paying attention and not being afraid to tell the truth."

"She didn't yell?"

"Not really. She said I should keep my head down and learn to pick my battles." Suze shrugged. "I think that means I should shut up unless it's *really* worth the trouble." She looked over at Dewey. "Is that why you didn't . . . ?"

"Pretty much," she said.

The sun woke Dewey a little after eight on Saturday morning. Suze was still asleep, a motionless lump under the covers of the other bed. She liked to sack in.

Dewey put her feet down for her slippers and took her glasses from the nightstand. Automatic gestures. But when she slid them on, she felt a soft *crack*, and held a piece in each hand.

She ran a finger over the broken edges and swore under her breath. The metal frames had broken in two, and she couldn't see for beans. She could read, close up, but the blackboard at school would be a blur.

The kitchen smelled like coffee and cigarette smoke and salty bacon. A shape recognizable as Mrs. Gordon sat at the table.

"Morning, kiddo. How'd you sleep?"

"Okay, but . . ." Dewey held out her glasses.

"Oh, no. When did *that* happen?"

"A couple of minutes ago." Dewey sat down. "Is the eye doctor here today?" Alamogordo didn't have an optometrist. A doctor from El Paso set up shop in the back of the jewelry store every other Saturday afternoon.

Mrs. Gordon leafed through the sixteen pages of the weekly *Alamogordo News.* "Nope, next week. He's in Tularosa this afternoon."

"Will you drive me there?"

"Can't. My car's in the shop and Phil just left for the proving grounds." She frowned. "How much can you see?"

"That big white thing's the fridge, right?" Dewey tried to make it sound like a joke.

"Damn. If we were on the Hill, a dozen clever fellas could fix 'em in a jiffy."

"That's it!" Dewey snapped her fingers. "I'll go ask Owen.

I know how to solder now, but squinting at molten lead's probably dangerous."

An hour later, Dewey stood in front of Parker's Fix-It, her thumb and forefinger holding her left lens to her face. The sign said CLOSED, but the door was ajar and she could see a wedge of light from the doorway at the back.

She stepped inside. "Hello?"

"Be right with you," a man's voice answered. Owen's dad?

Dewey waited. Keeping one eye shut made her head ache, but if she opened it, the blurry world made her dizzy. She closed both eyes to rest them.

"What can I do for you, young lady?" the man asked a minute later.

Dewey opened her eyes, startled. She hadn't heard his footsteps. She squinted into the face of a red-haired man sitting on the other side of the counter. He wore gray coveralls with *Jack* stitched over one pocket.

"Hi," she said. "Is Owen around?"

"He's in El Paso, getting his mouth rewired. Mr. Mobley's brother's a dentist down there. My wife does his books once a month, in trade for fixing Rusty's—oops, Owen's—teeth. We couldn't afford it otherwise, and—" He broke off in midsentence. "Huh. Long-winded answer. You just visiting, or can I help you?"

"My glasses broke this morning," Dewey said. "I was hoping he could fix 'em."

"You the girl with the intercom?"

"Yes, sir."

He smiled. "No need for that. I had enough 'sir's in the Marines to last me a lifetime. My boy says you solder like a whiz. Quick study. Come on back."

Dewey ducked under the counter and stopped in surprise. The left leg of Mr. Parker's coveralls was pinned up and only reached the edge of his wheelchair. *That* was why the counter and worktables were so low.

"Iwo Jima," he said. "Mortar round. Let me see your specs."

Dewey handed him both halves.

He shook his head. "Solder won't hold. I can braze a little fillet across, but they won't look pretty."

"They never have."

"Okay, then." He turned the chair in an easy circle and rolled back to a big gray tank.

"Will you tell me what you're doing while you work?" Dewey asked. "I can't see right now, but I'd like to know."

"Sure. Listen and learn. First I'm going to light this torch, then I'll take a piece of . . ."

Ten minutes later, a thin line of shiny brass ran across the nose bridge, fusing the two steel halves. She eased them onto her face and smiled. She could see again. "Great," she said. "What do I owe you?"

"You're Owen's friend? Not a red cent."

"Thanks. Tell him Sprocket Girl said hi."

A week later, Dewey sat in the back of Sorenson's Jewelers, waiting for the optometrist to finish with another patient. She'd never been inside that store before, just walked by and looked at the rings in the window. The diamonds used to be coal, and only millions of years of pressure—or Superman's hands—could squeeze black carbon into those glittering bits. Hard to imagine.

The boxes of lenses and gold frames didn't seem out of place among the watchmaker's loupes and tiny repair tools that lined the shelves of the narrow room. A pair of glasses, a necklace, or a brooch twinkling under the fluorescent lights? They were just pieces of metal people wore on their bodies.

"How long has it been since you had your eyes checked?" Dr. Halsey asked when it was her turn. He wore a starched white coat and had rimless glasses shaped like stop signs. She could hear the scold behind his question.

"About five years," she admitted. "Because of the war. We lived on an army base, and no one had time to pay attention."

"Your father's a veteran?"

"He died," she said after a moment.

The doctor's smile faltered. "I'm sorry."

Dewey nodded. Nothing else to say.

"Well, then," Dr. Halsey said in a hearty, get-on-with-things voice. "Let's take a look." He put his hands on both sides of her face and took her glasses off. It felt very odd for someone else to do that. Dewey felt exposed, in the middle of a room that was now a blur of brown shapes and horizontal lines.

She followed his instructions: "Cover that eye, read the top line on the chart. Now the next line." Ten minutes later he said, "Time to pick out your new frames."

"I can't keep the old ones?"

"No, after five years, they're much too small for your face. I suspect that's why they broke." He smiled. "Besides, I have a daughter about your age. I know how important it is to keep up with the fashions. I'll show you some samples."

Fashion? Yuck. Dewey made a face as he ran his finger down a stack of black cardboard cases and pulled out one marked GIRLS.

The case had three trays, each with a half dozen pairs of glasses, bows neatly folded. "What are *those* made of?" Dewey asked, leaning forward.

"The clear ones are a new material called Plexiglas. The others are Zylonite. Lots of great plastics developed during the war. Marvelous frames. Colors and shapes impossible before, and not as heavy on your nose, even with the lenses."

Dewey peered at the rows of frames, like empty eyes staring back at her. None of them looked right. Nana had picked out her old glasses and always chose ones that were cheap and durable.

"I don't know," she said after a minute.

"Well, let's see," Dr. Halsey said. He held her face between his hands for a moment, his palms soft and cool. "You've got an delicate face, oval, a little tapered at the chin. Dark hair, green eyes. With your coloring . . ." He took two frames from the case, tapped his lips with his finger, then added two more.

"Try these," he said. He pushed a round mirror, the size of a dinner plate, in front of Dewey and flipped it over in its metal stand. The other side was magnified. Dewey's face filled it like the Wicked Witch of the West in the crystal ball.

She picked up the first frames and put them on.

Dewey had worn glasses since she started school, more than half her life. They were the first thing she put on in the morning, the last she took off at night. In between, they were as much a part of her face as her nose and ears. Functional. Necessary. She didn't think much about what they looked like.

But when she tried the first frames on and looked in the mirror, she felt an odd dizziness. Suddenly, Dewey didn't look like Dewey. She saw a stranger, someone she'd never known before.

"Do you have any like my old—?" she started to ask, then stopped, because her old life was over. No one stood behind her, telling her which ones she was allowed to have, who she had permission to be.

"Never mind," she said, and tried on the other frames. The girl she saw in the mirror was different each time. She felt like she did in dreams, when she opened a door to discover rooms that didn't exist in her house, beckoning but unfamiliar.

New town, new school. "Brave new world," Dr. Gordon had said. Dewey wasn't sure how brave she felt. Her stomach fluttered. Scared or excited?

She narrowed her choice down to two and put one on, took it off, put the other on. After three switches, the doctor let out a small, impatient breath.

"Okay. These." She handed him a pair of plaid frames, actual fabric embedded in clear plastic. They weren't round or like stop signs, but curved around her eyes in a shape that had no simple name.

The doctor smiled. "That's a very popular style. Calico Hussy. Comes in polka dots and stripes, too. You can pick yours up in two weeks."

"Not today?"

He shook his head. "I have to place the order and grind the lenses to your new prescription. I can't do that in an hour."

"Oh. That makes sense." It did, but she was disappointed. In the last fifteen minutes, she'd turned an invisible page, had become someone who made her own choices. It felt like a lie to just put on her glasses and go home looking like the old Dewey, as if nothing had changed.

SEASON
OF
DISBELIEF

THE SHAPE OF THINGS

OCTOBER 1946

"Hey, where've you been?" Dewey asked when Suze came into the attic. "Your mom's been bugging me for an hour. I had to climb down from the Wall three times to answer the intercom. Did you have detention again?"

"Nope. I've been a saint. But I caught holy hell in the kitchen anyway." Suze dropped a brown paper grocery bag down on her table. "Ynez had band practice, and her grandmother wanted to play cards with some other old ladies, so I said I'd babysit Tony and Ray. I made them Halloween costumes."

"Oh. Did you get paid?"

"Better than that." She pointed to the bag.

"That's a *lot* of tamales."

"Better than *that*," Suze said. "Look!" She upended the bag, and hundreds of cork-lined bottle caps poured out onto the table and clattered to the floor.

"Wow."

"Yeah. At the Crystal plant, all the messed-up ones get tossed into a big bin. They can't go on bottles if they're printed crooked, or the wrong color. Ynez's mom brought a bunch home."

"Neat." Dewey kneeled down and picked up a handful— green, orange, purple, red, brown. "What're you going to use 'em for?"

"I dunno. Maybe that stupid project for Social Science."

"'*My* Alamogordo'?" Dewey said in a pretty good Mrs. McDonald voice. Dewey was working on a display about the hardware store. Mr. Stevenson's family had been around almost as long as the town, and he'd said she could borrow some old jars and pioneer stuff from the basement. "You're making a little bottling plant?"

"Nope. An Alamo box."

"Like a miniature town? A diorama?"

"I haven't figured it all out yet. But Doña Luisa showed me how to make hinges when she came back from playing cards. That's why I was so late."

"She makes hinges out of *those*?" Dewey stared at the pile of bottle caps.

"Out of leather. These are just decoration, like buttons. Sometimes she paints them and puts little pictures on the inside, so the cap's like a frame. I want to try that."

Dewey nodded and picked one up. "What's Delaware Punch?"

"Fruity grape drink. No fizz." Suze made a face. "Grapette's a lot better."

After dinner, Dewey did the dishes and finished her homework—writing all forty-eight state capitals on a blank map. It was easy, except for North and South Dakota. She always got them confused. She put the papers in her satchel and went upstairs to get *Amazing Stories*, a science-fiction magazine Owen had loaned her. It had rockets and people with special powers, and was even better than a comic book because she could read for *hours*.

She opened the door to the attic and heard pounding, then Suze swearing. A second later, a small projectile bounced into the stairwell and landed at her feet, spinning. A green Lemon-Lime bottle cap, all smashed up, a jagged hole punched through its center. Dewey pocketed it and climbed the stairs.

Suze stood next to her table, scowling and holding Dewey's hammer in one hand. Dewey stopped a safe distance away. "What's up, doc?" she said.

"Not in the mood," Suze said.

"Sorry."

"It's all stupid." Suze put the hammer down with a slam that made Dewey wince. *Her* hammer.

"Stupid how?"

Suze blew a raspberry in the direction of the pile of bottle caps. "I can't figure out how to stick them onto the box. Glue doesn't work, 'cause the inside isn't flat. I tried filling the whole cap, but it just runs out everywhere." She pointed to a congealing beige pool on a piece of newspaper.

"Drill a hole?" Dewey suggested.

"The drill slips off and scratches the paint. I hammered a nail through, but it just made a big dent in the cap." Suze took a deep breath. "*Then* I laid one facedown on one of those boring horse books, and nailed it from the back side."

"That should work."

"I thought so. But it punches through the front. That's really ugly."

"Good thing you got a lot of bottle caps."

"I'm fubaring them all up. I guess I'll have to wait and ask Doña Luisa next time I'm over."

"Want me to take a look?" Dewey asked. Sometimes Suze didn't. When she was really cranky, she just snapped.

Suze stared at the pile of dented, messed-up bottle caps. "Okay. I'm stuck."

"Lemme see a good one." The bottle cap's edges were flared and fluted, the back side about an eighth of an inch deep and lined with cork. Dewey turned it over, turned it back again. "Okay, now a snafu'd one."

"Which way?"

"A hammer one. From the back."

Suze pointed. "I got p.o.'d and threw it down the stairs."

"Oh. I've got that one." Dewey took it out of her pocket and

folded inward, pierced the center. She smiled, for the first time since Dewey had come upstairs. "Yeah, that's *exactly* what I wanted." She admired the cap for a moment.

"It's what I do," said Dewey.

"You're good." Suze stared at the Wall for a few seconds. "Um, by the way, I keep forgetting to tell you. Those are really swell glasses you've got now."

Dewey smiled. She'd had them for three days, and she knew Suze had noticed—new glasses were pretty obvious, lots more than a built-up saddle shoe. Maybe Suze had thought it would be rude to mention them? She sometimes got weird talking about personal stuff—underwear and the box of Kotex they shared in the bathroom.

"Thanks," she said, "they're—" But Suze was already fitting a new bottle cap onto the dowel. Dewey tucked *Amazing Stories* under her arm and headed downstairs to read in peace and quiet, away from Suze's now-happy pounding.

RELATIVITY

November 1946

Dewey came home from school on a chilly afternoon and stood inside the kitchen doorway. "Terry, are you busy?"

"Frustrated," she answered, without turning around. She ran her hand over a piece of white paper lying on a cookie sheet, smoothing it flat, and pulled it up by one corner. She made a face, crumpled the paper, and tossed it into the trash can.

"What are you doing?"

"I'm *trying* to make copies of this letter so I can mail some new packets out in the morning." She smoothed on another sheet of paper, pulled it off in one quick motion, and nodded. She laid it on the table.

Dewey sat down. The paper was damp and had bright purple words typed on it. The black letterhead said FEDERATION OF ATOMIC SCIENTISTS. "It looks like homework dittos, but those smell better. What's in the cookie sheet?" It was some kind of cloudy, acrid chemical Jell-O. Lines of purple type covered the rubbery surface, the letters backward.

"It's a hectograph." Mrs. Gordon nodded at a box of purple carbon paper. "I type onto a stencil, transfer it to the gelatin, and make copies. That way I don't have to go downtown to the Ink Well and have them mimeographed."

Dewey touched the sheet. Almost dry. "How many can you make?"

"It's not mass production," she said. "About a dozen, minus the ones that wrinkle or don't print right. After that the ink's too faded to read. Still, it's a *lot* faster than typing the same letter over and over."

"What's this one for?"

"New movie, *The Beginning or the End*, coming out from MGM early next year. It's about the project—the Hill, Oppie, the Bomb. It's got big-name stars, so it'll be in theaters all over the country. We want local groups to set up tables in the lobbies and hand out leaflets, so the public can actually get some accurate information. This mailing's to the League of Women Voters."

She pulled four more sheets off the gelatin, crumpling one. The ink on the last was just pale lavender. "Time to clean the slate. Stand back."

Terry Gordon poured a stream of rubbing alcohol onto the

pan, tilting it until the surface was covered. The purple letters blurred and ran. She lit a match and the film of liquid blazed for more than a minute, pale cool-blue flames flickering, then sputtering out. The gelatin was unchanged, but the words were gone.

Dewey whistled. "That's really slick."

"I thought you'd like it." She opened the window a few inches. The cool breeze smelled like pine and the possibility of snow, and wafted away the chemical smell. "You want a Coke?"

"Too cold today." Dewey shivered. "I'll make cocoa." She opened the cupboard and took out a tin of Hershey's powder. "Want some?"

"No thanks. I'll stick to coffee."

Dewey turned the gas burner on low and poured milk into the saucepan. "In Home Ec, Mrs. Winfield said by the time we're grown-ups, every kitchen will have an atomic-powered oven that'll warm milk up in thirty seconds, and pop popcorn in a paper bag." She stirred in sugar and cocoa powder. "Do you think that's true?"

"Atomic-powered? No, kiddo, that's just science fiction. Pie in the sky. I did read about an oven that uses high-frequency electromagnetic waves to produce heat, but I doubt it'll ever be a common household object." She took a sip of coffee. "Wouldn't that be nice, though? Instant dinners."

"That's what I wanted to ask you. Thanksgiving's in two

weeks. Are you gonna cook?" Dewey stirred the cocoa so it wouldn't get a skin.

"I suppose I could, now that we've got an oven that can hold a turkey. The Black Beauty on the Hill could barely handle chicken."

"I'll make mashed potatoes. You want to use Nana's carving set?"

"I like that. Adding to the family tradition. It's settled, then. We'll have a proper feast. Only four of us, though. There'll be leftovers for *weeks*."

"Um, that's kind of why I was asking. See—" Dewey turned the burner off. "See, Owen's dad'll be at the VA Hospital in Albuquerque again." She poured a stream of cocoa into a mug. "So could I invite Owen and his mom and his little sister? They'd bring stuff. Mrs. Parker even *bakes*."

"You suppose she could manage a pumpkin pie?"

"Yeah. She makes great crust."

"It's beginning to sound like a party," Terry Gordon said. "That may be just what we need around here."

"So I can ask them?"

"Better let me. It's more official that way, and I've been looking for an excuse to invite Mrs. Parker over for coffee. What's her first name?"

"Doris."

"Doris. Got it." She looked up at the clock. "I'll give her a call after supper."

━━━━━━━

Dewey pushed her chair away from the table. "I've got two more math problems," she said to Suze. "Then you want to mess with the new end of the Wall?"

"Sure. Half an hour?" Suze replied, and returned to her dessert. Usually she ate faster than Dewey, but this was butter pecan ice cream, and she liked scooping the nuts out one by one.

"I picked up the tickets for Cloudcroft, Ter," Dr. Gordon said. "The weekend before Christmas." He turned to Suze. "Your mom and I are going to take a little trip, by ourselves. You and Dewey are old enough to be alone for three days, right?"

"Of course," Suze said.

"That's lovely, Phil." Terry Gordon smiled at him. "But, Christmas. Egads. I've barely started thinking about Thanksgiving."

"You planning anything special?" Dr. Gordon poured himself another cup of coffee. Suze had been thinking the same thing. It was only two weeks away, and she loved turkey and stuffing.

"Funny you should mention it. Dewey asked if we'd invite Owen and his mother and sister. She said Jack Parker'll be back at the VA."

"He's having a rough time."

She nodded. "This may be the last round, and they'll finally be able to fit him with an artificial leg, after a year and a half in that chair. Poor guy." She lit a cigarette. "Anyway, do you mind putting another leaf in the table and inviting them?"

"Fine with me. Dewey's over there a lot, isn't she? Do you suppose the two of them—?"

"*Dad!*" Suze said.

"No." Terry Gordon shook her head. "She was pals with the boys on the Hill, too. I'd bet you dollars to doughnuts the only electricity involved is plugs and circuit boards."

"You're probably right." He cleared his throat. "So, how would you feel about adding *two* leaves to that table? Rudy Mueller, one of von Braun's crew, ballistics engineer. He's got a boy in high school. I thought we might give them an all-American meal."

"No wife?"

"She didn't make it through the war."

"Oh." Terry Gordon took a long drag on her cigarette. Suze could see that she was thinking, hard. So was she. Nazis—okay, maybe ex-Nazis—out at the proving grounds was one thing. But at their dinner table?

"I guess so." She blew out a stream of smoke. "They say the more the merrier." She didn't sound very merry to Suze.

"I'll buy a fruitcake. It'll be swell." Philip Gordon stood up and gave his wife a peck on the cheek. "One big happy family." He took his coffee to the den.

"Are you sure about this?" Suze asked, after her father was out of earshot.

"Not at all." Mrs. Gordon stubbed out her cigarette. "But I'm trying to keep an open mind. It'll still be Thanksgiving— turkey, gravy, stuffing, the works."

"And a Nazi." Suze shook her head. "What would Norman Rockwell say?"

THE VISITORS

The last Thursday in November was cool and crisp. Most of the cottonwoods had lost their leaves—only a few yellow pennants fluttered on bare dark branches, stark against the endless sky.

They had cleaned all week, moving piles of books and papers off the dining-room table, vacuuming the rug, ironing the creases from big damask tablecloth that had spent four years folded in a storage box. Mrs. Gordon bought candles and flowers, and Suze made placecards with small Thanksgiving pictures gleaned from her magazine scraps.

By noon the table looked like a magazine picture itself, nine places set with china and glasses gleaming in the sunlight. The house was rich with the smells of roasting meat and cinnamon.

The Parkers arrived a little after noon, bearing a pumpkin pie and a dish of cranberry relish. "Family recipe," Mrs. Parker said with a smile. "Wouldn't feel like Thanksgiving without it, right, Owen?"

Owen put down the pie, ducked his head, and mumbled something Suze couldn't quite hear, ending with "Dewey?"

"In the garage," Mrs. Gordon said. "She came home yesterday with a carton from the salvage yard. Treasure, I'm sure."

Owen nodded and mumbled again, then left the kitchen as if it were on fire.

Mrs. Parker set the glass relish dish down on the kitchen counter. "Now, Terry, what can I do to help?"

"Not a thing. Bird's in the oven, potatoes are mashed, green beans are on the stove." She knelt down at eye level with the small red-haired girl who clutched a Mickey Mouse coloring book. "You must be Betsy," she said.

The girl nodded and smiled, showing a missing front tooth. "I'm five."

"That's a nice age. This is *my* daughter, Suze." She straightened up and turned to Suze. "Take charge until dinner? Get her some grape juice, find a quiet place to color?" She raised an eyebrow and mouthed, silently, *Please?*

Suze nodded and went to the refrigerator.

"Are you sure you won't put me to work?" Mrs. Parker asked.

"Positive. Come sit and chat in the living room. Would you like a cocktail?"

"Oh my. This early? I don't—well, maybe just a small one."

"Good. I hate to drink alone." Mrs. Gordon took off her apron. "It must be hard, holding down the fort without Jack."

"No harder than the war. At least he came back."

"True. Whiskey sour?"

"Perfect."

Suze helped color in the flowers in Minnie Mouse's bouquet. When the doorbell rang, she looked over her shoulder and saw her father greet a man and a boy—the Muellers.

"Ah, Frau Gordon—excuse me, Frau *Doktor* Gordon," said Mr. Mueller. "It is a pleasure to meet you at last. I have heard much about you." He handed her a box of chocolates.

"Thank you, how thoughtful." Mom was using her very polite we-have-guests voice.

"Allow me to introduce my son, Kurt," he said. The boy looked down at his hands and nodded, once. Suze watched them out of the corner of her eye. They were both stocky and blond, although Dr. Mueller was nearly bald. He wore an ordinary brown suit and a patterned yellow tie. Except for his accent, she'd have never known he was a German.

Dr. Gordon ushered them into the living room and poured a drink for his colleague. The boy sat nervously on the edge of the armchair. He watched Suze and Betsy for a few minutes, then picked up the green crayon.

"Please," he said to Suze. His voice was almost a whisper. "What is the American word for this?" His accent was much heavier than his father's.

"Crayon. Green crayon," Suze replied. "What is it in German?"

"Ein grüner Wachsmalstift."

"Wow. That's a mouthful." He looked puzzled, so she said, slower, "That's a long word for a small thing."

"Yes." He laid the crayon on the table. "In German are many long words."

Suze nodded and wondered how soon it would be until dinner. "When did you come to America?"

"One year and two months," Kurt said. "We live now at Fort Bliss in Texas *mit"*—he shook his head, then said, slowly and precisely—*"with*—the others on the rocket team. I am a junior at the school there. At home, I would be at university, but I must study now more English."

He sounded sad, and Suze wondered if he was homesick. It would be hard, she thought, living in another country all of a sudden, being older than the rest of your class, learning a brand-new language.

"Your English sounds good to me," she said.

"Thank you." He gave a shy smile. "I work hard for it."

When their glasses were empty, the women went to the kitchen and the men continued talking about some kind of engine, leaving Suze with twenty minutes of awkward conversation and coloring pictures of mice. She had never entertained anyone, played the hostess before. What did boys like to talk about?

Through hesitant answers, she found out that Kurt did not read comic books, had not seen baseball, and thought America was nice, but very much hotter than Germany. Suze started to explain that New Mexico was very much hotter than just about anywhere, but Dewey came in with the message that dinner was ready.

"Gorgeous bird, Ter. Now, who wants white meat?" Dr. Gordon picked up the carving knife. He began to slice into the crisp golden skin of the turkey breast.

"Aren't we going to say grace?" Betsy asked. Her mother leaned over to whisper something, but Mrs. Gordon held up her hand.

"That's a lovely idea, Betsy. Would you like to lead us?"

The little girl shook her head.

"Doris? Will you do the honors?"

Mrs. Parker bowed over her hands. "Dear Lord, we give thanks for your bounty, for the food we are about to eat, for friends and family. We are thankful to live once again in a time of peace, and grateful for the loved ones who, through your grace, returned from battle. We ask your blessing on the souls of the dead, and for those who still suffer. On this day of thanksgiving, deliver us from any future evil, and help us to forgive our enemies. Amen."

Murmurs went around the table, some amens, some, like Suze's, just a murmur. It was an strange prayer, she thought, considering the company.

The food was good, Suze's favorite meal, but she was bored. None of the conversations at the table had anything to do with her. Owen sat next to Dewey and didn't say a word until the men started talking about rockets. Then they were both full of questions. Her mother and Mrs. Parker discussed the Alamogordo Women's Club and the recipe for the cranberry stuff, which was good. Sweet and tangy.

Kurt didn't speak, but he listened while Betsy told a story, nodding every few sentences, like an older brother. Suze shaped and reshaped her mashed potatoes with her spoon, as if it were very important not to let the gravy escape, and felt like the odd man out in her own house.

SUPERIORITY

An hour later, Dr. Mueller put down his napkin. "That was a most excellent meal," he said. "I will never need to eat again, I think." He inclined his head to Mrs. Gordon in a European bow.

"And now it's time for another American tradition, Rudy," Dr. Gordon said. "The men retire to the den to listen to the radio and smoke, while the gals clean up the remains." He stood and put his napkin on the tablecloth. "Join me?"

"Of course." Dr. Mueller stood, and a moment later, so did Kurt.

Dr. Gordon looked surprised. "Your dad and I are going to talk shop, son. You stay here, get to know the other kids."

Suze watched Kurt's face sag. His mouth twitched once, then he nodded, to show he'd heard. He watched the two men go off together, a longing look at his father. He was probably tired of speaking English, she thought, and hadn't liked being called a *kid*.

"You need help washing up, Mom?" she asked. The table was a pretty big mess now—dirty dishes and glasses, leftovers to be wrapped, a big stain where the gravy ladle had dripped. She crossed her fingers behind her back, for once hoping to go off with the women.

Her mother picked up a bowl with two green beans floating in a thin pool of juice. "Later. There'll definitely be a second shift of K.P. For now, you and Dewey take the boys upstairs. Read comics, play Parcheesi, show them your projects."

"Okay." Suze uncrossed her fingers with a small sigh. Betsy started to follow her up the stairs, but Mrs. Parker put a hand on the little girl's shoulder. "Let the big kids go, honey. You get Mickey and come keep me company."

Good. At least Suze wouldn't have to babysit.

Owen whistled. *"Nice,"* he said as he reached the top of the attic stairs and saw the Wall. "Can we get a demonstration?"

"Sure," Dewey said. "I'll turn it on."

Suze watched, which felt odd. The attic was hers and Dewey's. They worked on their own projects, or on the Wall, whole evenings of talking, sometimes just easy silence. It was different with the boys here.

Dewey rolled marbles and adjusted gates, flipping switches for the battery-operated parts. Kurt stood a few steps back, watching politely, but when Dewey started to explain a tricky bit to Owen, he sat down on the couch. He crossed and uncrossed his legs, picked up a comic book, looked at a page, put it down.

Kurt looked uncomfortable, and Suze wasn't sure what to do. He wasn't *her* guest, but she knew it was her job to start a conversation or suggest a game—something—and she didn't know how. Not without sounding bossy. Without being Truck. Maybe she should have paid more attention in Home Ec, watched the drippy movies, read the articles in *Seventeen*— "Casual Entertaining and You."

Across the room, Owen took off his clip-on bow tie and opened the top button on his white shirt. "Whew, that's better." He leaned against Dewey's workbench. "You know, Sprock, you really should join the Projection Club. You're a million times better with machines than Gilbert."

"It would be fun," Dewey said. "Except I'm a girl."

"Why should that matter?"

"I dunno." She shook her head. "Except it usually does."

"I'll ask. You finish this one yet?" Owen picked up one of his weird space magazines. *Planet Stories.*

"Yeah, last night."

"Whad'ya think of that Bradbury guy?"

"The story was okay, but the rockets seemed kind of fake. I've seen a real one."

Owen turned to Suze. "You s'pose your dad'll actually

take me to a launch?" He looked as excited as if her father had offered him a trip to Mars.

"Yeah, sure, if you remind him. He'll forget anything that's not work."

"Gosh. That'd be swell. I've been reading about rockets since I was *this* big." He held his hand out next to Dewey's head, and Suze laughed. Dewey made a half-annoyed face, like it was an old, tired joke.

"It was pretty nifty, when we went," Dewey said. "We got the whole tour."

"Ten feet away," Suze added. "I could even read the German writing on some of the parts."

"I have seen many launches," Kurt said from the couch. "One hundred or more." It was the first time he'd sounded confident.

The other three turned toward him. "Really?" Owen said.

"Yes. My father works very close with Herr Doktor von Braun." Kurt's speech was precise, but slow. Suze wondered if he had to translate each word in his head before he spoke. "At Peenemünde first, but I often came with him to the factory at Nordhausen also."

"Wow. What was *that* like?" Owen perched on the edge of the stairwell.

"Very hot and full of noise. It was *unter*—" He paused and closed his eyes. "*Under*ground, in—" He stopped again and mimed a long tube with his hands.

"A tunnel?" Owen said.

"*Ja*. Two tunnels. Very good factory. One hundred rockets each week."

"Wow," said Suze. "My dad says they're having trouble even making the parts over here. They've only got about twenty rockets left, and those are in pieces."

"Nordhausen was a—" Kurt stopped and Suze could almost see him searching for a word. "How do you say . . . ?" He closed his hands into fists and pumped his arms up and down, rhythmic and repetitive.

"Machine?" Suze guessed. Good. A game. They were playing charades.

He shook his head. "Many, all in one row."

"Assembly line?" Dewey tried.

"Yes, yes! Assembly line. Like your Henry Ford, *ja*?"

"Good old American know-how," Owen said, then added, "but German engineering is also pretty good, I've read."

Kurt nodded. "With rockets, very much. That is why my father and his men have come here to teach you."

Like Americans couldn't figure it out by themselves? Suze thought. *Hooey.* "My dad says that pretty soon we're going to make our own rockets, bigger and faster than V-2s." She stopped. Something Kurt said just rang a bell. She went over to her table and started looking through a pile of old *LIFE* magazines.

"It is possible," Kurt said. "But it will be a very long time,

I think. In Germany, many thousands work in the factory.
Twelve hours each group, two groups each day. "

"That's a long shift," Owen said. "I bet the workers got
tired."

"No." Kurt shook his head. "This was not allowed. Always
new workers came, each week. They were only—" He tapped
his fingers on his mouth, thinking. But this time he came up
blank, not even a gesture or a mime. "Only—" he started again,
but was interrupted by a screech from the intercom.

"Kurt?" Terry Gordon's voice was small and tinny through
the box's speaker. "Your dad wants to go. Long drive to El Paso.
Girls, K.P. in ten minutes."

Dewey pushed the TALK button. "Roger. We'll be down."

"Thank you for this American holiday," Kurt said formally.

"Ditto," Owen said. "It was swell." He pointed to the Wall.
"I oughta go, too. Can I come back, get a closer look?"

"Okay with you?" Dewey called over to Suze, who shrugged
without looking up from the magazines.

"Aces," said Owen. "Next week, some day after school?"

Dewey nodded. "Sure. Tell your mom thanks for the pumpkin pie. It was swell."

"Will do." The two boys went downstairs, Owen ducking
his head at the landing.

"Dishes," Dewey said to Suze's back.

"I know. Just—just a sec." Her voice was distracted and
unhappy.

"What're you—?"

"Just a *sec.*"

"Okay, okay." Dewey sat down on the couch.

Two minutes later, Suze found the issue she'd been looking for. May 7, 1945, the end of the war in Europe. Only a year and a half ago, but now it felt like ancient history. She turned the pages until she found *Nordhausen* in the caption of a full-page photo of rows and rows and rows of bodies, stacked like firewood. A few GIs in round helmets stared at the corpses; other soldiers looked away.

"Dewey? C'mere." Suze pointed to the page. "Look. This is where Kurt's father worked." She read the caption aloud:

At Nordhausen bodies of almost 3,000 slave laborers are laid out along a bombed street before burial by U.S. troops. These dead once worked at the Nordhausen underground factory which made parts for V-1 and V-2 bombs. The plant was started in September 1943 and its construction probably cost the lives of 20,000 slaves who died from starvation, overwork, and beatings.

"*Slaves?*" Dewey's mouth was open.

"Yeah." Suze was silent for a long time. She'd read about slaves in the Civil War, but that was a century ago, not last year. "Do you think my dad knows?" *No. How could he work with people who—*

Dewey nodded. "I think he'd have to. *We* know. And that's *LIFE* magazine. Kinda hard to miss."

"I guess." Suze remembered lying out at White Sands, watching the sky and listening to her father talk about going into space. He had sounded so excited. Now she looked down at the photograph, turkey and gravy churning in her stomach, and slowly closed the magazine.

Oh, Daddy . . .

ILLUSION

DECEMBER 1946

"Is it done?" Dewey asked. Their Social Science projects were due Friday, the last day of school before the Christmas break. She had finished typing the captions for her hardware history last night.

Suze had worked on her box every day for more than a month. Now it sat on her table, all her other junk cleared away, for once. She walked around and around, staring at it from every possible angle.

"Yeah. I just have to sign it. Like Maria Martinez cuts her name into the bottom of a pot before she fires it."

"So?"

"So I'm not sure what name to use." Suze opened her black sketchbook and laid it flat on the table. The page was covered with variations of her name: *Suze, Suze Gordon, Susan Gordon, Susan S. Gordon, S. Gordon, SSG, S. S. Gordon.*

"S. S. Gordon sounds like you're a boat."

"I know. None of them feel right."

Dewey considered the page of names. "Shazam," she said after a minute.

"Shazam," Suze said automatically.

"No, *Shazam.*" She pointed to the rock in the little alcove on Suze's shelf. "Because that's how you use your power."

Suze stared at Dewey as if she'd lost her mind, then looked at the Greek lettering on the rock. "Oh." She grabbed a pencil, turned the sketchbook to a blank page, and wrote *Susan Gordon*, *Suze Gordon*, and *Suze* in Greek:

$$\sigma\upsilon\sigma\alpha\nu \ \gamma\text{o}\rho\delta\text{o}\nu$$
$$\sigma\upsilon\zeta\varepsilon \ \gamma\text{o}\rho\delta\text{o}\nu$$
$$\sigma\upsilon\zeta\varepsilon$$

"The last one," Dewey said.

"The zeta is fun to draw," Suze agreed, "and my whole name's kind of long." She smiled. "My secret artist identity."

When she took the box downstairs ten minutes later, covered with an old towel, so her mother would be surprised, the back was signed in silver ink:

$$\sigma\upsilon\zeta\varepsilon\text{---}1946$$

She set it down on the kitchen table.

"Hey, Mom."

Terry Gordon looked up from a thick sheaf of papers. "Not now, Suze." Her voice was tight and the ashtray was full of cigarette butts.

"Please? It's my Social Science project and I have to I turn it in tomorrow."

"Oh. Well, okay."

Suze pulled the towel off and crossed her fingers.

The square pine box was fourteen inches on a side, five inches deep. Two hinged doors had bottle-cap knobs. She'd cut and painted a balsa-wood border across the top to look like the silhouette of the mountains, with a white capital *A* in the center. Underneath, between the closed doors, a thin strip of black-painted wood with vertical white letters said:

T
E
N
T
H

S
T
R
E
E
T

The left side was collaged with candy and gum wrappers, paper labels from soup cans, and other packaging that Suze had collected from the Gordons' trash and Dale's Piggly Wiggly, all varnished to a high gloss. The right side seemed to be the same, until her mother looked closer and saw that—except for a few Aunt Jemimas and Cream of Wheat's Rastus—the wrappers and labels were all in Spanish.

"Those are brands I've never seen. Where did you get them?"

"The *grocería* on Fourth Street, and the *tienda* on Delaware, mostly," Suze said. "Some of them I bought myself—the mango candy's really good—and the rest Ynez got from her family. Mrs. Esquero started saving stuff for me after she caught us wiping enchilada sauce off some wrappers from their trash can."

"Nice of her." Terry Gordon bent down, opened the two doors, and looked inside the box. Behind the divider was a pane of glass, secured on four sides by folded strips of copper. More labels covered the interior. Suze had pieced together the bits of paper so the colors and patterns led to the centerpiece, a one-quart milk bottle.

The reddish sandy dirt of their backyard filled the right side of the bottle from top to bottom. The left side held pale sparkling gypsum from White Sands. A mirror, reflecting the colorful labels on each side, divided both bottle and box.

Terry Gordon was silent for a long time, long enough to

make Suze uncomfortable. Very uncomfortable. Then her mother smiled.

"I'm proud of you." She put her arm around Suze and kissed her cheek.

"Really?" It came out as a little squeak.

"Absolutely. It makes a powerful statement without any words." She ran a finger across the varnished surface. "Beautiful work, sweetie."

She stepped back, cocked her head, looked at the box from a couple of different angles. "Okay, I'll bite. How'd you keep the two colors of sand separate?"

Suze grinned. "I couldn't. I tried everything. First a cardboard divider, but the neck of the bottle's narrow, so I had to fold it to get it in, and it wouldn't pop back again. Not stiff enough that the sands didn't leak." She opened the refrigerator and got a Pepsi, talking as she opened it. "I tried mixing the white sand with glue and pouring it into a bottle laid on its side." She made a face. "*That* was a mess."

"I can imagine. How many milk bottles did you go through?"

"I dunno. Half a dozen."

"Ah. That explains why there haven't been many empties for Mr. Quinn." She lit a cigarette and continued to peer at the box. "What *did* you do?"

"Cut the bottle in half," Suze said. "It was Dewey's idea. We weren't sure if it would just break into a million pieces, but the guy at the rock shop on the highway has a saw that spins *really* fast. Sliced it clean in two."

"So it's not a milk bottle? It's two half-bottles."

"Yeah. I traced the outlines on shirt cardboard and cut them out, then laid the half-bottles flat, like rowboats, and filled each of 'em with sand. I glued the cardboard covers on with model cement. It stunk, but it worked."

"Then you just glued the two halves together and— presto!"

Suze shook her head. "Nope. I glued the white one to its side of the mirror, then lined the other one up and glued *it*. You can't tell, can you?"

"Not even after I know. It's a great illusion." She tapped her cigarette into the ashtray. "Are you ready for what comes next?"

Suze sat down. "What?"

"Mrs. McDonald. Do you think she'll like it?"

"Probably not." Suze frowned.

"And why do you suppose that is?"

"It's not a diorama, or a display, or a painting about *My Alamogordo*."

"Why? Because no one talks about *your* Alamogordo?" Her mother smiled, an odd expression Suze couldn't quite read. "Remember what I said about picking your battles?"

"Yeah."

"You picked a good one."

"Even if I get an F in Social Science?"

"If that woman flunks you, I'll put on my good hat again and march down to the school so fast it'll make her head spin."

"You will?"

"In a hot second. She wants you to be a good citizen? I think you are." She shook her head. "All this talk about what a *marvelous* future science'll bring us? Art can change things just as much." She stubbed out her cigarette. "Maybe better."

"Why's that?"

"Art doesn't kill anyone," Terry Gordon said, and closed the doors of *Tenth Street.*

SUN
AND
SHADOW

NO PLACE FOR TEARS

JANUARY 1947

A week into the new year, the trees were bare and empty, the attic was chilly, and Suze was in a bad mood. Outside, the wind blew snowflakes against the window. Snow didn't stay long in Alamogordo, just dusted the ground for a couple of hours.

She paced around the attic. She'd looked at all the slides in the View-Master Dad had given her for Christmas, read three comics, even finished the book she had to read for English—*Junior Miss*. It was about a fat teenage girl; she'd put it off as long as she could.

Dad was at a rocket meeting, and Mom was downstairs getting ready to go to the women's club with Mrs. Parker. Suze thought it was dumb to get all dressed up on a Saturday—a hat and gloves and everything—for a lunch two blocks away. Dewey was with Owen, learning how to drive. In New Mexico, you only had to be fourteen to get a license. Suze punched a couch pillow. She wouldn't be fourteen until August, and by then they'd be back in California. It wasn't fair.

She picked up the physics book Dewey'd been reading. Maybe she'd find something she could use when her mother came home, start the kind of conversation that Mom sometimes had with Dewey.

Suze let the textbook fall open, put her finger on the middle of a page, then read: *Since all motion is relative, we should expect that if the magnet in Oersted's experiment were held fixed . . .*

None of that made sense. The beginning must be easier. But by the bottom of the first page, she knew she was in over her head. Even if Mom had time to talk, Suze would never understand what she was saying. She threw the book at the end of the couch. It landed like a tent, pages bending. She didn't care. She walked over to her worktable and fiddled with a stack of paper labels and folders she'd bought that morning, a new year's resolution to get her junk more organized.

She printed THE WAR on a label, and frowned. The problem was, Dewey and her mother *fit* together. Even Suze could see that. Two science peas in a pod. It wasn't really Dewey's fault, but—

"We got it!" Her father's voice boomed out of the intercom.

"What, Phil? You look like the cat that swallowed the canary." That was Mom. She must have forgotten to turn the kitchen unit off again.

"Funding for the whole fifty launches, is all," her father

said. "Through the end of forty-eight. They were going to pull the plug this June, after number twenty-five. But the big boys at GE say Washington's happy with the first seventeen, even with the duds. A hundred million dollars' worth of happy."

Suze went over to push the button and say, "Hey, the intercom's on," but when she was a few feet away she heard the sharp sound of something smacking down, hard, on the kitchen counter. She jumped back.

"End of forty-*eight*? Not on your life, Phil. We had an agreement." Her mother's voice was loud and tense. "One year."

"I know. But this is huge. This is what we've been waiting for."

"While I'm stuck here in the back of beyond? No, thank you."

"You've been busy enough. Saving the world with all those letters."

"How would you know? You're always out at the base, trying to blow it up again."

Suze froze. She heard her father sigh, not a sad sigh, but frustrated. "Will you climb down off your soapbox for a minute? I'm talking about a real space program here."

"Oh, save the fairy tales for the children." Mom's voice was angry now. "They're not giving you a hundred million dollars to go to *space*. Bigger rockets mean bigger bombs. Push-button war. Vaporize an enemy three thousand miles away. *That's* the future the big boys want you to deliver. And I want *no* part of it."

"Something's wrong with defending our country?""

"From *who*?" Mom shouted. "I went to the Hill to try and *end* a war, not get ready for the next one." A sharp click and an exhaled hiss. Mom had just lit a cigarette. "I won't stay here another year. I can't."

"What about my work?"

"What about *mine*? Last winter you asked me to choose: 'Which is more important, Terry? Your career or your family?' All right, buster, your turn. Same question. And don't you dare—"

Suze flipped the switch. Through the half-open door she could still hear the sound of her parents yelling two floors below. She sat down, her back to the stairwell, and put her hands over her ears, hugging her knees to her chest, staring at nothing. When the noises from the kitchen finally stopped, she didn't move, just stayed there until her butt was too numb to sit anymore. Then she tiptoed down the stairs, put on her coat and gloves, got on her bike, and sped away from the cold war on Michigan Avenue.

Up one street, down another. The raw wind stung her face, but she didn't want to stop anywhere. She didn't want to think. She rode aimlessly for half an hour before she crossed Tenth Street to see if Ynez was home.

Ynez was fun. They didn't do anything amazing together, like the Wall, just messed around, but Suze liked being at her house. It was warm and full of people and something was always cooking and smelled good. Maybe they'd practice Spanish. She could trill her *r*s almost as well as Ynez, and it made Ray clap his hands and laugh out when Suze said his name— R-R-R-R-Raymundo!, drawing it out so it sounded like a motor. She needed to hear *someone* laugh.

She let herself in the back gate, shooing away the chickens that clucked around her legs, hoping for corn, and knocked on the door before she remembered. Ynez's sister'd had a baby boy on Thursday, and the whole family had gone up to La Luz for a fiesta to celebrate.

Suze sat on the steps for a long time, watching the chickens, trying not to cry. She wanted to escape on her bike, as far away from her life as she could get, but the desert surrounded her as much as the barbed-wire fence on the Hill. She didn't need a pass to leave, but there was nowhere to go.

BATTLEGROUND

I t started with an innocent question.

"Can I use the hammer when you're done?" Suze asked, coming into the attic after school the next Monday. "I've got an idea for a new box, and I want to make holes in some bottle caps." Mrs. McDonald had put the eighth-grade Social Science projects on display in the case in the hall. Dewey's was right up front, but Suze's *Tenth Street* was all the way in the back corner, half-covered by a painting of the water tower and a plaque made out of White Sands gypsum.

Then she'd burned her finger on the stove in Home Ec.

Suze needed to pound something.

Dewey sat at her workbench with an open jar of nails and the hammer. She didn't seem to be doing anything, just staring at an envelope, but by now Suze knew that staring was part of how Dewey worked.

"You can have it now," she said without looking up. "I'm heading downstairs. I told your mom I'd meet her at four."

"It's *science* time again, huh?" Suze threw her books onto the couch.

Dewey shook her head. "No, she said she was going to that little stand north of town to get pecans, and I asked if she wanted company."

"I'll go with her," Suze said quickly.

"Sure, come along. She's going to let me practice driving."

Come along? That was when Suze snapped. "Practice with somebody else. She's *my* mother."

"Don't you think I *know* that?" Dewey stood up and slammed the hammer down onto her workbench so hard a dozen little tacks and nails jittered to the floor.

Suze stopped, dead in her tracks. "Well, if you know, then why do you always—?"

"I *like* her," Dewey broke in. "So I talk to her. Not always about science."

Dewey talked to Mom about other stuff? That was even worse. "Why don't you go talk to *O*-wen," Suze said in a girly voice.

"I do. But he's not a grown-up," she said, her hands on her hips. "Your mom helps me like Papa used to, and doesn't act like I'm some sort of freak."

"But you're not a freak anymore." It was true. Standing

there in her new glasses, in rolled-up blue jeans and a baggy sweater and saddle shoes, Dewey looked just like any other girl in town. "I hate that you're so—*normal.*" Suze made it sound like an insult.

"I'm the same person. My shoes just match. What's *with* you today? Are you on the rag?"

"No! That's got nothing—" Suze paused and glanced at the calendar. "Maybe. Wednesday. But that's not why. I just liked it better when *you* were the weird one."

"You did not. You hated me for being 'Screwy Dewey.'"

"But now people stare at *me. Look, here comes the Jolly Green Giant.*"

"How is that *my* fault?"

"Everything's your fault," Suze yelled. "Everything was fine before you came. I wish you'd go away so I can have my family back!"

Dewey stood very still. After a minute, she said, "You don't mean that."

"Yeah, I do," Suze said, but even with the scratchy feel of a good yell still in her throat, she knew she didn't, completely.

"You do?"

"Yeah." Even less conviction.

"Then you're a moron." Dewey turned to the stairs. "I'm not talking to you."

"But *I'm* talking to you!" Suze grabbed the nearest thing she could put her hands on—a piece of white chalk—and threw it at Dewey. Hard. It hit her on the shoulder, leaving a puff of dust on her red sweater, and clattered to the floor.

Dewey stared in surprise, at Suze, at the chalk. Then she smiled.

It wasn't her friendly smile.

"Fine," Dewey said in a cool voice, the *F* as explosive as if she'd bitten the word in two. "If that's the way you want it." She picked up the chalk, walked over to the top of the stairs, and squatted down, drawing a line down the middle of the attic floor, the chalk scraping audibly on the rough wood.

Suze stared. *Dewey* wouldn't—

Dewey did, right across the rug, leaving more of a flattened groove than a visible mark. She divided the last four feet of floor and drew a wobbly white line up the Wall, as high as she could reach.

"My side. Your side," she said. She stepped over the line, stood next to her workbench, then tossed the chalk in a hard, underhand arc. It landed on Suze's table and cracked into two pieces. "There's your chalk. You wanna go draw a line down your mom?"

"No. She's *mine*." Suze looked around. "And so is the couch," she said triumphantly. Hah. Now where would Little Miss Physics sit and read?

"Okay. But the switches for the Wall are on my side."

"No fair! I made half of that."

Dewey turned and considered the array of toys and art and

machinery. "I'll trade you. *You* can turn on the Wall if *I* can use the couch."

"Tuesdays and Thursdays after school," Suze snapped back. "And every other Saturday."

They stood across from each other, the thin white line between them, each with her arms crossed over her chest. They glared, neither of them blinking, for at least two minutes before Suze felt her lips twitch. A giggle started at the back of her throat. She swallowed. *No!* This wasn't funny. It was serious. This was war.

But once a giggle started, especially if she tried to stop it, it was bound to explode. She'd lost the battle in class often enough, suffered through *Miss Gordon, if the joke is that funny, I'm sure you'd like to share it with the rest of the class.*

She fought it for another minute, but the sound of Mrs. Winfield's voice in the back of her mind was the last straw. Suze burst out laughing.

Dewey stood motionless, fierce determination and anger on her face. But it was the contagious kind of giggle, and Suze watched Dewey's lips tighten and her eyes begin to crinkle at the corners—just as much against her will as Suze's had.

A little whistling snort escaped Dewey's nose.

They both doubled over.

"Nice chalk work," Suze said, when she had enough breath to speak.

"A skill I learned during the war."

That set them both off again. Suze looked away, but every time she caught Dewey's eye, the guffaws started anew.

"Ow," she said after five minutes of stopping and starting. "My cheeks hurt." She sat down on the floor with a thump and leaned her head against the leg of the table. "So. What do we do now?"

Dewey crossed the line and sat down in front of her. "We either talk or we start throwing things again."

"Talk. I guess."

Silence.

"Okay," Dewey said. "I'll start. You're my best friend, and you're a pain in the ass sometimes. It drives me nuts when you don't put my things away. Like the physics book. The pages got all bent." .

"You're just as big a pain," Suze countered. "You're *neat*, all the time."

"At least I can find things."

"Yeah, okay. But you line your boxes of screws up by size. Your bookshelf's alphabetical. How am I supposed to remember all that?"

Dewey was quiet for a minute. "What's really bugging you?"

Suze shook her head. She started to talk, then stopped, then—Finally she sighed. "*I* feel like the orphan. Dad's off with his rockets, and Mom's always busy. Then Saturday, she and Dad—" She pointed to the intercom. "Mom left it on. They had a big fight. They don't know I heard," she told Dewey. "I'm scared."

"Me, too." Dewey was silent for a minute, then said, "Go get pecans. I can practice driving later, and you really need to talk to your mom." A long pause. "You can say stuff about me, if you want."

"I don't think I do, anymore. It's just—oh, hell. I miss her. Even when she's here, she's working, and she yells if I bother her."

"She snaps at me, too. But that's why I do my homework in the kitchen. Sometimes she has another cup of coffee and we talk for a few minutes. You should try it, instead of stomping upstairs and moping."

"I don't *stomp*," Suze said with as much dignity as she could. "I'm just at 'that awkward age.' *Seventeen* magazine says so."

Dewey snorted. "Everyone in the eighth grade is at that awkward age."

"Maybe." Suze stared out the window. "You call her *Terry*," she said finally. "That bugs me."

"I know. But I *live* here. It's stupid to call her 'Mrs. Gordon.'" Dewey gave Suze a questioning look. "You'd hate it more if I called her 'Mom,' right?"

"Don't you dare."

"See. But I don't have a word for who she is. She's not my mother, and she's more than a friend. Terry's the only thing left."

"What am I?"

"Suze."

"No, I mean—" Suze tried to figure out how to say it. "I mean, people ask if you're my sister, and I don't have an answer. 'Cause you're not, really. But we share a room—and the Wall and tools and junk—and we talk every night, and—I don't have a name for *that*, either."

"It'd be easier to say we *are* sisters. Except it's a lie."

"And it's so hokey—*A Girl Scout is a sister to every other Girl Scout*," Suze said in a Church Lady voice. She made a face, then thought for a minute. "Wanna be my brother?"

"Huh?"

"Well, 'cause we're *not* sisters." The more Suze thought about that, the more she liked it. "And, after all, we *did* go through the war together."

"Brothers-in-arms," Dewey said.

"The Secret Brotherhood of the Shazam Club."

"'Oh, is that your sister?' 'No, ma'am. She ain't heavy, she's my brother.'"

Suze flinched. "You think I'm—?"

"No, sorry. It was just a line." Dewey looked at the clock. "Pecan time."

"You sure?"

"Yeah. Go on. Talk to my friend Terry." She buddy-punched Suze on the arm. "I think she likes you."

Dewey stood by the attic window until she saw the black Chevy pull out into the alley, gravel crunching under its wheels. Then she sat down at her table and picked up the envelope lying next to her hammer.

The mail had still been in the box when she got home from school, so she'd brought it all in and set it on the kitchen counter. A letter for "The Kerrigans" had been under some bills, and she'd taken it upstairs to open in private. It was postmarked from San Diego on December 15th, no return address. She didn't know anyone there, but Papa'd known other professors all over the world. It was probably nothing. But . . .

She looked for another minute at "The Kerrigans," written in black ink. FORWARD was rubber-stamped over the Hill's P.O. box, and someone had added the Alamogordo address in blue.

Dewey slit open the flap. Inside was a Christmas card, holly leaves with a banner that said SEASON'S GREETINGS. She opened it and drew in a little breath of stunned surprise. Her hand started to shake.

Three handwritten lines in the same black ink:

Jimmy—
I hope you and D. are well. I've been thinking
about you both.

—Rita

ASK ME ANYTHING

Suze told her mother that Dewey'd decided not to get pecans, because she'd gotten an idea that she *had* to write down, right now. Mom had bought it, then kept up a running monologue about how beautiful the snow had been up in the mountains last month, what a nice vacation she and Dad had. She was selling it really hard. Even if Suze hadn't heard them fight, she wouldn't have been convinced. Three days alone inside a little cabin. What fun was that?

On the drive back, Suze couldn't figure out how to begin. And by the time they got home, Mom said she felt like she might be coming down with something, and wanted to take a little nap. Suze sat in the kitchen and read *Newsweek*. Social Science homework. An hour later, she heard her mother get off the couch, go into the dining room, and begin to type.

Suze stood in the hall for five minutes before she was brave enough to go in.

"Can I ask you something?" She leaned one shoulder against the arched doorway. The dark wood of the table was covered—as usual—with stacks of stapled papers and boxes of envelopes. A coffee cup sat on the big blue dictionary.

"I suppose so." Terry Gordon looked up from her type-writer and pushed her glasses into her hair. "I'm not getting much done. Can't concentrate. Sit down."

"Not yet."

"Hmm. Okay." She picked up the manuscript and turned it over. "Shoot."

Suze still didn't how she was going to start, and was surprised to hear herself ask, "Do you love Dewey?"

Her mother looked just as startled. She touched the pack of Chesterfields, but made a face and didn't light one. "Yes," she said. "I do. How about you?" She looked directly at Suze.

"What?" Suze hadn't expected that.

"Do you love Dewey?"

"Most of the time." Suze sat. "When she's not a pain in the a—in the butt."

"More than you love me?" Her mother's voice was gentle.

"Huh?" Suze jerked, caught off guard. "No, of course not."

"Oh. Sorry. That's not my line, is it? That's what you wanted to ask *me*."

"How did you know that?"

"You've been sulking around for weeks."

So have you, Suze was tempted to say, but didn't. "You never said anything."

"I was waiting until you were ready to talk." She kissed her own palm and laid it on top of Suze's hand. "It's not easy having a sister. Trust me, I know. Your aunt Babs and I got into knockdown, drag-out fights as often as we were civil."

"Really?"

"Really. I broke my mother's soup tureen during a fight over a pair of socks. But Babs and I would defend each other to the death against anyone else." She put up her fists. "Stay away from my sister, you—"

"Dewey's my brother. We just decided."

Terry Gordon stifled a smile. "I see. Well, that's a little unusual." She reached for her cigarettes and lit one this time. "But I suppose I can live with it."

"It's good." Suze nodded.

"I'm glad. Because I do love Dewey. As much as if she was your real sis—sibling. But that doesn't mean I love you any less. You know that, don't you?"

"I guess so."

"Oh, *that* was convincing." She turned in her chair so they sat knee to knee. "You're my daughter, no matter what. Always will be."

"Even though I don't like science much," Suze said in a small voice. "You're not disappointed I'm not more like you?" She paused. "And Dewey."

"Not at all. Besides, you don't think figuring out how to fill a milk bottle with two different sands is an experiment?"

"I never thought about it that way."

"I have. You're a lot more like me than you think."

"Hah. How?" Mom was nothing like her. She was practical and precise. Scientists couldn't afford to be clumsy.

"Well—how about towering over the boys and feeling like a big galoot?"

"You think I'm a galoot?" Suze's voice got even smaller.

"No. But I suspect you do."

"Kind of. But how do you—?"

"Takes one to know one. Let me show you." She went into the living room and came back with the brown leather photo album, laying it on the table. She turned a few of the black paper pages. "Ah, here we are." She pointed to a snapshot, one corner ripped away. "I *hated* this picture. I tried to tear it up, but my mother took it and hid it until I went away to college. I'm glad now."

Suze leaned over and looked. A stocky girl in a square-necked dress, her hair in a pageboy cut, stood with her arms draped over the shoulders of two others.

"My best friends, Elsie and Caroline. Both as tiny as Dewey. Five minutes after this was taken, I tripped over my own feet and knocked half of Caroline's birthday dinner off the counter with my elbow. Succotash was *everywhere*, and I wanted to sink through the floor. That was ninth grade, not eighth, but—

details." She waved her cigarette in the air, dismissing them. "The Weiss women have always been tall and curious. You're following in the family tradition."

"Really?" Suze said again. She knew she sounded like a broken record, but she'd never have guessed the conversation would go like this.

"Absolutely." She tapped an inch of ash onto a saucer. "I have an idea. I've got to go up to Santa Fe next weekend to drop off some papers and talk to Phil Morrison while he's in town. Why don't you come with me? Dewey and your dad can fend for themselves."

"If Dad even comes home. He's got another launch and—" Suze hesitated. "Um—you left the kitchen intercom on Saturday morning."

"Oops. Sorry, I forget sometimes. What does that have to do with—?" She stopped, her cigarette halfway to her mouth. "Oh, no. Oh, sweetie, don't tell me that you heard . . . ?"

Suze nodded. "Enough. Before I turned off the upstairs box." She picked up a pencil and twirled it in her fingers. "Are you and Daddy going to—?"

Terry Gordon was quiet for a minute, then sighed. "I don't know *what's* going to happen. We've been married fifteen years, and it hasn't all been sweetness and light, but we've always worked things out before. Maybe we'll find some common ground before summer."

"I hope so," Suze said. "I don't want to stay here two more

years." She told her mother about Mrs. McDonald and the display.

"Oh, jeez. I'm sorry you've been having a rough time." She stubbed out her cigarette. "So we'll take a breather. You and me. Let's get out of Dodge next Friday. You can play hooky, just this once. It's a long drive, and we need to catch up."

Wow. "But won't you be in meetings the whole time?"

"Only a couple of hours. Friday night you and I can have dinner on the Plaza, spend the night in the hotel. In the morning, you can sack in while I talk *science*"—she rolled her eyes in a pretty good imitation of Suze—"then we'll go to the gallery with the Georgia O'Keeffe paintings in the afternoon. Sunday, we'll head back and both face the music refreshed."

"Super," Suze said. She kissed her mother. "Hooky, huh? You're okay."

"You, too." Terry Gordon smiled. "Don't suppose you'd be interested in a game of gin after dinner?"

"I could do that," Suze replied, and felt her shoulders relax for the first time in weeks.

MARGIN FOR ERROR

FEBRUARY 1947

Alamo Drugs had been crowded with people buying last-minute valentines after school. But Dewey managed to find a funny one with a pop-up parrot that said, "To My Brother," and hurried home to tape it to the Wall before Suze finished her shopping.

She opened the front door quietly and was surprised to hear chopping sounds coming from the kitchen. They'd had tamales three times last week, because Terry had napped until after six.

But today she stood at the kitchen counter, a pile of diced carrots and green peppers covering the wooden cutting board.

"Hey," Dewey said. "You're cooking."

"Don't stop the presses. It's only a casserole." Terry cut into an onion, then grimaced and put down the knife. She sank onto the kitchen stool, her hand over her mouth.

"You okay?" Dewey asked. She set her books on the counter and tried to make her voice sound normal, like everything was fine. It wasn't. Terry had been feeling lousy, off and on, for a couple of weeks. They'd all been pretending nothing was wrong, but she and Suze were worried. Worried enough that Dewey hadn't wanted to add to it by sharing the news about the Christmas card. That could wait.

Terry nodded. After a minute, she took her hand down. "Just a little dizzy. I couldn't sleep last night—tossing and turning." She pointed to the cutting board. "Can you finish up here? I need to rest my eyes for a little while."

"Sure," Dewey said. "No problem." That was a lie, too. She watched Terry walk slowly out of the kitchen, face pale and sweaty, even on a cold, blustery day.

Dewey chopped the last of the onion, seasoned the hamburger meat with salt and pepper and "just a smidge of paprika for color," as Mrs. Winfield would say. They didn't get to cook much in Home Ec, just read recipes, but Dewey's kitchen skills had improved since September.

She turned the flame up on the gas stove so the water would boil. She'd finish her English homework while the noodles cooked. Little bubbles had appeared on the bottom of the pan, one or two gliding up to the surface, when the phone in the hall rang, startling her.

"I'll get it," she called in the direction of the living room. She reached the phone in five running steps, catching it in the middle of the third ring.

"Hello?" she said. "Gordon residence."

"Is this Marjorie Gordon?" a woman's voice asked.

"No, she's in the other room. Hold on a sec while I get her."
Dewey lowered the receiver, then returned it to her ear. "May I
ask who's calling?" Home Ec was rubbing off more than she'd
thought.

"This is Laura from Dr. Cranshaw's office. We have Marjorie's test results."

"I'll get her." Dewey put the phone down gently, although
it felt like an anvil. Everything felt heavy. *Get a grip, Kerrigan,* she thought. The voice in her head sounded like her Trig
teacher, brisk and practical.

Test results can be good news. Right. That's why Terry was
on the couch in the middle of the afternoon, dizzy, why she
ran water when she went into the bathroom, so that Dewey
and Suze wouldn't hear her throwing up. Dewey had read the
radiation articles in the atomic packets. She knew what was
happening.

"Who's on the phone?" Terry leaned up on one elbow.

"Dr. Cranshaw's office," Dewey said, keeping her voice
steady. "Want me to tell them to call back? After you've
rested?"

"No, I need to take this one." She stood up, shook her head
to clear it, and went to the phone. She motioned Dewey back
into the kitchen with one—very insistent—hand.

Dewey went. The water was bubbling madly, but she didn't

put the noodles in. She stood between the stove and the doorway, holding her breath, listening.

"Hello? Yes, this is she." A long pause. "Are you certain?" Terry Gordon asked in a strained voice. "No chance that—Oh. I see. Yes. Yes, Tuesday at one thirty. No, I was just starting dinner. Thank you for getting back to me today." Another pause, then Dewey heard the receiver click back into its cradle. She had the package of noodles in her hand by the time Terry came in.

"Hold off on those a bit," she said. She sat down, looked at the pack of cigarettes lying on the tabletop, and shuddered. "Is Suze home yet?"

"She's still at the drugstore," Dewey said. "She should be here pretty soon."

"I'll wait, then." Terry put her face in her hands. "I need to talk to you both."

"It's bad, isn't it?"

"Well, it's certainly not a conversation I hoped to have at thirty-seven. But I'm not entirely surprised." She sighed. "I know the signs as well as anyone."

Dewey took a deep breath and asked the question she and Suze had whispered about, late at night, the question she'd heard in her head a hundred times in the last week. "It's radiation sickness, isn't it?"

Terry Gordon's eyes flew open. "What? How did you—?"

"I'm not a kid, Terry." Dewey sat down in the chair next to her. "I've read all the packets you've been mailing out."

"Oh, kiddo. I'm so sorry." She put her hand on Dewey's shoulder.

Dewey felt like the world was crumpling all around her, no room to breathe, no room for anything but cold sweat and tears. Even though she'd suspected, *knowing* was like being hit with a sledgehammer.

"How long have you been worrying about me?" Terry asked softly.

"A couple of weeks," Dewey managed. "We've heard you throw up, Suze and me. And your hands and feet are swollen. Just like"—Dewey's voice broke as she tried to remember the man's name—"like Lou Slotin, on the Hill. The one who tickled the dragon." She looked into her lap and began to cry.

"Oh, honey, no, no." Terry lifted Dewey's chin with a finger. "Look at me, kiddo." She smiled, a real smile. "It's not the most welcome news—the timing is *lousy*. But I'm not dying." She shook her head. "The rabbit did."

"Huh?" Dewey asked, bewildered. She took off her glasses and wiped her eyes with a napkin.

Terry Gordon sighed, smiled, sighed again. "I'm not dying. I'm not even sick. I'm pregnant."

"What? How did—?"

"In the usual way. The weekend in the mountains, I suspect." She looked at the calendar. "I'll find out more on Tuesday, but I'm pretty sure you and Suze will have a little sister—or brother—around the middle of September."

"Here?"

"Oh, God, no. Phil's still trying to convince me, but this is the clincher. We'll head back to Berkeley as soon as you two are done with school. I want my own doctor and a big city hospital, everything that modern medicine has to offer."

"What about teaching this fall?" Dewey asked.

"I'm just supervising research next semester. The grad students'll cope. Besides, Suze spent her first six months in a bassinet in the chem lab, and she turned out fine. I don't see any reason to treat this one any different. Except this time"—she smiled—"I'll have two built-in babysitters."

Dewey nodded. So many women on the Hill had been pregnant, she knew the routine. But she'd never lived with a baby before, not in the same house. *That* was going to be a brand-new experience. "That'll be . . . interesting," she said.

"You can say that again. Do me a couple of favors?"

"Sure."

"Get me a ginger ale. That usually settles my tummy."

Dewey went to the fridge and set the bottle down on the table. "What else?"

"Skedaddle for an hour or so? Suze'll be home any minute, and I'd like her to think she got the news first."

"Gotcha," Dewey said, heading for the back door. "I'll be at Owen's. He took care of Betsy when she was little. If he can teach me to solder, how hard can diapers be?"

MILK RUN

MARCH 1947

Saturday morning, Suze rode her bike down New York Avenue toward Dale's Piggly Wiggly to pick up groceries. Mom was working on notes for another lecture, and they were out of milk and eggs, hamburger and cereal, and cleanser for the sink. The February air was cold and dry, cold enough that she needed her heavy jacket and a scarf, especially riding into the wind. She felt grown-up and responsible, shopping for the family's food, practicing to be a big sister.

That had been a shock. She was relieved that Mom wasn't sick, but a baby? Everything would be so different next fall. She'd hoped the news would change Dad's mind about staying here, but after Mom told him, they'd had an even bigger fight, and he'd packed a bag and gone to the base. He'd called a few times, but hadn't been home in two weeks. It felt like he was punishing them, and Suze wasn't sure if she missed him.

Saturday morning shoppers crowded the sidewalk, and after a near miss with a lady who could barely see over all her paper bags, Suze got off and walked her bike, parking it against the brick wall next to Dale's. Inside, the store was warm and smelled like vegetables and floor wax and the sawdust by the butcher's counter. She took a striped cloth basket from the stack by the door and unfolded its metal frame. Then she walked up and down the aisles, looking at the colorful labels of cans and packages, her favorite part of shopping.

Most of what was on the shelves was familiar, brands that had been around before the war, things even the PX on the Hill had stocked: Jell-O and Campbell's soup and Ivory soap. But now every week, it seemed, she found something new—NEW! IMPROVED!—products she'd never seen before. Some of them were pretty useful—cans of frozen orange juice that you could have any time of year and didn't have to squeeze. But others were just stupid.

Like cleanser. They used Old Dutch, or sometimes Bon Ami. But today, next to those were bright red cans with spiky yellow flame borders around a roiling mushroom cloud. ATOMITE, it said. *With Atomic-like action!* It pissed Suze off.

The cleanser people hadn't been there on the Hill when the work was so secret, so serious. After V-J Day, Suze thought her parents should be heroes. But there were no parades. What had happened in Hiroshima was as awful as the concentration camps. It wasn't patriotic to say that about *American* science, so everyone made jokes—ha, ha, ha! Nobody could be scared of a cartoon cloud on a can of cleanser.

Songs, ads, comics—everything was "atomic" now, like just using the word would make stuff special? *Atomic-like action!* Who in their right mind wanted a cleanser that worked like the Bomb? It would blow up your sink, your kitchen, turn your whole neighborhood into ashes and rubble and radiation. Some way to clean.

She almost bought a can, just to take it home and share her exasperation—and to prove she hadn't made it up. But pictures of mushroom clouds made Mom mad, or sad. Last week Suze had come home from school and found her in the kitchen, crying. Nothing bad had happened, but—she'd said—no one really cared about what had already happened. Or what *could*, if people didn't listen.

Ynez said Gloria got all weepy when she was pregnant, too, but still . . .

Suze bought Old Dutch.

She put a quart milk bottle and a carton of eggs in the basket—good to eat, but boring to shop for—and got a pound of ground round from the butcher, glad he had meat again. She looked at the list and turned down the cereal aisle, thinking about breakfast. Not Cheerios—they'd just finished that box. Cornflakes were boring. Rice Krispies got soggy fast, but were fun for the first minute.

A bright yellow box of Kix caught her eye. Then she saw

the front: *Get this new amazing Kix Atomic BOMB Ring!* Suze groaned and reached for Rice Krispies, then stopped. Was it the same ring they were selling on *The Lone Ranger* last month? Weird episodes, about a meteorite from outer space, made of some mineral that scientists could use to harness the power of the sun. Sounded like more atomic baloney, except it was supposed to be in olden days. She turned the box over. No Lone Ranger. Just a bunch of bull. *See Genuine Atoms Split to Smithereens! Amazing Scientific Miracle!*

Would people believe *any*thing with the word *science* on it? *This* she had to show Dewey. Not only because they'd listened to *The Lone Ranger* together, but because she'd been on the Hill. That was why they were brothers. Suze put the box of Kix in her basket.

She rode her bike home in indignant anticipation, imagining sitting with Dewey at breakfast, making fun of the poor fools who believed you could see real atoms inside a plastic ring. It *was* neat-looking—gold with a red-and-silver "bomb" on the top. More like a rocket, if you knew anything about real science. But since last fall, Suze didn't think rockets were any better.

It had taken her a week, after Thanksgiving, to get up the nerve to talk to her dad about the photo in *LIFE*. He'd looked at it once, and sighed. "You and your mother." He shook his head. "Why do you insist on living in the past? The war's over. We won, and now we're moving forward." He'd closed the magazine and handed it back to Suze. "At least I am."

She didn't ask him again.

Suze leaned her bike against the back steps and brought in the groceries. Her mother's typewriter clattered from the dining room. No sign of Dewey. Suze put the perishables away in the fridge and the cleanser under the sink. She thought about leaving the cereal out on the counter, but it would be a better as a surprise. She put it in the cupboard sideways, so that it looked like an ordinary box of Kix.

In the morning, she would pull it out with a flourish— *ta-da!*

Riding her bike and looking at food had made her hungry. She grabbed the bread and poured a glass of milk.

Dewey came in the back door ten minutes later, fiddling with a black box with a big knob and some wires.

"What's that?" Suze mumbled around a mouthful of peanut butter sandwich.

"A transformer. It'll run parts of the Wall without batteries, and we can turn it off without having to unhook stuff. It used to be part of Owen's train set."

"He's a useful guy to know."

"Sometimes. This morning he was acting like a moron." She sat down and thunked the box onto the table. Dewey didn't thunk much, so it was either really heavy or she was annoyed. Or both. "Remember the *atomic* ring the Lone Ranger was hawking?" she asked. "On those meteor episodes?"

Suze almost swallowed her milk the wrong way. "Yeah."

"Well, Owen wasted fifteen cents and sent away for one. He's *sure* he'll be able to see atoms splitting." Dewey shook her head. "I thought he was smart."

Suze got up and opened the cupboard door. "I was going to surprise you at breakfast tomorrow, but—here." She put the Kix box on the table. "We can read the back out loud now, and eat the cereal in the morning."

Dewey turned the box around. "This is worse than I thought. Listen." She began to read in a dramatic announcer voice. *"Actual atoms—split to smithereens inside this ring, and you can see brilliant atomic effects."*

"Ri-i-ght," Suze said, and they both started to chuckle.

"Wait, it gets better. *You'll see brilliant flashes of light in the inky darkness inside the atom chamber. These frenzied vivid flashes are caused by the released energy of atoms. PERFECTLY SAFE! The atomic materials inside the ring are harmless."*

By the time Dewey got to the bottom, Suze was laughing so hard she was holding her sides and almost fell off her chair. Dewey wasn't doing much better.

"Is this a private joke, or can anyone join in?" Mrs. Gordon said from the kitchen doorway. She refilled her coffee cup and leaned against the counter.

"P-p-promise you won't get mad," Suze said between guffaws.

"Why would I get mad about a box of cereal?"

Suze didn't say a word, just handed her mother the box, back side first.

"Oh, for crissakes, not *another* one?"

"See. I told you you'd get mad."

"I'm not mad, sweetie. Just exasperated." She pushed her reading glasses down onto her nose. "What amazing powers are the atoms in *Kix* supposed to have, pray tell?" She began to read the box, glaring at it. A second later, her face changed to a kind of puzzled look. Then she smiled. "Interesting." She sat down.

"*Interesting?*" Dewey said.

"Ummm." Mrs. Gordon sipped her coffee and continued to read while the two girls looked at her, then at each other. After a minute, she handed the box back to Suze. "I think I've got fifteen cents to spare. Let's send away for one."

"What?!" Dewey and Suze said in unison. They stared at her.

"Who are you, and what have you done with my mom?" Suze asked.

Mrs. Gordon chuckled. "You don't believe what it says on the box?"

"Of course not," Dewey said. "No one can *see* atoms split."

"Technically, no. But if this is what I think it is, we *can* observe radioactive decay at an atomic level." She took another sip of her coffee. "Stop looking at me like I'm ready for the loony bin."

"Sorry." Dewey picked up the box again. "What did you mean, 'if this is what I think it is'?"

"It might be a little spinthariscope."

"I'll go get the dictionary." Suze stood up.

"I've trained you well," her mother said. "But it's a kind of a specialized term. I doubt if it's in Webster's. As long as you're up, though, get my smokes from the dining room table. I'll give you the two-minute lecture."

A minute later, Terry Gordon lit a Chesterfield and leaned back in the kitchen chair. "You know I got into this whole business because when I was about your age I fell in love with Marie Curie and her work, right?"

The two girls nodded.

"Well, in 1903, Curie gave a few grains of radium to an English scientist named Crookes, to experiment with. Very rare. Only minuscule amounts existed back then. Crookes knew that radium atoms constantly disintegrate and give off alpha particles—tiny, tiny, tiny bits of the nucleus. He went into a dark room to sprinkle some on a zinc sulfide screen, because it fluoresces—it glows—when the radium atoms decay. Then he spilled the radium."

"Oops," said Suze.

"Oops, indeed. He *had* to recover every last grain, so he put the screen under his microscope." She took a puff. "What do you think he saw?"

"Little glowing bits?" Dewey said.

"Better. Shooting stars. Teeny-weeny fireworks. Hundreds of green blips a minute, every time an alpha particle hit a zinc sulfide molecule. Flash, flash, flash."

"Wow," Dewey and Suze said in one voice.

Terry Gordon laughed. "I'll say. I don't know what the 1903 equivalent of *wow* was, but I'm willing to bet Crookes said something like it. He made a little brass tube with a magnifying lens at one end, a speck of radium salt and a zinc sulfide screen at the other. The first instrument for observing atomic reactions. He called it a spinthariscope, Greek for *spark*. I've got one in a box upstairs."

"And you think that the Kix ring is one?" Suze asked.

"That's my guess." She tapped the cereal box. "Why on earth did they have to make it look like a bomb?"

"It's *atomic*," Suze said, making a face. "You think it'll work?"

"It should. The eyepiece will be pretty small, and plastic, so the optics won't be great, but I imagine we'll see a bit of a show." She stubbed out her cigarette. "Are you two planning to catch the matinee today?"

"Not me. I'm going to wire up the Wall." Dewey pointed to the transformer.

"I'm meeting Ynez at the White Sands at quarter of one," Suze said. "*Holiday in Mexico* and *Son of Zorro*."

"Sounds more exciting than the laundry on my to-do list." She reached into the pocket of her slacks and tossed three nickels onto the table. "Cut out the box top and fill in our address, then tape these on. Stamps and envelopes are on the dining-room table. Suze can drop it in the mailbox on her way to the movies."

"Don't we have to eat all the cereal first?" Dewey asked.

"No, just cut carefully. I don't want Kix rolling all over my kitchen." She stood up. "Once I get the sheets and towels hung out to dry, I'll see if I can find my scope, and give you a demonstration tonight, after dinner."

"Neat," Suze said. "Will yours still work? The radium hasn't worn out?"

"Hardly," Mrs. Gordon said with a small, tight smile. "That's the problem. It's radioactive. It'll still be sparking away for another two or three thousand years."

THE DARK ROOM

"How was the movie?" Dewey asked. She stood on the step stool, a long trail of wire hanging from the little Ferris wheel at the top of the Wall.

"*Zorro* was okay. The other one was lame. Lots of music and kissing, and stars like Jane Powell, who's not even Mexican. The cartoons were good. Bugs Bunny and a mad scientist." Suze looked at the Wall. "Does it do anything new?"

"It will in a minute. This is the last connection, I think." Dewey tucked the wire through the jumble of ramps and tubes and tracks until the free end dangled behind the table. "Hold on a sec." She disappeared underneath. Suze saw the wire go taut. Then there was a sharp *pop!* and the air smelled like something burning. A wisp of smoke rose up, but nothing else happened.

"You okay?" Suze asked.

"Yeah." Dewey's voice was a little muffled. "I just forgot to unplug the transformer before I hooked up that last wire. Try the lamp for me."

Suze turned the knob on the floor lamp beside the couch, and the bulb lit up inside the shade. "It works fine."

"Good. I didn't blow a fuse this time."

A few mechanical sounds from under the table, then the whole left side of the Wall suddenly burst into motion. The Ferris wheel turned, dropping marbles through gates, and a little whirligig spun round and round, its arms hitting a set of graduated bells that rang in a sort of clangy harmony.

Dewey backed out. "Not bad," she said, still on her knees. "Next week I'll get an extension cord, so we can turn it on and off without crawling under there." She lay flat and reached an arm out. The Wall came to a stop, the marbles rolling to the bottom, the whirligig slowing. *Clang. Clang . . . Clang.*

She stood up and brushed dust off the front of her pants. "Whad'ya think?"

"Super. You did all that this afternoon?"

"I'd been thinking about it for a couple of weeks. When's dinner?"

"About an hour. Ham and potatoes. Oh, and Mom found her—" *Rats.* Suze had repeated the word over and over, but five hours of movies had erased it from her brain. "—her scope thing."

"Spinthariscope," Dewey said.

Of course she *remembered.* "Yeah. It only works in total

214

darkness, so she said we can go down to the basement after we eat."

Dewey glanced at the stars outside the window. "It got dark an hour ago."

"I know. But she's taking a nap and said not to bother her."

After dinner, Suze did the dishes as fast as she could without breaking anything. Dewey read a magazine with a big, bug-eyed monster on the cover, carrying off a spacewoman who wasn't wearing very many clothes. Mom did the crossword puzzle and smoked. Suze didn't see any sign of an atomic instrument.

She wiped her hands on the towel that hung over the faucet. "So, where is it?" she asked. She rolled down her shirtsleeves and put her sweater back on.

"In my pocket." Her mother pulled out a little hinged box covered in pebbled black leather. She set it down next to her coffee cup.

"It's not very big," Suze said. She reached for the box.

"Don't open it!"

Suze jerked her hand back. "How come? Is it dangerous?"

"No, just *very* sensitive to light. It'd be useless for twenty-four hours."

"Oh. Sorry."

"My fault. I should have warned you. Didn't mean to snap." She ground out her cigarette. "Ready?"

Suze turned off the kitchen lights and they trooped down

the steep wooden steps by the back door, single file, Mrs. Gordon bringing up the rear with the big silver flashlight and the little box. She shut the kitchen door behind her.

It wasn't a full basement, just a root cellar and some storage shelves. The walls were thick stone and the floor was hard-packed dirt, cool and a little damp. Suze remembered her father saying it stayed the same temperature year-round, about sixty degrees, which was nice in the summer, but chilly on an early March night.

"Sit down and get comfortable," Terry Gordon said. "We'll be here at least twenty minutes." She unstrapped her wristwatch and put it in her pocket. "The hands glow," she explained. "Dewey, it'll be easier to see the effects without your glasses, so go ahead and stow them before I douse the lights."

They sat in a rough triangle, legs folded Indian style. Suze's mother reached up and tugged on the string from the single ceiling bulb.

The basement went totally dark.

For a minute, Suze could still see blue-green floating shapes, afterimages of her mother's white sweater and Dewey's socks. Those faded and it was pitch black. She held her hand in front of her face. Nothing. She could feel her fingers wiggle, and knew exactly where they were, but she couldn't see them. A strange sensation.

"I figure it'll take ten or fifteen minutes for our eyes to dark-adapt," her mother said, a disembodied voice to her left.

Suze's senses felt like they were on alert, because sight had gone missing. She could feel her mother's leg—a few inches away, radiating more heat than the cool air—and smell the smoke on her skin. She could hear Dewey breathing softly on her other side, a faint whiff of ham and potatoes on her breath. Was this what it was like to be blind? No colors, no shapes, no depth, no direction. Just space, all around her.

The three of them sat in silence, mostly, and after what seemed like a lot longer than ten minutes, Suze heard a small click as her mother opened the latch on the little leather box.

"Okey-dokey," she said a few seconds later. "It's working like gangbusters."

Suze felt a warm hand around her wrist, and something cool and rounded slid into her palm. She picked it up with her other hand and ran her fingers over it, thinking of the blind men and the elephant. It felt like a metal tube, about an inch long. She grasped it between her thumb and forefinger and held it up to her eye.

"I don't see anything," she said, disappointed.

"Give it thirty seconds." Mom's voice.

Suze did. "Nope, nothing."

She smelled hand cream when her mother took it back. A pause. A chuckle.

"Wrong end, sweetie." Her mother guided it back into Suze's fingers.

"Oh." She touched the smooth, convex curve of a glass lens,

a different smooth, a different curve than the metal. She held it up to her eye again, like a stubby pirate telescope, and the universe exploded with tiny pinpoints of light.

Her field of vision filled with stars in an infinite, three-dimensional space where there had been flat, featureless black a second before. They twinkled and flashed, over and over and over, dozens every second, winking off and on faster than any real stars ever would, so fast she couldn't tell what color they were. Greenish-white? Gray? So many. So fast. Everywhere.

"These are actually atoms." She said it in a hushed voice.

"Yes," her mother replied in a whisper.

All the news. All the pictures and articles and big words talking about atomic this and atomic that, and here they were. Not a cartoon, not a diagram.

Atomic particles.

"Can I see?" Dewey asked.

Suze nodded, even though it was dark. But she didn't have words right then. She reached over and found Dewey's hand, slid the little tube into it.

"Oh my God," Dewey said a few seconds later. Then she was silent, too.

They sat on the floor for a long time, passing the spinthariscope until Mrs. Gordon groaned. "Okay. The old lady's getting a bit stiff. Let's head back up."

Suze lowered the scope from her eye and gave it back. She

heard the snap of the little case and a rustle of fabric as her mother stood up.

"I'm not going to turn on the bulb," Terry Gordon said. "Too much of a shock. There should be enough moonlight for us to make it to the kitchen table."

"Can I take the scope out and look at it then?"

"Sure. We're through for the night."

Once they were upstairs, Suze could see pretty well, even though the lights were off. Her mother got the cocoa out of the cupboard. "Cover your eyes. I'm going to open the fridge and get the milk." Suze did, and when she took her hands away, the walls danced with strange flickering shadows from the blue flames of the gas burner, like a kitchen monster movie.

She opened the box and examined the brass tube. It looked so ordinary. She held it up to her eye. Nothing. "The sparks— that's *always* going on in there?"

"Always." Her mother stirred the cocoa.

Suze stared for a moment, then returned the scope to its case. Even when no one was looking, the radium atoms in the tube kept disintegrating, giving off particles. All day, all night. All year. All century. Two thousand years from now—in 3947, a Flash Gordon, made-up year—the little speck would still be losing bits of itself, one by one.

PATENT PENDING

Spring flowers were pretty, no matter where you lived, Suze thought, looking out at the crocuses that had appeared at the edge of the driveway. She stood at the kitchen sink rinsing spilled root beer out of the dishtowel. A moment later, she saw Owen Parker leap the irrigation ditch on Eleventh Street and run down the alley. His feet barely seemed to touch the ground. He skidded to a stop at their back door, gravel flying. Rutherford, who had been snoozing on the steps, leaped up, his orange-striped tail big as a puffball, and hissed once.

"Sorry, fella," Owen said. "Didn't mean'ta scare ya." He reached down to scratch the cat behind the ears, but Rutherford walked away with wounded dignity and collapsed onto another sunny spot. Owen rapped his knuckles on the pane.

"It's open," Suze called.

"Hey," Owen came in. "Dewey home?"

"Upstairs, working on the Wall."

"Hey," Owen said again, this time to Ynez, who sat at the kitchen table rolling a pair of dice across the board of a Sorry! game.

She waved her fingers.

"She's got blue," Suze said. "I'm pretty much sunk." She pointed to the intercom box. "Wanna call, or just go up?"

"Up," said Owen. "Can't wait. Thanks." He raced out of the room and Suze heard him take the stairs two—maybe three—at a time.

"Wonder what he's in such a hurry about?" Ynez said. She rolled a five and sent Suze's last man back to Start. "Hah! Uncle?"

"Yeah, I give. That's three in a row. Let's go listen to *The Shadow*."

Dewey stood on the step stool, looking at the Wall, close up, trying to figure out where to put a row of tiny flashlight bulbs. Terry had given her a soldering iron for her birthday, which made it easier to assemble parts before hanging them up. The bulbs were in individual sockets, mounted on a strip of tin, the batteries on the back.

She turned at the sound of footsteps on the stairs, coming up fast. Faster than Suze's usual thuds.

"I saw one!" Owen said when he got to the top. "I saw a *television*, Sprock!"

He lifted Dewey off the table and twirled her once before

setting her onto the floor. She wasn't really in the mood to be twirled, but Owen was so happy, grinning from ear to ear, revealing pale rubber bands stretched between his braces. They hadn't been there when she'd been at his house two days ago.

"In El Paso?"

"Yep. The dentist got done with me sooner than usual. Ma was still working, so I walked around town for an hour, just killing time, ya know, and there it was, big as life, in the Popular's front window—a DuMont with a *ten*-inch screen."

It was the longest sentence Dewey'd ever heard him say. "What was on?"

"Nothing." He shrugged. "No station in El Paso yet. Nearest one is Los Angeles. But if they're in stores, it can't be long."

True. No one would buy a box that didn't do anything. "How much was it?"

"Four hundred dollars."

Dewey whistled. "You're kidding."

"Nope. Almost two months' work for my dad. Good months. But it's *real*! Ain't that the bells?"

"It's pretty exciting," Dewey agreed.

"And that's not all. Pop found out the GI Bill will pay for the repair course—the one I showed you, in the magazine?—so we'll do it together. He's gotta fill out forms to get the dough, but the VA says that'll only take a month or two. Then we'll put one of those babies together, and good-bye Alamo High."

"Right. Only two months till school's out."

"I'm not just talkin' summer vacation. Come September, when all those suckers are sitting in junior English class, I'm gonna be a working man."

"You'd quit *school*?" Dewey stared as if Owen had just grown two heads.

"Yessiree Bob. I know enough math, and I don't need geography and Shakespeare and all that bull to fix machines."

"What about college?"

"Why would I want to go away? I'm gonna be the go-to guy here in Alamo. Four years from now, I bet I'm making enough to open my own shop."

Dewey took a step back, so she could look up at his face without craning her neck. He was really excited, but she didn't get it. She liked school. "Have you told your dad?"

"Last night. First it was no. Not on your life. But I said, 'Look, Pop. Nothing like this's ever happened before. I wanta be in from the get-go. Television's gonna change the world, Pop,' I said." He pumped his fist. "Took some convincing, but he finally said he'd sign the permission."

"Oh." Dewey felt disappointed. She wasn't sure why. It wasn't *her* life, and by next fall, she'd be in Berkeley.

"What's the matter? I thought you'd be happy." Owen looked baffled. "Pop's gonna make me a partner. That's why I came over. I want'cha to help me paint a new sign—PARKER AND SON, TELEVISION REPAIR." He spread his hands over his head, as if it were going to be blazing neon instead of paint on wood.

"I can't this week," Dewey said quickly. Once the sign got painted, Owen would never change his mind. "Um, I've got cramps," she lied. *Oops.* She forgot it wasn't an excuse that worked with boys. Owen blushed to the roots of his hair.

"Oh. Oh. Sure. Yeah." He rubbed the side of his cheek, and she wondered if his mouth hurt. It usually did, after he came back from El Paso. "We can wait. I mean, you'll be okay in a couple of . . ." He let the untouchable subject drift away and picked up a screwdriver, fiddling with it nervously, then put it down with elaborate care. "I should go, let you rest, or whatever you do when . . ."

Owen looked like a hangdog turtle, not the hare who'd raced up a few minutes before. Part of her wanted to shake him, make him come to his senses and not do anything permanently stupid. But another part wanted to reach out and touch him, because he was her friend, and she felt bad, wrecking his excitement.

"Hey," she said.

He looked up.

"If we wait a couple of weeks, the weather will be warmer, and maybe we could rustle up a work party? You ask some guys, and I'll see if Suze'll help. She's good with paint, and tall enough to reach without a ladder. It'll be lots faster." And with other people around, maybe he wouldn't notice if she was less than enthusiastic.

"Okay. That sounds swell." He stopped a few feet from

the stairs. "Oh. I almost forgot." He lifted the back of his shirt-tail and pulled a magazine out of the waistband of his jeans. "I picked up the March *Weird Tales* in El Paso. It's got a story by that Sturgeon guy you like."

She hesitated, because she'd lied to him about having cramps and didn't feel like she deserved a present right then. "Thanks." She took the magazine.

"No prob. Um—feel better." He ducked his head and loped downstairs.

Dewey stared at *Weird Tales* as Owen's footsteps grew distant.

Sometimes bug-eyed monsters made more sense than real life.

WHEN
IT
CHANGED

THE TROUBLEMAKERS

APRIL 1947

On Monday mornings, the magazine truck came to Corner Drugs. The driver dropped off big twine-wrapped bundles of new issues, and took away the covers of the ones that hadn't sold. The drugstore got a refund for every cover they sent back. Just the covers, because whole magazines were too heavy to ship once they were out-of-date and useless. That was what Ynez had told Suze.

Monday afternoons were the best days to find treasure, because the manager dumped all the stripped magazines into the big metal trash cans in the alley behind the store. Perfectly good magazines—for free. The color pictures inside were fine, so Suze could live without the shiny covers. The trick was to get there as soon as the school bell rang. After that, the pickings could be pretty slim.

It was even better than the dump, Suze thought, as she

watched the clock tick toward three thirty. Home Ec was so boring. Yesterday's lecture was about polio again, and how you shouldn't come to school if you had a cold, because you were a threat to other students. Today Mrs. Winfield was going on and on about vagrants and tramps. Now that it was warm again, they loitered near the highway. Talking to strangers was dangerous. Suze wasn't listening. Anyone older than six knew *that*.

The hand on the big black clock ticked once more, and a second later, the bell rang. Suze jumped up and was out the door and on the first stair before the clanging stopped. She'd taken her binder and her books home at lunch, so she'd have her hands free. Ynez met her at the front entrance.

Only a block and a half to the drugstore, and if they hustled, they could make it before any of the other kids got there. Unless *they'd* cut class. The older boys sometimes did, to grab *Field & Stream* and *Football Stories* first. Suze didn't care. She wanted *McCall's* and *Good Housekeeping* and *The Saturday Evening Post*. The articles were boring, but there were big glossy color ads that she could cut out and add to her growing files and sorted boxes: MEAT. LADIES IN HATS. DOGS. Even, this spring, TELEVISIONS. Ynez wanted *Modern Screen* and *Movie Mirror*.

They ducked into the narrow walkway beside the drugstore, breathing hard, and turned the corner into the brick alley at the back, then stopped suddenly. No high-school boys pawing through the trash cans, but they weren't alone.

By the far wall, near the driveway that led to the Plaza Bar, a motorcycle sat parked with its kickstand down. A woman reclined on the leather seat, her booted feet up on the handlebars, her bare muscular arms propped on saddlebags that hung on either side of the rear wheel. A black leather cap tilted back on her head, curly auburn hair spilling over the collar of her white T-shirt, the sleeves rolled up to her shoulders. A pack of Lucky Strikes peeked out of the top of the right sleeve.

She was reading *Cosmopolitan*, which seemed odd to Suze.

"Holy smokes," Ynez whispered. "Margarita Carmen Cansino. She's a dead ringer."

She *was* really pretty, Suze thought. Glamorous, even in a T-shirt. She moved back a step, her feet scuffing in the gravel, and the woman looked up.

"What's cookin'?" Her voice was low and a little husky, like Lauren Bacall.

Suze stood still, her mouth open.

The woman chuckled. "Don't worry, kid. I don't bite." She smiled, showing nice white teeth, except there was a gap, a missing tooth, way back on one side, which sort of spoiled the movie star effect.

"Good. That's good. Okay," Suze said. She backed up another step anyway. The woman nodded and went back to her magazine. *Zowie!* That had to be, hands-down, the most dangerous—and interesting—person in Alamogordo. Suze had never seen a lady like that anywhere, not on the Hill, not even in Berkeley.

She and Ynez looked into the trash cans. *Eureka!*

A whole pile of ladies' magazines, their bottom corners crumpled, but otherwise fine, lay on top of the heap. Suze bundled them into her arms. Most Mondays she sorted through her finds right there in the alley, but today she thought she'd do that at home. She was too aware of the woman on the motorcycle behind her.

"Find anything?" she asked Ynez.

"A few." She held up three magazines. "There may be some more farther down, but the boys never take the movie ones, so"—she moved her chin in the direction of the far wall—"I'll just come back later."

"I was thinking the same thing." Suze shifted the stack of magazines, cradling them all in one arm, and turned toward the passageway. On New York Avenue, there'd be other kids, in front of the drugstore and heading home from school. *Safety in numbers,* Mrs. Winfield had said.

Just then five boys barreled around the street corner, hell-bent for leather and the trash cans. Suze stepped back into the alley, out of the way. Bobby, the kid who'd sent them to the salvage yard, had seen Suze here before. He nodded as he passed, but checked out her magazines, in case there were any he'd claim dibs on.

"Va-va-va-voom!" the boy behind him said, and gave a long,

low wolf whistle. "Check out the sassy chassis on the Harley."

The woman looked up from her magazine. "Can it, junior."

A tall, dark-haired boy stepped forward, a big-shot senior whose father owned the car dealership out on the highway. He pulled a comb out of his pocket, slicked back his hair, then held out his hand. "What's your pleasure, treasure? You crack the whip, I'll take the trip."

The woman looked him up and down. She sighed and shook her head, like she'd seen *that* before, and closed her magazine without a word, tucking it into the left-hand saddlebag. Then, in a graceful motion that Suze envied, she swung her long legs down off the handlebars, straddling the bike, her boots on the gravel.

"Hey, hey, hey," the boy said. "What's your hurry? You're not giving *Johnny* the old brusheroo, are ya, Red?" He smiled a tight, confident smile.

"Ah, for crissakes." She shook her head again and shrugged on a black leather jacket. "Back to the nursery, cream puff."

The big Harley roared into life as she gunned the engine and expertly turned it, then hit the gas again, spraying gravel across Johnny's Keds. She sped down the driveway onto Tenth Street, leaving five startled boys and a blue haze of exhaust.

Shazam, thought Suze. Now *there* was a lady you'd want on your side in a fight. She stared, fascinated, for a moment, until Johnny turned, a scowl on his face.

"What're *you* lookin' at?" he said.

"Come *on*!" Ynez grabbed Suze's arm and tugged her around the corner.

"You wanna come over?" Suze asked, when they were safely back on New York Avenue. "Look through this stuff?"

"Okay. You got real Cokes? I'm sick of the Crystal sodas from the plant."

"Prob'ly. Or Pepsi." Suze wasn't sure what was in the fridge. She was thinking about the stash of *Popular Mechanics* in the attic. Maybe Dewey'd let her cut out just one page? She remembered seeing a Harley Davidson ad, and had the glimmer of an idea for the Wall that would need a new folder: MOTORCYCLES.

SORRY, RIGHT NUMBER

"It'd be real exciting, riding something like that," Suze said as she and Ynez turned the corner onto Michigan Avenue. The branches of the cottonwoods were full of small green leaves, and the two girls had their sweaters tied around their waists. "You could go *any*where."

"You can do that in a car, and it's a lot safer."

"Cars are boring."

"Only 'cause *you* can't drive yet." Ynez sidestepped Suze's elbow and changed the subject. "How's your mom?"

"Okay. She says none of her pants fit, but she's not throwing up anymore." Suze opened the front door. "I'm home," she called.

No answer.

They put the magazines down on the table, next to a note that said: *Shopping. Back ≈ 5:00. xoxo. TG.*

"Looks like we've got the place to ourselves," Suze said. Dewey was at Owen's, borrowing tools. Suze got two Cokes from the fridge and found a package of Hostess cupcakes in the breadbox.

"I like the traditional food of your people," Ynez said, biting into hers. "My mom only buys the ones from the *panadería*. They're too dry."

Suze peeled the dark cap of frosting off in one piece and stuck her tongue into the moist, dark cake. She licked the creamy center out.

"Why do you eat it that way?" Ynez took another bite, frosting and cake and cream all together.

"I always have. I like to taste the textures separate."

"*You're* strange." Ynez wiped chocolate from the side of her mouth. "Have you done the Home Ec assignment yet?"

"A chart of all my 'Daily Dainties'? No." Suze made a face, as if the very idea were poison. "I'd rather barf."

"Why do you always make such a stink? It's easier to just do what she asks."

"C'mon. Six weeks on *good grooming*?" Suze stuck out her tongue. "That's—" She couldn't even think of a word. The stupidest of all stupid *girl* stuff.

Every week Mrs. Winfield handed out another checklist of dos and don'ts that were even worse than Girl Scout rules had been. *Do* scrub your face with soap and warm water every night.

Don't share your toothbrush. *Don't* eat too many sweets. And pamphlets from some women's magazine: "Let's Be Lovely." "Mirror Magic." "Facts About Figures."

The other girls at her table read them right away. Mary Sue even *underlined* parts, like it was an instruction book handed down from God. Suze pretended to be interested, if Mrs. Winfield was watching, but after class she threw them to the bottom of her locker and tried to forget they existed.

"Are you doing it?" she asked.

"Sure. It's no big deal. I brush my teeth at night anyway, so why not write it down? And Mama and Doña Luisa and my sister Gloria and I do each other's hair every Sunday afternoon. It's fun."

"Fun?"

Ynez nodded. "Mama calls it our Señoritas' Siesta. We sit and yack and drink sodas and take turns with the brush. It feels nice." She studied Suze's hair, straight and blonde and pulled back into a ponytail. "Lots of movie stars are blondes. Real different hair than mine. If I practice on you, you could put it on your chart."

"Nah, that's okay." Suze backed up a step and finished her cupcake.

"Big baby," Ynez said. She thought for a minute. "Tell you what. Instead of lookin' through magazines, let me brush your hair—two hundred strokes, like Mrs. Winfield wants—and give you a shampoo. Then, while your hair dries, I'll teach you all the bad words in Spanish, the ones my brothers don't think I know."

"I dunno," Suze said. She didn't pay much attention to her hair, now that it was long enough for a ponytail. She washed it in the shower Sunday nights, then put a rubber band around it and let it dry. But curse words her mother wouldn't understand? That was tempting. "Okay," she said with a sigh.

"Line up the firing squad, boys," Ynez yelled to an invisible army.

Suze smiled, a little, because Ynez was in her actress mood, and because that was pretty much what she'd been thinking.

They went upstairs and Ynez assembled supplies: hairbrush, comb, rubber bands, shampoo, and a big bath towel. "We'll do it in the kitchen. Bigger sink, easier to get the suds out. And the booklet says blondes should rinse with lemon juice, 'to keep your golden tresses shining,' and I've been wanting to try that."

"So now I'm an experiment?"

"*Bwah-hah-hah.*" Ynez did a pretty good evil-scientist laugh.

Suze cracked a smile. "Too bad. We're out of lemons."

Back in the kitchen, Ynez laid everything out on the table, sat Suze down on a chair, facing backward, "so you can lean on your arms, and I can brush all the way down," then stepped back. "Zo," she said in a fakey French accent. "Madame Ynez will now proceed to make you bee-yoo-ti-ful." She kissed her fingers with a loud smack and draped the towel over the back of the chair.

"Now what?"

"Something my mom taught me. Close your eyes."

Suze did, but was wary and alert for tricks. Ynez began to rub her shoulders, kneading the muscles, which were pretty tight. Both shoulders, then up the back of her neck, to the top of her head, strong, nimble fingers massaging her scalp.

"Mmmm," Suze murmured. That felt better than any beauty shop. She eased down onto the chair in front of her.

"Okay?"

"Mmmm."

Ynez ran both hands down the back of Suze's head, then untucked her ponytail through the rubber band, so fast it didn't even hurt. Suze was impressed. When she did it, she always pulled out a few hairs.

She held her breath when Ynez began to brush the ends, remembering when she was little and Mom tried to get out tangles. But the way Ynez did it, the brush didn't pull all the way to her scalp.

"Do you raise rats in here?" Ynez asked.

"Shut up." Suze turned her head and felt a hand on her chin, gentle but firm.

"Sit *still*."

Suze sat. Ynez began to brush with long strokes, from the

top of Suze's head to the ends of her hair, lifting it up and out and brushing back the other way. Suze could feel air on the back of her neck. "Are you counting? Two hundred strokes?"

"Don't need to. I can tell when it's 'lustrous and more manageable.'"

It did feel nice. The motion of the brush was regular and soothing. A line from one of the Home Ec booklets drifted into Suze's mind—*Take time to pamper yourself*—and for once that sounded okay. "You and your mom do this every Sunday?" she asked in a slow, sleepy voice.

"Since I was a little girl. I'll miss it when I leave."

"You're going somewhere?"

"Hollywood. I told you. But not till I graduate." She gave Suze's hair a few more strokes. "Then I'll walk down to the depot with my suitcase, right up to the ticket window, and say 'Los Angeles, please. One way.' Why would I want to stay around here? There's nothing but desert and—*Chihuahuita.*" She said it with a hard edge to her voice—and the brush.

"Ow," said Suze.

"Sorry."

Ynez worked in silence for a minute, then swept the brush from Suze's forehead to the tips of her hair, three times. "There. Ready for your shampoo?"

"Sure," Suze said. She knew she had a dopey grin, but didn't care. She felt like she could float across the kitchen.

Ynez ran the water until it was warm, but not too hot, and uncapped the shampoo. She flipped the towel open and draped it around Suze's neck, fastening it with a clothespin. "Okay, lean over the sink."

Suze felt the first rush of water just as the doorbell rang. She jerked upright and felt a trickle run down her collar, under the towel. "Probably the mailman with a package. Or a Jehovah's Witness. Everyone else uses the back door and knocks."

"I'd get it," Ynez said. "But I hate it when people think I'm the maid."

"Why would they?"

"Lots of Mexican girls drop out and go to work for you north-side *gringos*."

"Oh." Suze hadn't known that. "Hold on," she yelled. "I'm coming." She rubbed her hair so it wasn't dripping, and draped the towel over the post at the end of the stairs. She opened the door. "Hel—"

Suze stopped, her mouth open. The motorcycle woman stood on the front porch, a scrap of paper in her hand. She had put on deep red lipstick and wore a beige sweater over her blue jeans. The leather jacket and cap lay across the seat of the Harley on the front walk.

Standing, she and the woman were the same height. Suze stared. Mrs. Winfield hadn't said what to do when dangerous strangers came to your *house*.

"Whoa." The woman stared back, then shook her head. "I can't believe I didn't recognize you. I guess you changed more than I expected."

"Huh?" Suze said, confused. "My hair's just wet."

The woman smiled, a sad little smile that went all the way to her eyes, and made her look even prettier. "You don't even remember me, do you?" Her voice was still husky, but softer than it had been in the alley.

"Jeez-Louise, it was forty-five minutes ago. Of course I remember." Suze reached for the doorknob. "But if you're selling something, we're not interested."

"Wait." She looked at the paper. "This *is* 1229 Michigan Avenue?"

Suze nodded, feeling her shoulders tense again. "How did you get my address?"

"It wasn't easy. I had to jump through a lot of hoops to track you down, DeeDee."

DeeDee? Who the hell was DeeDee? "Sorry, lady. Right house, but we're just renting. I don't know any DeeDee. My name is Suze."

"Oh. I wonder why—?" She sighed and folded the paper into her pocket. "Well, sorry to bother you." She held out her hand. "I'm Rita Gallucci."

PALACE OF DARKNESS

After the bell rang, the main hallway of Alamogordo High School was loud with students talking and laughing, the hollow clang of metal locker doors slamming shut, the scuffling of hundreds of leather-soled shoes on the linoleum floor.

Dewey stood next to Owen's locker, waiting for him to get out of English. Suze had sprinted out of Home Ec to go trash-picking with Ynez.

"Hey, Sprock." Owen reached around her and opened his locker.

"Hey. Can I borrow your socket wrench set for a couple of days?"

"Sure. I'm goin' to the shop in an hour or so." He put his black marbled composition book onto the shelf and tucked a sheaf of purple homework dittos into his binder. He still talked about quitting school, but they hadn't painted a new sign yet.

He said it was because he and his dad couldn't agree on a color, but Dewey hoped Mr. Parker was trying to change Owen's mind.

"But right now," he continued, "I've got auditorium duty. Coach is screening some new Driver-Ed films for the principal and folks. Might have a real class next year." He closed the door with a soft but solid thunk. "Come along and keep me company?"

"Okay," Dewey said. "Then I'll walk you home."

"Carry my books?" Owen teased.

"Sure. As long as you carry *me*."

"Oh, my achin' back." He looked at Dewey's empty hands. "No homework?"

"I finished it in Home Ec." She made a face. "It's Personal Grooming month, and Janice was in the catbird seat. We were supposed to be watching *exactly* how she rolls her hair every night, but who cares."

"Your hair's curly enough." Owen unhooked the ring of keys from his belt loop. "I thought you girls were learning to cook? Something practical."

"Last month. But Mrs. Winfield said food prices are too high. All we ever did was read cookbooks and make white sauce. Even that took a week—twenty girls and only one stove. Home Ec's pretty useless."

"I'll say." Owen dangled the keys. "You want to run the projector today?"

"Sure." She'd spent a whole Saturday in training, but Mr. Knott hadn't put her name on the rotation list for projectionists yet, or given her a set of keys. She could run all the machines and do repairs—tighten loose fittings, change the bulbs, strip new leader onto old film—but it was still Owen and Gilbert and Everett who wheeled the cart to classrooms. Was it because she was the new kid, or because she was a girl? If she asked anyone—even Owen—she didn't think she'd get a straight answer.

The classroom equipment and carts were stored in a closet on the second floor. The big projector in the auditorium stayed in the booth, a tiny room with a wide glass window, high above rows of varnished wooden seats. Owen unlocked the door at the back of the last row. Dewey climbed the narrow stairs.

At the top, he had to duck to get through the doorway, and when he stood up straight, she could hear his hair brush the acoustic tile ceiling. The booth was Dewey's favorite place in the whole school: tucked away, hidden and secret, like a room in a Nancy Drew mystery. In the winter, when it'd been too cold for anyone to go home at noon, kids ate lunch in the auditorium and they'd shown movies—Flash Gordon serials and Woody Woodpecker cartoons. But now that it was spring, she borrowed Owen's key sometimes to have a quiet lunch by herself.

She turned on the lights. From up here, she could control almost everything: the house lights, the PA system, and the screen that rolled down from a gray tube hanging over the stage. At the flip of a switch, it lowered slowly, ponderously, gears turning and echoing across the empty seats until a blank white rectangle blocked the center of the heavy maroon curtains.

Owen handed Dewey the flat film can. She slid the reel onto the machine and threaded the perforated celluloid through the gates and onto the take-up reel.

"Ready, Coach," Owen said into the microphone of the PA system.

"Let her run, Parker," came the reply from below.

Dewey killed the lights, and Owen slumped into the chair to the right of the projector. Standing, she was an inch or two taller than he was, for once. She flicked the switch and the beam of the projector's lamp angled out over the auditorium onto the screen, dust motes dancing in the expanding cone of light. When the announcer's voice began—*Speed, sinister and deadly, beckons to the impatient and the thrill-seeker*—Dewey turned off the booth's speakers. On the screen, colorful toy cars careened silently out of control on painted toy streets.

The motor of the projector whickered, loud and continuous, like a mechanical Bronx cheer. Loud enough that when Owen spoke, Dewey wasn't certain that she'd heard him say, "My dad walked me to school this morning."

She turned.

"Seven blocks. Only a cane."

His voice broke, and in the flickering light she saw his mouth tremble. He wiped his eyes with the back of his hand, and a lock of hair fell onto his forehead.

Dewey reached over and brushed it back with her fingertips. He looked so sweet, so happy. Her hand smoothed his hair and rested on the back of his head. She leaned down and kissed him, right above his eyebrow, where the stray lock had been. "That's so great," she whispered.

Owen tilted his head to look at her, his expression both startled and pleased. Dewey bent lower, and kissed him again. His lips were soft and a little dry.

"Jeepers," he said.

"Shhh." Dewey kissed him once more, then leaned her head against his. He smelled like soap and spearmint gum. They stayed like that, without another word, alone in the shifting darkness high above the Alamo High auditorium, until THE END filled the screen.

THE NAMING OF NAMES

S uze put out her hand, to be polite, then froze, fingers in midair. *Gallucci. That was—No.* She *couldn't be—* "Gallucci, not Kerrigan?"

The woman's face changed, her eyes narrowing. "It used to be," she said slowly. "And that was way too good for a wild guess. What do you know, kid?"

Oh jeez. This was Dewey's mother? A million thoughts went through Suze's head and she didn't know what to say. It was too late to lie—she'd blurted out *Kerrigan* without thinking. But she had to warn Dewey, stall for time. "Well, there's no DeeDee here," she said after a minute. "But have a seat." She pointed to the glider. "I'll be right back." She shut the door and went to the kitchen.

DeeDee? That had been so weird to say. But she hadn't wanted to say Dewey's name out loud. Like in fairy tales. If you tell the witch your true name, it gives her power. You can never be too careful.

"You look like you just saw a ghost," Ynez said. "Who was that?"

"I'm not sure yet. She says she's"—Suze paused—"an old friend of the family." She picked up the rubber band and redid her ponytail.

"Hey. What about your shampoo."

"It's gonna have to wait. I need you to do me a favor, right away."

"What?"

"You know Parker's Fix-It Shop?"

"Yeah. He got our toaster popping up again."

"Good. Dewey's over there with Owen. It's his dad's place. Go tell her she needs to come home?"

"Okay, but why don't you go?"

"'Cause my mom isn't here, and we've got *company*."

"Oh. Gotcha. You want me to come back, after?"

"Not a good idea. I'll catch up with you tomorrow."

"You sure?" She looked toward the front door. When Suze nodded, she just said, "Okay, then," and went out the back.

Ynez had been gone about two minutes when the black Chevy pulled up onto the gravel driveway. The sweetest sound Suze had ever heard. She'd bounded down the back steps before the motor had stopped.

Her mother got out. "Suze? Why on earth is a motorcycle parked on our front walk?" She reached into the car for the groceries.

"She says she's Dewey's mother."

Terry Gordon dropped the ten-pound sack of potatoes. *"What?"*

"The lady on the bike. She's Rita Gallucci and she used to be married to Jimmy Kerrigan and she's 'DeeDee's' mother." Suze made quote marks in the air. "She's on the porch."

Her mother swore, a word Suze was surprised she knew. "Where's Dewey?"

"Owen's. Ynez went to get her."

"Did you . . . ?"

"No, I just said she should come home." She hesitated, then gave her mother a hug. "I'm glad you're here. I don't know what to do. Is she going to take Dewey *away?*"

"I have no idea, sweetie." Terry Gordon shook her head. "I suppose she—I mean, she might—Oh, hell. I really don't know." She patted Suze on the arm. "Bring in the eggs and the milk so they don't spoil. We'll take it one step at a time." She picked up the sack of potatoes.

A minute later, they stood in the front hall. Terry Gordon took a deep breath and put an arm around Suze's shoulder. "Well, here goes nothing."

Or everything, Suze thought.

They stepped out onto the porch.

"Hello. I'm Terry Gordon, Suze's mother."

"Ah. *Gordon*. That explains it." She stood up. "I'm Rita Gallucci."

"That's what Suze said. I knew your husb—Jimmy—during the war."

"You worked on the A-Bomb?"

"That's right. But these days I'm helping to control the demon."

"Glad someone is."

A long silence.

Suze watched the two women size each other up, like Rutherford and a strange cat, circling and sniffing the air.

Rita broke the silence. "Do you know where my daughter, DeeDee, is?"

Suze watched her mother hesitate, then say, "Dewey's at a friend's house. I expect she'll be home soon."

"Dewey?"

"That's what she calls herself now."

"Oh. DeeDee was what we—Well, her whole name was kind of long for a tiny baby. Jimmy named her. Means twelve, in Latin, and—" She stopped in midsentence and pulled a pack of Luckies out of her pocket, then lit a kitchen match with her thumbnail. She exhaled blue smoke through her nostrils. "Anyway, she *does* live here?"

Terry nodded. "She's been with us for a little over two years."

"Since Jimmy died."

"And a few months before." She lit a cigarette of her own. "You know about Jimmy, then."

"I found out a couple of weeks ago. Kind of a one-two punch, after the news about my mama. I'd gone to St. Louis to try and mend some fences, but I was too late. The only address her lawyer had for Jimmy was some P.O. box in Santa Fe."

"Sixteen sixty-three," Suze supplied.

"That's the one. I rode a thousand miles and just got the army runaround—all hush-hush and secret." She shook her head. "One look at me, full leathers and dusty, and everyone clammed up."

"That happen a lot?" Terry asked.

"I'm not your typical housewife." A pause. "But neither are you."

"True enough." Mrs. Gordon took a slow drag on her cigarette and leaned against the railing. "So how did you manage to—?"

"A nice old gal in an office off the Plaza. McGubbin? Something like that. She gave me a cup of coffee and told me Jimmy was gone and a family named Gordon had taken DeeDee in. I had to sweet-talk for an hour before she'd cough up this address."

"You just came here for Dewey's money, didn't you?" Suze

asked. Her voice was too loud and angry for normal conversation, but she didn't care.

"*Suze!*"

Rita frowned, then held up her palm. "I suppose that's a fair question." She turned to Suze. "It *was* my mother's house. But I hadn't been back in years. If she wanted the money to go to Dee—to Dewey—well, fair is fair. About time the kid had some luck break her way. What I *came* for? Well, with Mama and Jimmy both gone"—she shrugged—"I'm all she's got. You do what you gotta do."

She stubbed out her cigarette on the heel of her boot and started to toss the butt onto the grass, then rolled it between her fingers and stuck it in her pocket. "I imagine you've heard plenty of stories about me." It wasn't a question.

"A few," Terry said evenly.

"If you can spare a cold beer, I'll fill you in on the rest."

"Don't you want to wait for Dewey?"

Rita shook her head. "I'm not sure how much she needs to know. I could use a dry run." She jerked her head in Suze's direction. "Without little pitchers?"

Little—? Of all the nerve. "Hey. I'm plenty old enough to—" Suze said, but her mother shook her head.

"Bring a six-pack from the fridge and give us a few minutes, sweetie. Stay in the kitchen and keep an eye out for Dewey, okay?"

Suze shot her mother a look, then sighed and obeyed.

Mostly. After she'd delivered the beer, she did go back into the house, but not all the way to the kitchen. She slipped into the sheltered triangle behind the open front door and eased herself quietly to the floor. Through the space above the hinge, she could see both women. She watched her mother take a sip of beer, and waited to hear what Rita Gallucci had to say.

HISTORY LESSON

"I guess the place to start is the summer of 1931," Rita began. "That's when I left school, went to New York to be a dancer. I was only sixteen, but I was a looker, and I knew all the steps—Charleston, Black Bottom, you name it. I got work at a dime-a-dance place and waitressed days at a diner near Columbia.

"Jimmy came in about four most afternoons. Black coffee, scrambled eggs, and hash browns—extra crispy. Funny what you remember." She lit a cigarette. "He wore specs and did the crossword with an *ink* pen. Smart guy. After a week or two, we'd chat, just 'Hi there,' at first, 'How's your day?' He was in math, and a nut for music—longhair, classical stuff, but jazz, too." She paused to take a drink of her beer.

"January, he came in and put two concert tickets down on the counter and blushed—I swear to God. The man was twenty-four, but shy. . . . I bet I was the first girl he'd ever gotten up the nerve to ask out."

Terry Gordon frowned. "Did he know how old—?"

"Are you nuts? I'd told him I was twenty. Like I said, I could pass." She looked around, then flicked her ash over the edge of the railing. "Next night he came to my rooming house with a brand-new haircut and a white carnation for my dress. Took me to Town Hall to hear a Bach canon, the Duodecima." She shrugged. "No mystery why I remember *that*.

"So we went out, off and on. Music, a movie, a cup of coffee and a piece of pie. Then one Saturday he showed up at the dance palace. Boy, could that man cut a rug." She smiled. "Coming from him and me, Dee—sorry, *Dewey*—must be a helluva dancer, huh?"

"Not exactly." Terry Gordon's voice was low and cool.

"Damn. Go figure." Rita sat for a moment, looking out at the dark shapes of the cottonwoods. "Jimmy took me to a speakeasy after. First time I'd ever had hard liquor. After two cocktails he looked so handsome, I leaned across the table and kissed him. Surprised us both. He bought another round, and his place was only a few blocks away, so—well, you know . . ."

Suze knew all about the birds and the bees, and was pretty sure what Rita meant, but was hoping for more details, the kind grown-ups never talked about. She held her breath. Nothing but silence, then the hiss of a cigarette hitting the last few drops at the bottom of the bottle.

"I kissed him first," Rita said after a minute, "but the next morning he wouldn't stop apologizing. After that one time, we never—only movies and music and coffee. But come April, I was late." She swore, the same word Mom had used in the driveway. Suze wasn't surprised *she* knew it.

"The last thing I needed was a kid. I'd just turned seventeen and I was starting to get auditions. I thought Jimmy might give me money to get rid of it—her—" She looked at Terry and bit her lip. "But instead he got down on one knee, right there in the diner. A real gentleman. What could I say? We got married at City Hall in June, after he got his diploma. There I was, Mrs. Doctor Kerrigan. Mama was thrilled. Jimmy thought I was twenty-one."

She popped the cap off another beer. "DeeDee came six months later. Jimmy graded papers in the waiting room. You'd think a Harvard professor would make good money, but not so much, starting out. We had such a tiny apartment, she slept in a dresser drawer.

"It was *cold* in Boston that winter. I'd stay in bed most days, me and the baby tucked under the covers. At least she was good, didn't cry much. Cute as a button, all those dark curls and big gray eyes. But . . ." Rita drank an inch of her beer.

"But I couldn't dance, or even waitress. I was stuck while Jimmy went out every day, taught his classes, talked to people. He'd come home around dark and give the baby a bath while I made supper, then sing her to sleep. All he had to do was walk through the door, and you shoulda seen the way her eyes lit up."

"I have," Terry said. "She adored him. Jimmy was a great guy."

"Sweetest man I ever knew," Rita agreed. "But it wasn't much of a marriage. After supper, he'd pour himself a glass of bootleg whiskey and sit on the couch. I wanted to talk. About anything. Just to hear another voice. Half the time he fell asleep before he'd finished his drink.

"Look, I tried," Rita said in a near-whisper. "I really did. Once we bought a stroller, I could at least take DeeDee to the park, or down to the river to watch the ducks. Then she started to talk and—Jesus Murphy, there was no stopping her. It was Jimmy who read to her, taught her numbers before she could walk. Once *that* happened, she was into everything. Cupboards, kitchen drawers—she'd try to take apart whatever she got her hands on."

Terry smiled. "She's still like that."

"Damn. Hope *you've* been keeping up. I'd put the pots and pans away and—*crash!* Jimmy's books were all over the rug, and there was DeeDee grinning and pretending to read. Hell, maybe she *was* reading. Smart as a whip, and wore me out before lunch, just trying to stay one step ahead."

"I know the feeling."

Rita nodded. "I don't remember the first morning I put a

little knock of Jimmy's whiskey in my coffee, to smooth things out. After a bit, I hid my own bottle under the sink, behind the cleanser. I'm not saying it was right, but—hell. I was eighteen and scared and lonely." She reached for the pack of Luckies, then crumpled it. Empty. "Can I bum a smoke?"

"Here." Terry held out the pack of Chesterfields. Rita lit one and took a deep drag, staring at the glowing tip for a long minute before she spoke again.

"Jimmy told you about the accident?"

"Not much. Said you were drunk and dropped Dewey on the stairs. Broke her leg in three places."

"*Three?* Jesus." Rita winced and looked down at her hands. "I'd had an extra cup of my special coffee, 'cause she was teething and fussy. I thought running around in the park might help. I had that big stroller in one hand and DeeDee on my hip, kicking and screaming and"—Rita blew out a long stream of smoke—"she slipped out of my arms. Down to the landing."

Silence.

Terry Gordon gave Rita a long, cold look. "And then you *left?*" she asked in an angry voice. "How could you just walk away from your baby?"

"I couldn't stay," Rita said. Her voice was so low Suze could barely hear it. "Not the way Jimmy looked at me when he got to the hospital. She was Daddy's girl, and we both knew it was my fault she—" She stopped and gazed out at the now-shadowed yard.

"It wasn't like I didn't think about them. I wrote to Jimmy, from New York, then Chicago, but after a while my letters came back: 'Not at this address.' I even called Mama in St. Louis, long distance, a year before the war. All she said—before she hung up—was that DeeDee was with her, safe and sound, and did *not* need the likes of me."

She'd pitched her voice higher, and Suze was startled by how much she sounded like Dewey, when *she* talked about her nana.

"To tell you the truth," Rita returned to her regular voice, "that was kind of a relief. I mean, if Jimmy left her, too, I was off the hook a little. And with Mama watching after her, I knew she'd be okay. So I hit the road to California. Tended bar on and off, rode courier during the war, until the men came home and put me out of a job. It took me a year to get up the nerve to go back to St. Louis and check up on things. But by that time—well, you know the story from there."

Rita dropped her cigarette onto the others that lined the bottom of the smoke-filled beer bottle. "If you don't mind, I need to use the little girls'—?"

Suze slid out of her hiding place and was in the kitchen by the time her mother answered, "Down the hall, under the stairs."

"Thanks. Back in a sec," Rita replied.

From beside the fridge, Suze saw her come in, heard the bathroom door open, then close. A minute later, shoes crunched on the driveway gravel.

"Mom!" she called, heading for the attic stairs. "Dewey's home!"

FIRST CONTACT

Dewey skipped down the alley from Owen's house cradling a flat metal box of socket wrenches against her chest, feeling the vibration as the pieces inside rattled with each step. She kicked pebbles just to watch them skitter, tiny dust trails marking their trajectories, thoughts bouncing around her head.

She'd borrowed the tools to finish an addition to the Wall, a cantilever arm that would lower a little dumbwaiter box down to the bottom of the stairwell. That would be useful when they started packing next month. She envisioned the construction, how the parts would fit together, but underlying all that was a faint memory of spearmint that made her skip and skitter stones.

In *Seventeen* stories, a first kiss was supposed to be in all capital letters, violins playing, that sort of mush. Dewey knew she wasn't a magazine kind of girl, but what happened in the projection booth was really nice. She just hadn't expected it to change anything.

On the way home, Owen had started acting like a magazine *boy*, serious one minute, then goofy in a way he'd never been before. He called her "my girl," two or three times, like she belonged to him now.

He was sweet, but she wasn't "sweet on him." Not that way. And she certainly didn't *belong* to him, like a book or a truck or a set of wrenches.

She imagined telling Suze, later that night, when the house was quiet. Would Suze understand, or get all weird about it? *Dewey and O-wen, sitting in a tree. K-I-SS-I-N-G.* It hadn't been like *that*.

Her shoes crunched on the pea gravel when she turned into the Gordons' driveway. The Chevy was parked by the back door, and a potato lay near the front wheel. *Must have fallen out of the grocery bag.* Dewey picked it up, wedging it under her arm, and opened the screen door to the kitchen.

Terry Gordon stood by the sink, an expression on her face that Dewey didn't recognize. She looked serious—very serious—but not sad, or at least not crying.

"You dropped this by the car." Dewey put the potato on the counter. She laid the metal box down beside it.

Terry nodded. She started to say something—Dewey could see her mouth move, then close, her lips in a tight line, like she was trying to keep the words from coming out.

Dewey stopped smiling.

"Dewey?" Mrs. Gordon said, smoothing her hand on her pants. "Honey—?"

Dewey felt her armpits prickle with sweat, felt her throat tighten. She'd only heard those words, that tone of voice, once before, the afternoon that Oppie told her Papa was dead.

But there was no one left to die, no one who mattered *that* much to Dewey. Terry was here, standing in front of her, and if anything had happened to Suze—or Dr. Gordon—she'd be sobbing. And they were all the family Dewey had.

"Terry? What's wrong?"

"Nothing's *wrong*, exactly. It's just, well, we've had a surprise, and—"

Dewey didn't hear the rest of the sentence, if there was one. A woman in blue jeans and a light brown sweater walked in the door from the front hall. A stranger.

With the same gray-green eyes as hers.

No one needed to say a word. She knew who this was.

Everything had changed.

Dewey stands in the Gordons' kitchen, light from the setting sun slanting red-gold through the window, her hand on the rough skin of a potato. She stares into the face of a stranger who is a version of herself and feels as if she is looking through the wrong end of a telescope, the life that had been ordinary a moment before now very far away.

Bye baby bunting, Daddy's gone a-hunting, a faint voice sings in the back of her mind. It's a soothing song, a lullaby, but it makes her stomach knot and flutter. The voice is not Papa's and not Nana's, and who else ever sang to her that way?

She knows that when this familiar stranger speaks, she will hear that voice, and she doesn't want to. Dewey stands as still as a statue, but she can feel herself quivering. She does not want to get any closer. If the smell of Brylcreem at the drugstore can make her eyes sting, can conjure Papa, unbidden, what will *her* scent unleash?

She looks at Terry Gordon, standing next to the sink, and wants to run over and throw her arms around her, bury her head in that soft plaid shirt. *You said no one could take me away. You promised.*

But she does not move, because even Terry can't help. This is the one person, the only person, who can claim that Dewey *does* belong to her, no questions asked.

"DeeDee," the woman says, and inside Dewey, the ice breaks. Not a melting, but a glacier shearing off and floating away from safe anchor into the open sea. She tastes applesauce, and her leg aches in memory. She feels as if her skin is too tight, and will never fit again.

"Mama," she replies, without thinking, and is startled by the word.

FAMILY RESEMBLANCE

Dewey stared at the woman who had once been her mother, waves of feelings crashing through her, crushing her. Dread and the sting of tears, oddly mixed with curiosity. Nothing she expected.

Shouldn't she hate her, for the hospital, for the ugly brown shoe and the limp and the stares of other children? For leaving?

Shouldn't she love her, instantly, because that was how nature worked? A baby reaches for its mother. But mothers are supposed to care for their children, too. Could there be one without the other?

"I'm Dewey now," she said, when she remembered how to breathe again.

"Hello, Dewey. Let's go for a walk."

"I don't think—" Dewey shook her head.

"I'm not going to kidnap you. Just a walk." Rita reached

into her pocket and pulled out a set of keys on a leather fob, laid it on the kitchen table. "There. That's everything I own, except what I'm wearing." She looked at Terry Gordon. "Call it a deposit on a pack of smokes?"

"Now." She turned back to Dewey. "We need to talk. Do you want to take a walk with me?"

"Not really," Dewey said. "But I guess I should."

"I'll settle for sitting on the porch."

"That would be better." Dewey looked at the clock.

"Dinner in an hour or so," Terry Gordon said. "Meat loaf and mashed potatoes. Ask Suze to come in and give me a hand." She opened a drawer and tossed Rita a pack of Chesterfields.

Dewey kept her eyes down as they walked into the hall, out onto the porch. Each footfall sounded hollow.

Suze stood by the steps, tall and straight, for once, like a bodyguard, her hand an inch away from her hip, ready to draw an imaginary pistol.

"It's okay," said Dewey. She didn't know if that was true. "Your mom wants you in the kitchen to help with dinner."

"You sure?"

"No, but I'll yell if I need you."

"I thought you might want this." Suze pressed Dewey's Shazam stone into her hand.

"Thanks." The weight of the smooth dark stone was the first comfort she'd felt since she walked in the back door. "It helps."

"What is it?" Rita asked.

"Do you read comic books?"

"Not really. The Sunday funnies, sometimes."

"Then it's just a rock." Dewey slipped it into her pocket and turned back to Suze. "Give a holler when dinner's ready?"

"Should I set another place?"

Dewey shrugged. "I don't know yet." Suze went inside.

Rita sat on the porch swing and patted the seat next to her. Dewey shook her head and leaned against the railing. She wanted to perch on it, the way Suze did, but she wasn't tall enough to ease onto it, and her leg made jumping awkward. Things were awkward enough.

Dewey waited, conscious, for the first time in months, of the glasses on her face, of the built-up shoe on her right foot, even if it wasn't as obvious as the brown one. She wondered if she was what Rita had imagined, if that worked both ways.

"You don't seem very happy to see me," Rita said.

I'm sorry, Dewey started to say, but stopped. That was what she wanted to *hear. I'm sorry I broke you. I'm sorry I left. I'm sorry your papa died.*

Rita leaned forward, her hands on the knees of her jeans, and waited. She looked more puzzled than angry. After a minute she opened the pack of Chesterfields and lit one, blowing a cloud of blue smoke into the twilight. After another minute she sat back. "I guess that's an answer. I can't say that I blame you—after what I did."

It was almost an apology. Dewey could hear that. It was a

gesture she couldn't ignore, and it wasn't enough. She waited to see if there would be more, but Rita just popped the cap off a bottle of beer and took a long, slow drink. Dewey took a deep breath and asked the one question that Nana and Papa would never answer. "Will you tell me what happened?"

"It's about time, isn't it?" Rita Gallucci said.

Dewey felt as if she were listening with two different ears. One heard the low, husky voice of an oddly familiar stranger, a woman who wasn't a Church Lady or a teacher or a scientist, not like anyone she'd ever met. The other heard, for the first time, a story about Papa and Nana, people she'd always thought she'd known, with details that were almost memories, like fragments of dreams.

Every few minutes, Rita stopped and lit another cigarette, for punctuation, breaks in the story. And because she was nervous. Dewey could see that. Her hand shook, just a little, when she snapped a match on her thumbnail, a trick that one of the listening Deweys wanted to try.

It was fifteen minutes before Dewey asked her next question.

"What would you have done if Papa—if Jimmy Kerrigan hadn't married you?"

Rita let the match burn almost to her fingers before she answered. "I don't know. Girls at the dance palace knew doctors who would—who would make the problem go away." She took a long drag and blew out a stream of smoke. "But

I've never been sure if I could. All those years with the nuns. If Jimmy hadn't been a stand-up guy, I guess I would have given the baby—given you up. Let some family adopt you, make you a real nice home."

"You wouldn't have kept me?"

"A seventeen-year-old waitress, living in a rooming house on forty-two bucks a month?" She shook her head. "What sort of life is that?"

Even though she looked tough, Dewey thought, her eyes could be kind. Not gentle, but kind. Dewey wondered if that was always true.

The sun had gone down and moths fluttered against the porch light by the time Suze came to the door. "Dinner in five minutes."

Dewey hesitated, then asked Rita, as politely as if she were an ordinary guest, "Would you like to stay for dinner?"

"Yes. Thank you," she replied in the same tone.

Another quiet meal. Dewey and Suze exchanged glances— hand gestures answered by nods and shrugs—but didn't say much. Dewey couldn't eat. Her stomach fluttered with the uncertainty of what would happen next. She watched Rita and Terry make grown-up small talk about the news—commu- nists, French Indochina—as if that would keep the immediate reality at bay.

"I'm curious," Terry said as she mopped up the last of her gravy with a piece of bread. "Why a motorcycle?"

"I got tired of Greyhound, and I couldn't afford a car. But after that first one—you ever ridden?"

Terry shook her head.

"Nothing better. I go where I want, when I want, on nobody else's schedule. Some mornings I toss a penny onto the map, and wherever it lands, that's where I'm headed," Rita said. "I'm just a gypsy, I guess. I like the feel of the wind in my hair, the road humming under me."

"Wowza. I'd like to try that," said Suze.

"Be my guest," her mother said. "As soon as you're eighteen."

Rita laughed. "It's worth the wait. Last week I rode right through a thunderstorm, out into a blazing sunset. Nothing but me and a sky full of clouds colored like Broadway."

"Don't you get lonely?" Suze asked.

"Not really." Rita put her napkin by her plate and lit a cigarette, thinking. "I can take care of myself. And waiting tables, tending bar, I talk to people all the time. Part of the job. I like being alone when I ride."

Suze nodded and stood up to clear the dishes.

"Thanks," Rita said when Terry put a cup of coffee down in front of her. "I haven't had a home-cooked meal in a while."

"It was only meat loaf."

"Yeah, but under the circumstances . . ." She looked into her coffee. "I told you, my own mother hung up on me. I wasn't sure what kind of welcome to expect."

"Not the sort of thing you can look up in Emily Post."

"Got that right. And then there's how to thank you for taking care of my little girl these last coupla years." She shook her head. "I don't even know where to start."

Terry frowned, her cigarette halfway to her lips, but before she could say anything, Rita turned to Dewey. "I bet you want some time to think about all this."

"That's for sure," she agreed. In the last two hours, Rita had filled in a lifetime of blanks, and now Dewey had solid facts instead of guesses. It would take a while for all of it to sink in, but order had replaced chaos.

"Good, 'cause I've got to go back to Albuquerque, pick up some parts for my bike. I ride, but I don't wrench." Rita shrugged. "The repairs'll take a couple of days, Friday at the latest. So I'll come over Saturday morning and we'll get your gear stowed then. You'll have to ride double as far as Tucson, but—"

"Wait. You want to take me *with* you?" Dewey said. The three sips of milk she'd managed at dinner felt like acid in her stomach as chaos reappeared. Suze sat with her mouth open, like she'd been sucker punched.

"Of course. You didn't think I rode a thousand miles just to say hi, did you?" Rita took a drink of coffee before she noticed the look on Dewey's face. "Hey, now. No need to worry. I'm going to take real good care of you. There's a nice sidecar waiting in Tucson—red leather seats. We'll use a little of Mama's money, get you set up in style."

Dewey stared at Rita. "That's my college money."

"*College?*" She shook her head. "You're Jimmy's kid, that's for sure. But we'll cross that bridge when we come to it." She picked up Terry's Zippo and lit a cigarette. "Back to *this* week, I've booked cabin seven out at the motor court for Friday night. I'll probably get in pretty late, so why don't we say I swing by after breakfast the next morning?"

"Terry?" Dewey heard the plea in her voice.

"No, I'm sorry. That's out of the question," Terry Gordon said.

Rita sat very still. "And why is that?" she said. Her tone was even, but her eyes were no longer kind.

"Because the girls still have another month of school." She looked at Suze. "Your last day's when, the middle of May?"

"Yeah, the sixteenth, I think."

"Is that important to you?" Rita asked Dewey.

"Yes." She could hardly believe the question. "You want me to graduate the eighth grade, don't you?"

"Like I said on the porch, kid, this time around—I promise—I only want what's right for you." She picked up her keys and stood up. "Another month of school, that's jake with me. Vacation starts early, that's even better. You think about it. We're gonna make up for lost time, have some fun this summer." She reached out a hand to tousle Dewey's curls.

"Don't." Dewey flinched, moving her head just out of reach.

"Okay, okay." Rita was still for a moment, then put both hands into her pockets. "We'll—well, we'll talk more on Saturday." She turned to Terry Gordon. "Thanks again. For everything."

She left the kitchen.

"Saturday," Dewey said, when she finally heard the roar of the motorcycle's engine. The word had the same fearful edge as when radio announcers said *Alamogordo*. The beginning of the end.

UNEASY LIES THE HEAD

Suze woke up in the middle of a nightmare, sheets damp with sweat, and couldn't get back to sleep. Her bed felt wrong. Everything felt wrong.

They'd sat in the kitchen and talked for a long time after dinner. Dewey hadn't said much. Mom had even called Dad, out at the base, but came back from the phone shaking her head. What was happening? Dad had become a stranger and pretty much disappeared into the desert. And now Rita Gallucci had shown up out of nowhere—after twelve years—and wanted to take Dewey away, too.

Suze tossed and turned, thinking about the afternoon they'd had a fight. She'd said out loud that she wished Dewey would go away. Tonight, she'd give anything to take that back, because it had come true. Dewey wasn't an orphan anymore, and that meant—

"Hey, Dewey? You awake?" she asked, staring at the ceiling.

No answer. Suze turned over. The other bed was rumpled, but empty. She got up and went into the dark hallway. A pale sliver of light flickered under the attic door.

She padded up the stairs in her bare feet. Dewey sat cross-legged on the floor, rocking slowly. A string of tiny Christmas lights across the top of the Wall was the only illumination, pulsing on and off, filling the room with strange shapes and shifting shadows. It reflected off the lenses of Dewey's glasses, faceup on the carpet, and revealed thin silver lines trickling down each cheek.

Dewey was crying, without a sound, and Suze wasn't sure what to do. She sat down, a few feet away, and watched the Wall. In the year they'd lived here, it had grown, piece by piece, never the same from one week to the next. But tonight it felt like the only thing in her life that *hadn't* changed. "I couldn't sleep," she said finally.

"Me neither."

How many nights had they started conversations that way? Both of them leaning on their elbows, talking across the space between the beds, night black outside the windows, the house quiet. It was as if their words drifted away on the moonlight, honest and real, but from the same world as dreams. At night, in the dark, the truth came out in whispers.

"Don't leave me," Suze said, and felt her own tears well up.

"I'd miss you." Dewey's voice was tiny, as if even three words was an effort. A long silence, then a deep, rattly sigh.

"Everything's upside down. If this was a movie, it would be a happy ending, right? My mother returns. Happily ever after."

"But it's not, is it?"

"No."

The room was so quiet that Suze could hear the tiny ticks as the bulbs turned on and off.

Dewey stopped rocking. "You know why?" she said. Her voice was still soft, but stronger. "My whole life, people made that *tsk-tsk, isn't-that-a-shame* sound when I said she'd left when I was a baby. But even at Nana's, I wasn't sure that was a bad thing. If she'd stayed, she might have hurt me again." A longer silence. "I don't trust her."

"You just met her."

"Exactly. And she expects me to go off and *live* with her?"

"You didn't trust me when we first met, and we're good, right?"

"Yeah," Dewey said. "We're good. But you never got to run my life." She paused. "Even when you wanted to."

"I tried."

"I know."

They sat and watched the Wall go from dark shapes to bright colors, over and over. "That penny-on-the-map thing sounded like it might be fun," Suze said, breaking the silence.

"For a day or two, maybe. I bet a lot of kids would give anything for a mom who didn't believe in rules. It'd be like one big day of playing hooky."

Suze thought about the weekend she and Mom had spent in Santa Fe. They'd laughed and talked for three days straight. It had been great, as if four years of labs and labels and I'm-too-busy had fallen away and she had *Mom* back again. Suze had never felt closer to her. But every day? She tried to find the bad part of that, but it sounded exciting and fun. An adventure. She debated a long time before she said that out loud.

"Yeah, I could tell from how you watched her at dinner. But I'm tired of that kind of 'adventure,'" Dewey said. "Papa putting me on the bus to Nana's, the train ride to the Hill. I hated that."

She hugged her knees to her chest.

"I like to wake up and know that the bathroom's next door, and where the box of cereal is, every morning. I like having my hammer on the hammer hook, and my jars where *they* belong."

"That'd be hard, on a motorcycle."

Dewey sighed again. "I'd lose things. Screws and little parts. Pieces'd get wrecked, 'cause I wouldn't have a place to work. I'd have to do my homework in a bar. If I was even in school."

"Do you think it'd be that bad?" Suze asked.

"I don't know. Out on the porch, before dinner, she promised she'd settle down and stay in one place. She promised a lot of stuff. She sounded like she meant it, but—" Dewey shook her head. "You saw her when she talked about being on the road."

"Yeah. Her whole face lit up."

"See. So how long would it take before she missed that? Before she started feeling trapped, like she did when I was a baby, and decided to take off again?"

"What're you gonna do?"

"I don't know." Dewey reached over and put on her glasses, as if they might help her think better. "She keeps saying she's gonna do the right thing, like it's suddenly her job to come and save me. Save me from what?"

"Got me. At least Mom said she'd put her foot down about school, even talk to the principal, if she has to. That gives us a month to figure something out."

"No," Dewey said. "I'd spend the whole time worrying. Like on the Hill, waiting for the war to end, wondering if I'd have to go to an orphanage. That was awful. I have to tell her—something—on Saturday. If she'll listen. I'm afraid she might *make* me go with her."

"Me, too. I mean, she *is* your mother. She's the only family you've got left."

Suze wasn't prepared for the punch. "Ow! What was *that* for?"

"You are such a moron," Dewey said. "*You're* my family. She's only 'my mother' because a long time ago she—accidentally—got pregnant, and Papa married her. But your mom's—"

"*Mom,*" Suze supplied.

"Yeah." Pause. "You okay with that?"

Suze had to think, but only for a second. "I am." She scooched over and put her arm around Dewey's shoulder. "You're my brother. *I'd* adopt you, if I could."

"Thanks. I wish you could."

Silence. Then Suze snapped her fingers.

"What?"

"R-R-R-R-Raymundo!" Suze said. "I've got an idea."

HAIL
AND
FAREWELL

OPERATING
INSTRUCTIONS

Suze caught up with Ynez by her locker a few minutes after the bell rang the next afternoon. "Do you have band practice today?"

"Nope." She picked up her clarinet case. "We got new music in class, but we have to work on it at home this week." She made a face. "It always sounds terrible the first time we try it together. No one's on beat. Why?"

"I need your help."

"Dewey again?" Ynez rolled her eyes.

Suze sighed. She liked Dewey, and she liked Ynez, but neither one understood what she saw in the other. "Yeah, but it's important."

"That's what you said when you sent me to the Fix-It Shop, and she wasn't even there."

"She *wasn't*?"

"Nope. Wild-goose chase. But buy me a *paleta,* and I'll think about it."

Suze checked her pocket. Two dimes, a nickel, and a penny. "Deal."

A wooden cart piled with fruit stood beside the front door of the little *grocería* at Eighth and Florida. Today it held mangoes, three kinds of bananas, and some greenish yellow fruit Safeway didn't carry. Suze wasn't sure what they were, but they cost six cents each.

"*¿Qué es esto?*" she asked Ynez, holding one up.

"Papaya."

"*¿Qué es, en ingles?*"

Ynez gave her a funny look. "Papaya."

"Oh." Like *banana*. Same, same. Suze liked Spanish. It felt more fluid than English, rolling off her tongue in an easy cadence. *Yo quiero dos paletas, por favor*. But the family that ran the little two-aisle store replied so fast that she could only catch some of the words, and Ynez had to translate the rest.

Suze scanned the candy rack. Any she hadn't tried? Some were great, mostly fruit flavors, but one packet had turned out to be fruity *and* salty. Nice wrapper, but she never bought that again.

She could read most of the labels, at least the words in big print. Her vocabulary didn't stretch to all the ingredients and descriptions. Even here, lots of packages boasted *¡Nuevo!* in starbursts. *¡Todos son Nuevos!* Everything Is New! One or two even said *¡Atómico!*

A small knot of dark-haired women chatted near the counter. Suze caught *radio* and *beisbol* and *Jaqui Robinson*. Everyone in town was talking about him, but these women sounded happier than the men in the hardware store.

"I took the last mango one," Ynez said. Suze bought her second favorite, pineapple. *Paleta ananas.* She pulled the paper wrapper off the pale-yellow Fudgsicle-shaped bar. They walked down the street, juice dripping onto their fingers. At Ynez's house, Tony and another boy knelt in a bare patch of the backyard, playing marbles. Ray crouched by the hen coop, trying to grab one of the fuzzy yellow chicks that cheeped around his bare feet.

"*¡R-R-R-R-R-Raymundo!*" Suze yelled.

The little boy looked up and grinned. "*¡Suz!*" But she was not the big draw today. He returned his attention to the chicks.

Doña Luisa smiled when they came in and added a handful of onions to a fragrant pot of beans simmering on the stove. They tossed their *paleta* sticks into the trash and washed their sticky hands.

"So, what do you want from Esquero's House of Favors?" Ynez asked as she sank onto her bed.

"Remember the lady on the motorcycle?"

"Yeah. Hard to forget *her*."

"Well, she's who rang my doorbell yesterday."

Ynez whistled. "How come?"

"She's Dewey's mother." Suze sat on the other bed. "She left when Dewey was a baby, and just showed up."

"Wow. She came back to get her, after all that time?"

"Yeah, but Dewey doesn't want to go. That's why I need your help. How did your folks end up with Ray?"

"What does that—?"

"Trust me. It does."

"Okay. Like I told you, the guy who knocked up my aunt Linda, my mother's youngest sister, was real bad news. He stole a car. Linda was sixteen and he was in jail, so when Ray was born, my folks adopted him."

"Did they have to get a lawyer and go to court and everything?"

Ynez shrugged. "Lawyer, maybe. I think that was all. Linda's not the brightest *chica*, but she knew Ray'd be better off here. She signed some paper."

Suze grabbed a pencil. "*That's* what I need. What's it called?"

"How should I know? I was ten. I'll ask my mom later. Anything *else*?"

Suze nodded. "Can you get one of them for me? From Mr. Mobley, downtown?"

"No way, José. You go."

"What if he guesses it's about Dewey and calls in some social-work lady?"

"He might." Ynez nodded. "So tell him it's you."

"I can't. Owen's mom works for him, and she's in the women's club with *my* mom, so he knows I have parents. And I can't pretend *I'm* in that kind of trouble, 'cause it'd already be hot gossip from every Church Lady in town."

Suze waited for Ynez to answer. She wasn't prepared for a cold, hard stare.

"So that's it? You think if *I* go, he'll figure—oh well, nobody cares if one more *Chihuahuita spitfire* got herself knocked up, huh?" Ynez turned away. "Trust you, huh? Fat chance. You're one crappy friend, Gordon."

She couldn't see Ynez's face, but heard the tears and anger in her voice. "C'mon. That's not what I—"

"Sure it was. Get out."

Suze didn't move. She felt like she'd become "Truck" again, big and clumsy and pushy, treating Ynez the way she used to treat "Screwy Dewey." And she *knew* better. The hardest part was that when she'd made her *Tenth Street* box and went to the *grocería* and tried to speak Spanish, she'd felt special, like she was becoming part of Ynez's big, friendly family. But she wasn't. No one would ever mistake *her* for the maid.

"I can't believe I just did that," she said to Ynez's back. "I didn't mean to. You're only person I know with an adopted kid, that's all." She waited. No reaction. "But I didn't stop to think about how you'd feel when the lawyer—" She sighed. "I'm really sorry." She stood up to leave.

"Wait." Doña Luisa stood in the doorway. "Why do you need a made-up story, Suzita?"

"My friend—my other friend, Dewey—is in trouble, and we're afraid it could get worse if people start asking a lot of questions about her."

"She is having a baby and your mama wants to raise the child?"

"Oh, jeez, no." Suze shook her head. "Dewey *is* the baby. Well, was. Her mom left, and then her dad died and she lived— *lives* with us. Now her mom's back, but we want to keep her." She saw Doña Luisa's confused look, and explained what had happened yesterday.

"Ah. I understand now." She tapped Ynez on the shoulder. "Suz said she was sorry. She didn't use her head, but she has a good heart. Make nice with her."

Ynez sat up. "Why should I?"

"One, you will not lose a friend. And two, your grandmother will not beat you." She shook a scolding finger at both girls and left the room.

"I really am sorry," Suze said.

"Okay. But if you ever ask me anything like that again, I'm gonna deck you so fast—"

"I won't. Cross my heart."

A few minutes later, Doña Luisa returned and handed Suze

a piece of paper. "This is what Linda signed for Raymundo. The woman who works for the lawyer, she is a friend of your mama?"

"Yes."

"*Bueno.* Then you don't need stories and play-acting. Go home and ask your mama to make the phone call. Her friend can bring another paper home from work, and the lawyer will not have to know." She turned toward the kitchen and stopped. "But, Suz, it is only a paper. If the lady really wants to take your friend . . ." She shook her head. "It may not be enough."

THE WIND BETWEEN
THE WORLDS

Dewey sat on the couch in the attic, her Trig book in her lap, staring at the numbers and symbols without seeing them until she heard Suze on the stairs.

"How'd it go? Will Ynez help?"

"Nope. She got pretty p.o.'d at me." She sat on the stairwell wall. "I deserved it, too. But Doña Luisa thought of something easier." She explained about the form.

"Wow. *We* should've thought of that. If your mom calls this afternoon, I can pick it up at Owen's tomorrow afternoon."

"Hey. Ynez went over to get you yesterday, but she says you weren't there."

"Not until later."

"Where'd you go after school?"

"Right after? Um—I was helping Owen run a movie in the auditorium. For some teachers." That was true, but Dewey felt her face flush. *Now or never.* "And I, well—I kind of kissed him."

"You *what*?"

"I kissed Owen."

"Where?"

"In the projection booth."

"No, I mean—on the lips and everything?" Suze stared at her.

"Yeah. But it wasn't goopy and lovey-dovey. He told me some good news and looked so happy that I just, you know, kissed him."

"Oh. Like my mom, when I do something she likes?"

"Not exactly. Better than a mom kiss, but not smooching. It was nice."

"You gonna do it again?"

"Maybe. To say good-bye, when I leave for Berkeley. Or the 'open road.'" Her shoulders slumped. "He doesn't know about Rita yet. I was gonna tell him tonight, but they're having another 'family meeting' about him quitting school. I'm not going anywhere *near* that."

Owen was leaning against Dewey's locker when she got out of Home Ec Wednesday afternoon. He wore a plaid jacket over a gray hooded AHS sweatshirt.

"How'd it go last night?" she asked.

"It's complicated. Wanna take a drive? I'll tell you on the way."

"Way where?"

"White Sands. Play Day's this weekend—every April, big picnic. Buses come from El Paso, Las Cruces, all over. Four thousand people last year. I said I'd take a couple dozen cases of soda out. The Boy Scouts sell 'em for a nickel, raise money for the troop. Nice weather, they make a bundle, but it's s'posed to stay cold and windy all week, so who knows."

At the civic center, Owen loaded the heavy cases onto the truck and lashed everything down with rope. They headed for the highway.

"So, did your dad sign the permission?" Dewey asked as they passed the CITY LIMITS sign.

"Nope." He didn't say anything for a mile. Dewey knew him well enough to wait. They'd passed the roadhouse near the airfield before he gave a little huff and spoke again.

"One more year," he said. "Once I turn sixteen, I can quit without his okay."

"I thought you'd talked him into it?"

"I did, too. But . . ." He flicked his finger against the steering wheel. "Heck, maybe he's got a point. Until there's a station close enough to get a signal, there won't be any sets in Alamo to repair."

"That makes sense. Who'd spend that kind of money to watch gray fuzz?"

"That's what Pop said. He did promise that if El Paso starts broadcasting this fall, he'll give the idea another chance."

"Sounds reasonable."

"I guess. And they're giving an Aeronautics class next year, so it won't be too bad."

They turned off the highway. "Scoutmaster didn't know where they'd be setting up, said to leave the sodas here." He parked behind the adobe administration building. The wind flapped his jacket open and blew his hair straight back as he unloaded the truck.

"Not the best weather, but you wanna go for a little walk when I'm done?"

"Sure," Dewey said. She'd only been out to White Sands once, a school field trip. They'd spent the whole morning taking notes about desert plants—yucca, rosemarymint, creosote bush—and she hadn't gotten to see much else.

The fine granules blew against the side of the truck like whispers. Overhead, low clouds massed so tight together there was no blue sky, just a gray ceiling on the world. It matched how Dewey had felt since Monday night.

A hundred yards from the entrance, army men were unloading a V-2 from a flatbed truck. "Kurt thought they might have one on display," Owen said. "He's gonna come up from El Paso Saturday morning."

"The kid from Thanksgiving?"

"Yeah. When Mr. Gordon took me out to the launch in

December, Kurt was there with his dad. We yakked, and I gave him an *Astounding*, so he could practice English on something fun. He's written me a couple of times."

A mile farther in, a sign blocked their way: ROAD CLOSED. Beyond it was nothing but white sand, a foot deep, stretching from dune to dune.

"I guess we stop here," Owen said. He pulled the truck into a turnout.

They scrambled up the white slope as the wind whipped the grains against their skin, hard enough to sting. Once they were over the crest and in the lee of the dune, it was better. Parallel ripples striped the top surfaces, undulating like a field of invisible snakes. Below them lay a steep slope, a playground slide of sand two hundred feet long.

"Race ya!" Owen shouted, and took off full tilt, half running, half falling, sand cascading down in front of him. After a moment, Dewey followed. She ran and then slid sideways, rolling and tumbling, fast and out of control, out of breath—not from exertion, but excitement.

"Wow!" She came to a stop at the bottom of a huge, curved bowl. The wind was merely a breeze down here.

"I used to do that all day, when I was a kid." Owen grinned. "And this. Watch *this*." He lay down on a spot as smooth as a sheet of paper, and moved his arms and legs in wide arcs. He stood up carefully.

"A sand angel!" Dewey had a sudden memory of being

bundled up in a padded suit and boots and mittens, snow crystals sticking to damp wool. She lay down and made an angel of her own, then stood back. A tiny angel, wings spread.

They sprawled against the slope of the dune, side by side, the sand conforming to the shapes of their bodies.

"I never brought anyone here before." Owen looked away for a minute. "I never kissed a girl before, either." He looked back at Dewey.

"Hey. I kissed you."

"Technically. I'm glad you did."

"So am I." Dewey hesitated. "I really am. But it doesn't mean we're—"

"—getting married?" Owen nodded. "I know. I went a little nuts, huh? We can't even go steady. You'll be a thousand miles away." He reached over and took her hand. "But I'm glad it was you, the first time. A friend, not just some girl."

They lay in the stillness, the wind the only sound, holding hands and watching the landscape change around them, sands shifting moment by moment.

"I have a present for you," Owen said after the crest of the dune across from them had suddenly crumbled in an quiet avalanche.

"You didn't have to—"

"Hey. Save your complaints until you *see* it." He reached into the pouch of his sweatshirt and pulled out four folded pages, stapled together and typed in purple ink.

"It's my fanzine," he said. "First issue. I reviewed three stories from last month's *Astounding*, and printed some letters from guys who're my s.f. penpals." He laid it on Dewey's stomach.

The cover was a design of interconnected gears, titled THE SPROCKET. "It's—it's great. You did a lot of work," she said, sitting up. "Hectograph or mimeo?"

He looked surprised. "Hectograph. How do you—?"

"Terry uses one for her mailings."

"Ah. Gotcha. Anyway, I've got ten guys signed up so far, but *you* get subscription number one. It'll come right to your mailbox in Berkeley every month. Well, maybe every other month, once Pop and I start the repair course."

"Thanks. It's really swell." Dewey looked at the fanzine in her lap. "Trouble is, I may not have a mailbox in Berkeley."

"You guys are *staying*?" Owen sat up like a marionette whose strings had been pulled. "But I thought—"

Dewey shook her head. "Looks like Dr. Gordon'll be here, at least for the summer. Suze and Terry are going home for sure. I just don't know if I'll be with them." She drew a slow spiral in the sand with a finger. "Remember when I told you about my shoe, and how my leg got broken?"

"Natch."

"Well, my mother showed up Monday afternoon."

"Wow." He looked at her face. "Is that good?"

"Not really. She rides a motorcycle."

"Your *mother*? She's, uh—different." Owen said nothing for a minute. "Where does she live?"

"That's the problem. Nowhere. Anywhere. She's a gypsy. A waitress, sometimes. And she wants to take me with her." Dewey shook her head. "I feel like I'm dry cleaning she dropped off—twelve years ago—and just forgot to pick up."

"Just like that? What about your tools?"

Dewey almost smiled. It was such an Owen question. "That's on my list to worry about."

"Do you *have* to go with her?"

"I don't know. Maybe not. Terry asked your mom to help."

"She will. She likes you. Almost as much as me." Owen took her hand and kissed the back of it, like a knight out of King Arthur. "I hate it that you're leaving, Sprock. But say the word, and I'll do anything. You only go where you want to go."

"Thanks." She held his hand and they lay side by side under a gray, rumpled sky, watching for a break in the clouds.

CHAOS, COORDINATED

S aturday morning, after breakfast, Dewey waited for two hours. No Rita. At eleven, she picked up the phone in the front hall, the slim directory beside it open to the page with "Tourist Courts." She started to dial, put the receiver down, picked it up, put it back in the cradle. Finally she took a deep breath and dialed 2-3-4, the number of the motor court out on the highway.

"Parkview," a man's voice answered.

"Cabin seven, please?"

"Cabins got no phones. Who you lookin' for?"

"Gallucci," Dewey said, then added, "The woman on the motorcycle?"

"Oh. *Her.* Hang on."

Dewey stood in the hall holding the heavy black receiver to her ear, listening to footsteps and a door opening, then nothing but the sound of cars swishing by, ten blocks away. A minute later the man came back on the line.

"She never showed. Wanta leave a message?"

"I guess." Where was Rita? Dewey had assumed she was still sleeping, that her idea of "breakfast" was later. "Um, tell her to come over to Dewey's house."

"Dewey, like the governor?"

"That's right." She hung up the phone and went out to the porch to wait. Every time her life had changed, she'd come home and found out, blind-sided and stunned. This time, she was ready. She didn't know *when* Rita would get there, but she'd see her coming.

She turned the pages of *Amazing Stories*, but wasn't in the mood for imagining and what-if. Real life was too full of what-ifs right now. Instead, she grounded herself in the practical instructions and how-to tips of *Mechanix Illustrated*, reading about the long-playing records and ballpoint pens and car-phones that every household would have in 1948.

Diagrams of jigsawed bookends and plans for television cabinets occupied her while she rehearsed what she wanted to say. But how would Rita respond? Even Mrs. Parker said that the law would be on Rita's side if she insisted on taking Dewey with her. Blood was stronger than anything else.

For almost two years, the world had been rocked by the power that came from splitting the atom. It had changed everything, even the way people thought about the future. Either they would all be blown to bits, or it would be a paradise where cars could run for a year on the energy in a cup of water. Nothing was too fantastic, because the strongest force in the universe had been undone.

So how could ordinary blood be stronger?

Dewey longed for a magazine to answer that question. *Because she's your mother* wasn't a real reason. It wasn't science or logic or even feelings. It was an accident of birth. There were all kinds of accidents, things nobody planned. Bad ones, like her leg, and the car that hit Papa, and good ones, like penicillin and Goodyear rubber—and the Gordons. They were an accident, too. An accidental family.

Terry came out onto the porch a little before noon and set a peanut-butter-and-jelly sandwich and a glass of milk on the steps beside Dewey. "I thought you might be hungry," she said. "I cut the crusts off, the way you like them."

"Thanks." Dewey took a drink of milk but didn't reach for the sandwich. "I'm not sure I can eat, though. My stomach's all scrunchy."

"I'm not surprised. She should have been here hours ago." She laid a hand on Dewey's shoulder. "Are you sure you don't want me to talk to her?"

Dewey shook her head. "I need to do it."

"Okay, kiddo. But I'll be in the kitchen, if you need backup."

"I know. Thanks. I'll come get you if I have to."

When Rita Gallucci rode her Harley across the wide planks of the moat an hour later, the sandwich had two bites out of it.

Dewey watched as her mother stopped the big machine and swung her long legs down to the ground. She wore boots and a white T-shirt tucked into her jeans and carried a carton of Chesterfields.

"Thank-you present for Terry," she said, holding it up. "For taking such good care of you."

"That's nice." Dewey stood. "But where've you been?"

"Just got in. Late start, so I stayed in Carrizozo instead. Why? What's up?"

"I've been waiting."

"Oh. Sorry." She looked around. "Where's your stuff?"

"Inside," Dewey said. That was true. Nothing was packed, but it *was* inside. "First I want to show you the Wall."

"The *wall*?" Rita looked confused.

"You'll see. C'mon in." Dewey held the front door open. "It's upstairs."

At the landing just below the attic, Dewey stopped. "Hold on to the railing and shut your eyes," she said. "It's four steps up, then six steps in."

"Lead on, Macduff." Rita closed her eyes.

When they stood near the end of the workbench, Dewey said, "Okay, now turn to your left and open 'em."

"*Jesus* Murphy," she said, and let out a long whistle. "What the hell *is* that?"

"The Wall. Watch."

Dewey climbed onto the step stool and took a handful of marbles from the blue box with the brass gears. She set the first one at the top of a red ramp and let it roll through the gates, across a trestle, and down two different chutes before it rattled to a stop and plunked into the bucket in the bottom corner, eight feet away.

"Wow. That's a neat trick."

"That's nothing." Dewey flipped the switch on the transformer that now sat on the edge of her table, and the Wall came to life. The Ferris wheel turned, the conveyor belt of Dixie cups made its slow circuit across the bottom, and lights blinked on and off. She released half a dozen marbles into a tube at the top. Bells and finger cymbals rang as the balls clattered down the maze, hitting switches and releasing springs, so that they traveled down six different pathways before they reached the bucket.

Rita sat down on the arm of the couch, her mouth open. "Don't tell me you *made* that," she said when the noises had stopped.

"Suze and me. She does the colors and the pictures and figures out how everything'll look together, then I make it move."

"Nice work. That Suze of yours has got a keen eye."

"Yeah." Dewey nodded. "We make a good team. Do you want to try?"

"I guess. What do I do?"

Dewey pointed to the collection bucket. "Those are marbles. We've got two sizes of ball bearings, too. They all sound a little different."

Rita took a few marbles and walked over to the left side of the Wall. She didn't need the step stool. "Where do I put them?"

"Anywhere you want. I haven't done all the calculations, but there are a couple dozen paths, depending on where you start, and what they hit."

"Sounds complicated." Rita dropped two marbles—one on a ramp, one into a tube—and watched as they took diverging routes before meeting at the bottom and dropping into the bucket. *Clang. Clang.*

"Nice rhythm," she said. "You could almost dance to that." She smiled at Dewey, her eyes kind again.

"Rhythm, sound, motion. It's all physics." Dewey looked at Rita. "So is dance."

"Nah, I got you there, kid. Dance is art, not science."

"I bet you an ice-cream cone it's both."

A raised eyebrow. "You're on."

"Okay. You know about music being full of math and patterns and stuff, right?"

"I guess." Rita nodded slowly.

"Well, I can talk about a dancer the same way. You're mass—weight—moving through space. That means you're affected by rate of spin, center of gravity, coefficient of friction."

"You lost me on that last one."

"Sneakers on dirt or leather shoes on a marble floor? When you change the surface, you move different."

"Sure."

"That's coefficient of friction. It's physics."

Rita Gallucci stared at her daughter. "I'll be damned. I owe you an ice cream." She raised her arms, bent one leg, and pirouetted gracefully, one booted toe on the worn attic floor. "Physics. Who knew?"

"Papa did," Dewey said. "There wasn't very much he couldn't explain." She switched off the transformer, and the Wall slowed down, then stopped.

"I'm glad you showed me this," Rita said.

"It's what I do. That's a pretty big part of my life, so I figured you should know."

"Right. Too bad we can't take it all with us. Maybe you should pick out a couple of your favorite pieces, ones that'll fit in the saddlebags. Get you started once we settle down somewhere."

It wouldn't be the same. Half the Wall is Suze. Dewey bit her lip and stared at a metal tube, pretending to think about the idea. "I'm not sure," she said. *That* wasn't a lie, either. "Why don't we get ice cream first."

"Works for me."

When they walked into the kitchen, Terry Gordon sat at

the table, her glasses down on her nose, glancing from a sheaf of typed pages to the lined pad of paper in front of her.

"Hey, Mom," Dewey said.

Rita jerked in surprise and dropped the carton of Chesterfields onto the counter.

Terry looked up, her eyes soft. "What, kiddo?"

"We're gonna go get ice cream. Can I borrow the car?"

"Sure." She reached into her pocket and tossed the keys, underhand.

Dewey caught them and turned to Rita. "C'mon," she said. "I'll drive."

THE ANSWER

Rita looked even more startled, but nodded. "Okay. You know the territory."

They could have walked to any soda fountain downtown, but it was a Saturday, and Dewey didn't want to see anyone she knew, didn't want to have to explain. At the highway, she turned the Chevy north, toward Tularosa.

"You mind?" Rita held up a pack of Lucky Strikes.

Dewey pointed her thumb at the ashtray half-full of Chesterfields without taking her hands off the wheel. "No, I'm used to it."

She drove intently, her head only a few inches above the dashboard, her eyes on the road, hands at ten and two, as she'd been taught. She'd driven alone before, without Owen or Terry coaching, but only around town. When she passed the blind school and the fairgrounds and was out on the desert highway, it was as if she'd crossed a border. She was in charge.

That felt good, but her arms were all goose bumps.

"How long have you been driving?" Rita asked. She cranked her window down an inch, and the smoke from her cigarette plumed out and back.

"A couple of months. I got my license in February, but there aren't many places I need to go that I can't walk. Terry lets me drive when we run errands."

Tularosa was fifteen minutes from Alamogordo. At the intersection where the road through the mountains angled off to the east, Dewey pulled into the gravel parking lot of the Frosty Bar. Three picnic tables sat in the shade of a pair of cottonwoods next to a small creek.

"What kind do you like?" Rita asked. They stood side by side, Dewey's head just clearing Rita's shoulder, scanning the list of flavors above the screened window. They were both slim and wore blue jeans and had the same curly hair, but Rita's shone red in the spring sunlight, and Dewey's was darker, like Papa's.

"I'm thinking," Dewey said. "You go ahead."

A man in a white paper hat slid the screen open when Rita stepped up to the counter to order, "One peppermint stick, please."

When he handed her the cone, he glanced at Dewey. "Your sister made up her mind yet?"

"My sis—? Oh." Rita turned. "Dewey?"

"Pistachio."

"Can do." Rita handed the man two dimes, and brought the cones over to the picnic table where Dewey sat. "Here you go."

Dewey licked a pale green drip. "He thought you were my sister?"

"Easy mistake. We could be, under different circumstances. Mama raised us both, for a while." She shook her head. "She wasn't the easiest person to live with."

"She was kind of bossy," Dewey agreed. She evened out the edges of her cone, swirling it into a rounded mound. "Did she wash *your* mouth out with soap?"

Rita nodded. "All the time. You?"

"Only once. And it wasn't even a very bad word." Dewey thought for a minute. "When you met Papa, you were only two years older than I am now."

"About that."

"No wonder the man thought we were sisters. By the time Terry's baby is my age, Suze and I will be almost thirty. It's about the same difference."

"I thought she looked pregnant. When's she due?"

"September." Dewey looked away and busied herself with licking the surface of the ice cream smooth and flat to the edges of the cone.

"You like her a lot, don't you?" It was a soft but loaded question.

Dewey nodded. "She took care of me, after Papa died, and ever since. And she's a scientist, like he was."

"Why's that important?"

"I ask a lot of questions."

"Like what?"

"Well—" She held out her cone. "How much ice cream do I have left?"

"A coneful." Rita shrugged. "Minus the scoop part."

"How much is that? A cup? Five tablespoons?"

"I have no idea, kid." Rita bit into her own cone. "Why does it matter? Can't you just eat it?"

"Sure. I usually do. But measuring the volume of a cone is the kind of question Terry helps me with."

"And that's useful for . . . ?"

"Lots of things." Dewey pointed up. "The sky goes up forever. Infinity. But Suze's dad is out in the desert, shooting up rockets to measure *that*." She bit into the side of the cone and chewed thoughtfully. "Papa used to say that science is just people figuring out the instruction manual that should have come with the world. Like God left it out of the box, and our job is to keep measuring and experimenting until we know all the rules."

"Whoa. You *like* rules?"

"Mostly. Some of the Church Lady ones are annoying, but other ones tell me where the edges are." Another bite. The cone was now a miniature version of its former self. "I like knowing stuff."

Rita said nothing as she ate the rest of her cone. She wadded up her napkin and tossed it overhand, straight into the trash barrel. "What about your wall and your experiments?"

"What about them?"

"Do you always know what's going to happen?"

"No," Dewey said slowly. "If I did, they wouldn't be experiments. They'd just be like problems in a textbook. I wouldn't find out anything new."

"Okay. That's how I feel on the road. I never know what'll happen next."

"It's not really the same," Dewey said. "If a gizmo it doesn't work, I just mess with it until it does. But—" She bit her lip, afraid to say what she was thinking.

"But?"

Dewey finished her cone and walked over to the trash barrel. Distance. Just enough to give her the courage to turn around and say, "But in real life, that doesn't work. I can't do the last twelve years over."

"No." A very long silence.

Dewey walked back and sat on top of the picnic table, both feet on the bench. "I didn't show you this on Monday. There was too much else. See my right shoe?"

Rita looked, puzzled for a moment, then noticed the difference. Her face tightened and she closed her eyes. "I had no idea. How bad is it?"

"It's better, now." Dewey wiped her fingers on the last paper napkin and told her mother about her limp and the ugly shoe, the accessories of her childhood.

"I'm so sorry," Rita said. "Now I know why Mama used to say that her favorite teapot—"

"—was the one with the mended lid," Dewey finished. "What the hell does that *mean*?"

"That when you break something, you find out how much it means to you. Then you fix it, and try to take better care of it." She smiled at Dewey.

Dewey tried to smile back, but the muscles in her face felt shaky. "I need to ask you a question," she said after a moment.

"Ask away."

"When you were at the hospital—after—were you scared?"

Rita hesitated, then said, "As scared as I've ever been in my life."

"Is that why you left?"

She winced, and when she didn't say anything for a minute, Dewey continued. "'Cause I ran away once, right before the war ended. I thought the Gordons were leaving—without me—and I couldn't stick around and watch that happen. I wasn't that brave."

"Brave enough to go back."

"No. Suze had to come and find me." Dewey shook her head. "I guess what I mean is, I kind of understand."

"Thank you for saying that," Rita said in a soft voice.

"I never knew the whole story before. It makes a difference."

Dewey watched Rita's face relax a little, at the same time

as she felt her own body tensing. She knew what she had to say next. She'd talked to Suze and Terry until late last night. But now she was alone, with no one to reassure her that she was making the right choice. Once the words came out of her mouth, she couldn't take them back, and she had no idea what Rita would do.

Another car pulled into the parking lot and three teenage girls got out, laughing and talking. Dewey waited until they'd walked up to the ice-cream window, until they were too far away to overhear her. Then she took a breath so deep it felt like it went all the way to her toes and let it out in a long, slow sigh.

"I don't want to come with you." *There. She'd said it.*

Rita frowned. "But why, if—?"

"I like my life the way it is. And you like yours."

"It'll take some adjusting," Rita agreed. "But we'll work it out." She lit a cigarette. "I promise."

"Like you said you'd come by first thing this morning? I waited four hours on the porch."

"I told you. I had a little change of plans, that's all."

"But *that's* what I'm afraid of—your plans will keep changing." Dewey's voice faltered, barely a whisper. "Then, one day I'll get hurt again."

A long pause. "Well, that was honest," Rita said. She put her hand on the table, next to Dewey's, not quite touching her. "Dewey, listen. I'm going to do things right this time. I really mean that."

"I believe you. But . . ." Dewey's mind raced with a dozen things to say. None of them felt right. *How can I—? What do I—?* She drew her hand away, clenching her fists in her lap so tight she could feel her fingernails digging into her palms, until she finally blurted out: "I don't need you to be my mom. I already have one."

"Oh. Is that so?" Rita stared at her for a long moment, then blew out a stream of smoke and stood up. She began to pace, her hands in her pockets, five long strides toward the fence, five back, over and over.

The giggling girls, cones in hand, got into their car and drove away as Dewey watched and waited, fists still tight. After what felt like forever, Rita stopped pacing. She put one booted foot on the bench on the far side of the table, leaning an arm on her knee. "Okay. My turn?"

Dewey nodded and held her breath.

"I gotta admit, some of the guys who ride can be pretty rough. They don't give *me* any trouble—not more than once—but with you around? I'd have my hands full trying to tend bar and keep an eye on them all the time."

She paused to light a Lucky Strike. "So maybe it *would* be better if—"

"—if I stayed with the Gordons?" Dewey's hands relaxed and she let out a relieved sigh.

"I think that'd be easier for a while." Rita nodded. "Don't you?" She sat down.

Dewey's sigh stopped with a little choke. A while? A while wasn't yes or no. A while was like "the duration." A while could be *any*time. She hesitated, then reached into the pocket of her jeans, pulling out a folded piece of paper, and smoothed it flat onto the tabletop between them.

"I didn't know if I'd need this, but—read it? Please?"

Rita took the page and scanned it, her eyes widening with surprise. "What the hell?" She read it again, slower this time. "'Termination of Parental Rights'? You gotta be kidding. You want me to give you up for *good*?"

"You said you would have, when I was a baby."

"That was different." The cigarette in Rita's hand burned down to her knuckles as she stared at the paper. She jerked, then flipped the butt into the dirt and ground it out with her heel.

"Not really." Dewey pulled Papa's fountain pen out of her pocket and set it on the table. "Once I'm eighteen, it won't matter. I might even go on the road with you one summer. But for the next four years, all I want is to know—for sure—that I can live with Suze and go to high school and no one can take that away."

"And if I don't sign it?"

"I've had to take care of myself before," Dewey said, trying to sound much calmer than she felt. "My friend Owen's mom works for a lawyer. I guess I'll ask her what happens next." She stood up. "But only if I have to."

Dewey walked over to the fence and listened to the rhythmic sound of the creek, willing it to smooth away the tension of waiting while Rita Gallucci sat and stared at the paper. She lit a cigarette, smoked it, lit another one off the butt. "You're sure?" she asked when that was gone.

"Yes." Dewey came over and stood by the picnic table.

"You know, fifteen years ago, I would've done this in a heartbeat and felt a big load off my shoulders." Rita uncapped the pen. "Maybe you're right. Maybe it's not so different now." She paused for just a moment, then inked her signature across the bottom of the form.

"Thank you," Dewey said, picking it up. She kissed Rita on the cheek and felt her twitch in surprise. She hadn't planned that. It had just happened. But it felt right.

"So what happens next?" she asked.

"Well, I don't know about you, but I'm starving." Rita stood up. "So how 'bout we get a couple of burgers and you can tell me more about that penny arcade up in the attic. What else d'you like to do?"

"Some interesting stuff," Dewey said, and felt her own stomach growl.

"I'll bet. I think I saw a café when we drove into—where are we now?"

"Tularosa, New Mexico."

"Tularosa. Okay, then. Why don't we start here?"

THE SKY IS FALLING

MAY 15, 1947

Late spring in Alamogordo looked like the town was having a giant pillow fight. The puffy fibers that gave the cottonwoods their name floated through the air, and pine trees, bushes, even the cactuses were flecked with white tufts. The bottoms of some ditches looked like snow.

On a Thursday afternoon in mid-May, a couple of boys stood in front of opposite ditches and tossed a baseball up and over the electric wires that crossed Indiana Street. Dewey sat on the tailgate of the Parkers' pickup truck, her legs dangling, reading *Planet Stories*, an adventure with a Martian and a ray gun that could vaporize anything. Owen sprawled in the bed of the truck, his legs bent, his knees level with Dewey's chin. He twisted the tail on his Kix ring around and around as he turned the pages of a fanzine that had come in the mail.

Every few minutes he'd huff and shake his head. Sometimes he'd keep his indignation to himself, but once or twice he'd begin to read aloud. Dewey nodded, not that interested in arguments over a story she'd read months ago. They were moving next week, and it was hard enough to keep her mind on the pages she was reading *now*.

"Listen to this," he said. "Harry Warner reviewed a story from *The Saturday Evening Post*, for crying out loud. 'The Green Hills of Earth.' Some guy named Heinlein who must think *anyone* can write science fic—"

"Hey!" One of the boys in the street shouted, "What the heck is *that* about?"

Dewey looked up and saw the electric wires swinging back and forth in a wide arc, as if in a big wind, a storm coming. But the sky was clear and calm. *That's strange,* she thought, *what could—?*

BOOM!

A huge explosion rattled the windows of every house on the block. The wires whipped in the air, and fountains of cotton-wood fluff erupted from ditches.

"It's the Bomb!" the boys yelled in unison, and dived under the wheels of a parked car. Owen tucked himself into a ball, his hands over his head, the way they'd been taught in school drills.

Like that would help? Dewey leaned back and stared into the sky, her eyes following a line of smoke that angled down toward the mountains. Not a cloud, definitely not a mushroom, more like an airplane's contrail.

She poked Owen. "Look."

"You're not supposed to look," he said, his voice muffled by his folded arms. "It'll burn your eyeballs out of your head."

"I've *seen* an atom bomb," she said. "This isn't even close." She poked him again, harder. *"Look."*

Owen peered out beneath his elbow, then sat up. The trail of smoke and vapor was still visible, but wisping away. "What is it?" he asked.

"I dunno. A plane?"

"Looks like it went down by the Indian Wells," Owen said. He jumped off the tailgate. "Let's go see."

Dewey hestitated, but curiosity won and she joined Owen in the cab of the truck. "Hang on," he said. "It's three miles, not much of it paved."

He took Fifteenth to Florida, the old highway, up to the north edge of town, then turned east toward the mountains. No houses out that far, just sand and scrub. Asphalt turned to gravel as the road climbed.

A pillar of smoke and dust rose from behind a small ridge on the rocky hillside. Owen parked the truck next to an old Model A Ford at the side of the road. "We gotta hoof it from here," he said. "Those ruts'll bottom out the tranny, and Dad'd have my hide." He tossed her a baseball cap.

Dewey climbed down from the truck and put on the cap, tucking her hair underneath. No shade. No trees, just low fringes of bushes, and the flat prickly pear cactus that looked like Mickey Mouse ears with two-inch spines. Lizards skittered out of sight, too fast to register as anything but a long-tailed blur, and a jackrabbit bolted when Owen slammed the truck door.

The ground sloped up, rocky and uneven, a hundred shades of gray and brown. Sand and pebbles, flat shards of flint, boulders the size of footstools, all surrounded by plants on the defensive, prickly and vicious. Dewey stumbled once and Owen caught her arm.

"Careful," he said. "Cactus'll *get* you. I fell onto one once and Mom never did get all the stickers out of my jeans. Had to throw 'em away."

Two hundred feet up from the truck, Dewey could smell the smoke and hear a soft hissing, like a teakettle slowing down. She stepped onto the low flat ridge and looked down into a steep-sided arroyo, a small natural canyon. Fifteen feet below, crumpled and flattened, lay a V-2 rocket in the center of an unnatural crater. Bright raw wood shone through the branches of broken bushes, and long scrapes of paint colored jagged rocks. Parts of the tail fins were missing, and twisted pieces of metal littered the ground for fifty yards.

Dewey stared at the black-and-white checkerboard pattern, too precise and geometric against the jumble of the desert landscape. The end of the arroyo was a wall of rock with crumbly diagonal layers. It looked like the Lone Ranger should come down the trail any minute, riding Silver, looking for rustlers or Apaches. Not a rocket ship. It had landed in the wrong story.

"Jeez-sooey. It's a rocket!" Owen exclaimed from behind her. "I wonder if the Reds shot 'er down?"

"From where?" Dewey asked, just as two older boys appeared on the far side of the nose. They each carried a heavy black box. One of them shaded his eyes against the sun and waved. "I got a camera," he yelled. Dewey wondered if he could see them, or if they were just silhouettes against the sky.

"You want anything more, you better scramble," Owen called down. "The cavalry's coming." He pointed. Far off across the desert, Dewey could see tiny plumes of dust from the cars that raced along the highway from the proving grounds.

"How soon?" the boy shouted. Dewey could only see his head as he inched along the far side of the V-2.

"Twenty minutes!" Owen turned back to Dewey and pointed down the slope. "You coming?"

"Not this time."

"Okay. Give a holler when they turn off the highway." He scrambled down the side of the arroyo, dust and pebbles following in his wake.

Dewey found a patch of flat ground with no cactus and sat, watching the boys pull the siding off the rocket to search the interior. She liked taking machines apart as much as anyone, but not a bomb.

Fifteen minutes later, the plumes of dust on the road angled toward the mountains and she could see the dark shapes of cars. "They're coming!" she shouted.

Owen made it up the side first, one arm for balance, a black box under the other.

"You gonna keep that?" Dewey asked.

"Nah. Wouldn't know what to do with it. But Eddy couldn't climb and carry two." He reached his hand down and pulled the boy up the last few feet. "You better hightail it," he said.

"You got that." Eddy pulled his friend up, then the two boys cradled the camera boxes as if they were footballs and raced down the hill. The square-backed Model A pulled away a scant minute before the first jeep screeched to a stop.

Dewey and Owen sat and watched the army arrive in half a dozen jeeps, a handful of round-fendered civilian cars, and a long flatbed truck with a white star. A man with a rifle sprinted up the steep slope as if it were level ground, his thick-soled boots getting good purchase on the hardscrabble surface. He didn't see them sitting on the dirt until he crested the last ridge.

"Stand up—now! Back away from the perimeter!" he ordered.

They obeyed, and watched as the rest of the men arrived and spread out, ten feet apart, rifles angled across their chests, cordoning off the crash site.

"How are you going to get it out of there?" Dewey asked the nearest soldier.

"Look, son—" He stopped, baffled when he realized the

face under the baseball cap was a girl's. "Sorry. Ma'am. This is no place for kids. Scoot."

"Okay," Dewey said. She'd lived on a secret project for two years. No sense arguing with a man on guard duty. "Are you going to pull it out tonight?"

"No time. It'll be dark in an hour," he said, looking west. The sun was a few inches above the far mountains, rays slanting through some clouds like the fingers of God in a Sunday School book. "My orders are to stand watch till morning."

"Then what?"

"Got me. Some engineer has to figure out how to get *that*"— he gestured down at the rocket—"onto *that*." Another gesture, this time to the flatbed truck at the end of the road, two hundred yards down the rocky hillside.

Owen whistled. "Can we come back and watch?" He pointed to Dewey. "Phil Gordon's one of the rocket scientists. That's his kid."

Dewey gave him a funny look, but said nothing.

"What about it, Sarge?" the soldier called to a man standing at the edge of the arroyo, muttering swear words. "They don't look like commie spies."

"Okay," he replied after a minute. "But up *there*." He pointed to a rocky outcrop another hundred yards up the mountain. "No closer."

"Yes, sir," they said in unison, and the sergeant almost smiled.

LET THE FINDER
BEWARE

By dinnertime, the news was all over town. Pieces of the rocket had landed as far away as First Street, on the far edge of Little Chihuahua. The boys who had gotten the cameras sat on drugstore stools, impressing their friends with first-hand tales of danger and adventure.

"It just went a little off course," Philip Gordon told Suze later that evening when he called home to make sure they were okay. "But we learn something from every snafu. Pitch was wrong. It went end over end till it hit the atmosphere and blew. Put your mother on now, okay?"

Suze wanted to talk to him longer, but she put down the receiver. "Mom! It's Dad!" When the Michigan Avenue end of the conversation got angry, and her mother started to yell— again—she went upstairs to bed.

The next morning, the last day of school, they had an assembly in the auditorium. The principal talked about the rocket, and how dangerous it was to go up to Indian Wells. Federal agents from El Paso had arrived the night before and recovered some stolen cameras. No charges were filed, but everyone needed to respect government property. A few minutes after ten, he dismissed them for the summer.

"C'mon. Let's go," Owen said, catching up to the girls outside the auditorium doors.

"Go where?" Ynez asked. She linked her arm in Suze's. "We were gonna get sodas to celebrate. No more school."

"Up to the crash site. The sergeant said we could watch them pull the rocket out, from up the hill. There'll be great stuff left when they're done."

"I doubt it," Dewey said. "The army'll take all the interesting parts, so they can find out why it went wrong. It'll just be broken scraps."

"Of a *rocket*," Owen said.

"We saw it yesterday. Besides, it's gonna be *hot* up there."

"Aw, c'mon, Sprock. You leave next week. One last picnic? I got drinks and sandwiches in my knapsack. And a blanket to sit on. Even a tarp for the sun." He looked at Suze. "You coming? It's your dad's rocket. I brought an extra hat."

Maybe Dad would be there, Suze thought. He was one of the tail-fin guys. He'd come by the house a dozen times to pick up more of his stuff but hadn't slept there in months. She turned to Dewey. "I haven't seen it. You can explain the science stuff to Ynez and me."

Dewey rolled her eyes. "It's going to be a giant tow truck."

"You're the one who says *everything* is physics." Suze held out her hands. "C'mon. School's over. If we go home, Mom'll put us to work all day, wrapping plates in newspaper."

"Good point," said Dewey. "Okay."

Dozens of booted feet had worn a path up to the arroyo, but the next hundred yards were hard going. The sun beat down from a crisp blue sky, and a column of white clouds loomed on the other side of the mountains, towering a mile above the rough brown pinnacles. All four of them were out of breath and sweaty by the time they got to the outcrop. Owen wore a padded appliance blanket around his neck like a stole. "This oughta be thick enough to save our butts from stickers. And red ants. They bite." He spread it out on a relatively rock-free space.

They sat on the slope, feet angled downhill, and watched uniformed men scurry around the wreckage below them. From up here, Suze could see the scoured path the rocket had made when it crashed, a wide scar of reddish sandy dirt edged with uprooted bushes and tumbles of rock.

"Good thing it was only carrying cameras," she said.

"Good thing it didn't go any farther," Owen added, pointing toward town.

Suze tipped her khaki cap down to her eyebrows and scanned the landscape. She'd never been this high up before.

The giant A on the mountain looked like it was lying on its side, a few miles to her left, with the town spread out below. The middle ground was green—tree-lined neighborhoods, the park, and the golf course. Then the flat brown of the desert, and a thin bright line of White Sands, like a stripe painted along the base of the hazy Organ Mountains.

Nothing blocked the sky—no houses, no buildings, no trees. Suze felt very small, but at the same time, like a giant sitting on the rim of the world. She could reach out and touch a mountaintop with a finger. A fifty-mile finger. Last month a V-2 had gone up so high that when its cameras took pictures of the earth, they showed it curving, proving the earth was round. Like no one had known that? Still, it sure looked flat from here: dry, brown, unchanging.

Suze looked up. The sky was never the same, not for a day, not for a minute. A geography that couldn't be mapped. Puffy clouds floated like a fleet of zeppelins waiting to moor. Their shadows made darker brown patches on the desert below, a two-dimensional herd creeping slowly west. Farther out, a long line of clouds hovered, their tops rounded like cauliflower, bottoms flat and gray. A range of sky mountains, waiting to descend, as if one day the Organs would sink into the ground, and it would be their turn to become solid.

She was glad they were leaving, going *home* after four years away, glad that Dewey was coming with them, to stay. But she knew she would miss the desert. The view from the hills above the UC campus was great, too—the tree-lined town stretching to the bay, the distant stone towers of San Francisco—but it was nothing like the endless vista that surrounded her now.

Shouted commands carried up, like far-off radio. A crew of army men dragged heavy cables up the hill. They looked like toy soldiers, tying wires onto a toy rocket. Suze squinted and held out her arm, once again pinching a V-2 between thumb and forefinger, transferring it effortlessly to the toy truck. Simple, for a giant.

Not as simple for the army. It took forever for the men to attach the cables and winch the rocket, foot by rocky foot, to the far end of the arroyo. Owen and Suze sat on the outside of the blanket and draped the tarp over their heads, making a lean-to with the shorter girls in the middle.

They had a picnic—chicken sandwiches and potato chips, root beer warmed by the sun, fizzing over the tops of the bottles when Owen opened them—and watched the slow progress of the rocket: to the raw scar of sand, then up the steep bank, pieces falling off, men swearing and leaping out of the way. It disappeared over the side of the ridge, and Suze closed her eyes, afterimages of clouds blue-green against her lids, the other kids' voices fading as she drifted off.

"There it is." Ynez touched Suze's arm twenty minutes later.

"Huh? Wha—?" Suze woke with a jerk.

"They got it to the road."

Suze reached for the binoculars. A handful of men in shirt-sleeves, civilians, stood near the flatbed. None of them was Dad. She sighed and handed the glasses back to Owen, then half watched as a crane slowly lifted the rocket onto the truck.

Owen stood up and folded the tarp, then put the remains of their picnic into his knapsack. "Let's go see what's left."

He shouldered the blanket, and they scrambled and slid and sidestepped down the slope while the men lashed the battered, flattened rocket onto the truck. By the time they reached the arroyo, the convoy was on its way to the highway and the proving grounds.

"Can we take a look now?" Owen asked a different sergeant. The last of the soldiers had packed up their gear and were filing down the hill.

"Help yourself. But watch out for two things," he said, holding up his fingers in a **V**. "Nothing liquid. Hydrogen peroxide will burn the bejesus out of you."

"That's from the steam turbine that drives the fuel pump," Dewey said. "Chemical reaction."

The sergeant gaped at her, a small curly-haired girl casually explaining rocket science. "Ri-i-ight," he said.

"What's the second thing?" Ynez asked.

"Insulation. Looks like spiderwebs. It's glass wool, and it *will* cut you."

"Got it," Owen said to the soldier. "You need help down?" he asked Dewey.

"Too steep for me," she said. "Even in sneakers." Owen wore a pair of war surplus combat boots. "I'll wait up here and watch the stuff."

"Me, too," said Ynez. "I'm not big on climbing over cactus."

"Well, *I'm* going," Suze said. "I sat there too long to leave without *something*." A few desert rocks would do. She'd started a shoe box of mementoes—matches from the Lariat, Alamento ticket stubs, a paper bag from the Piggly Wiggly, a jar of white gypsum sand—talismans to conjure up this year of her life.

She clambered down the bank, sliding and crab-walking, hands on boulders for balance, and joined more than a dozen boys who had been up on the hillside or had waited on the road until the army had left. Everyone walked across the shallow crater, heads down, scanning the ground for pieces of a real, honest-to-God rocket to take home.

The boys formed a bucket brigade to pass the bigger pieces up. The wires bristling from a shattered control panel, one boy explained, were just the right gauge for model airplanes. Suze filled her pockets with rocks and a dial with German markings. Owen carried a heavy metal bottle, almost two feet long.

"What are you going to do with that?" Dewey asked as he staggered back to the truck, cradling it in both arms.

"It's half-inch steel, with a threaded neck. High-pressure stuff. Pop and I can make a portable welding rig from it. On-site repairs."

As the truck bounced over the rutted gravel track, Suze looked at the dial in her hand with mixed feelings. She had taken it because the V-2 launch had been her first experience of Alamogordo. A whole day spent with her dad, a good memory, before the rockets had taken him away. The dial was still warm from lying in an American desert, but it had been made in a concentration camp. If a rocket did go to the moon one day, far in the future, most people probably wouldn't remember that. She'd save this piece, along with her white sand and green glass, so she wouldn't forget.

AND THE WALLS CAME TUMBLING DOWN

"That's the last of it," Dewey said. She removed a bolt from a two-foot board and pulled it off the attic wall. Cut-out heads of Billy Batson, Captain Marvel, Clark Kent, and Superman, alternating by secret identity, bordered the red-painted surface. She handed it down to Suze, who settled it onto the top layer of crumpled newspaper in the cardboard carton on the floor.

Suze stuffed more newspaper around the delicate structure on the left side of the board. A slanting tube—six metal film canisters with marble-sized holes cut into them—led to a cascading ladder of bottle caps. The right side was empty except for the screw holes where the Ferris wheel had been. They'd removed the biggest pieces first, the wheel and the merry-go-round and the cigar boxes of Shazam Theater, and packed them separately.

The Wall was gone. Dewey surveyed the now-empty studs

and plaster that had become an ordinary wall again. But they had the whole summer to rebuild it, the North Wall, when they got to Berkeley.

"You forgot those." Suze pointed. Half a dozen paper Dixie cups hung down one side of the window. The bottom one held a few blue-green marbles.

"I thought I'd leave them. They'll just rip if I try and pull them off the nails, and it's easy to get more." She sat down on the edge of the table and wiped her sweaty face with a bandanna. It was *hot* in the attic, but there were too many loose pieces and piles of newspaper to risk turning on the big fan.

"Besides," she continued, "if we leave them here, it might give some other kids ideas. They might build their own Wall."

Suze nodded. "Should we write down instructions?"

"Nah. Figuring it out is the fun part."

"That's true. I've already got some ideas for the new one." Suze put two more layers of newspaper on top of the last board and sealed the box flaps with paper tape. She took the grease pencil from behind her ear and wrote WALL, 12 OF 12 on the sides and top of the carton.

Dewey sat in the dry, stuffy attic and looked around the room. A dark rectangle, outlined in dust, marked the spot where her pegboard had hung. Her tools were wrapped and packed away. Over on the kitchen table that had been Suze's art space lay a small carton filled with random junk they'd found behind the bookshelves or under the couch, too late to go in any of the organized boxes. A red box of chalk lay on top of the jumbled assortment. It gave Dewey an idea.

"When you finish one of your art boxes, what's the last thing you do?"

"After the varnish?"

"The very last thing."

"Sign it." Suze wiped her face on the bottom of her shirt.

Dewey nodded. "So we need to sign the Wall."

"Yeah, like those Indian rock paintings. 'Dewey and Suze Were Here.'"

"There's chalk in that box."

Suze climbed up onto the table. She stood next to Dewey, facing the wall, and handed her a piece of white chalk. "You wanna go first? It was your idea."

Dewey printed her name in capital letters, as high as she could reach.

Suze wrote SUZE GORDON below it.

"In English?" Dewey asked.

Suze shrugged. "It wasn't all *mine*, and it was just as much science as art."

"Okay." Dewey held a white chalk stub an inch away from the wood and studied the Wall. "It needs one more thing. Shazam."

Suze smiled and took the chalk. She reached up and wrote

$$\sigma \eta \alpha \zeta \alpha \mu$$

in letters six inches high, just below the edge of the ceiling.

"Perfect," Dewey said.

They sat on the workbench, side by side, for fifteen minutes, not saying anything. Sweaty and dusty, each gazed at a room that was no longer there, like an afterimage that had not yet faded.

The next morning, muscular men in Bekins coveralls loaded furniture and boxes into the big truck. Dr. Gordon carried suitcases and the ice chest out to the black Chevy.

"You're sure you'll be okay?" he asked Mrs. Gordon, handing her a folder of maps. He glanced at her belly, visibly round under her light cotton maternity smock.

She didn't answer for a minute. "Not at all," she said finally. "But the drive home will be fine."

Dewey heard a little emphasis on the word *home*.

"It's a long way, just you and the kids."

"I'm pregnant, not crippled, Philip." Mrs. Gordon shot him a look. "Besides, they're hardly *kids* anymore. Dewey will drive part of the time, and if we get a flat, Suze can use a jack and change a tire."

"What if something worse happens?"

"The auto club card's in the glove box." She crossed her arms over her chest. "If you're so worried, why don't you come along?"

"You know I can't. We've got a launch in a couple of weeks, and with the last two duds, the brass is breathing down our necks."

"Well then, you'd better let us get going." She threw the maps onto the front seat and lit a cigarette, snapping the Zippo shut with a loud click.

"Is that all right, for the baby?"

"Oh, for crissakes, Phil. *Now* you're being ridiculous." She blew an annoyed stream of smoke in his direction. "Look, I'll call you when I can. There should be long distance in Albuquerque, but Flagstaff and Bakersfield are pretty well out in the boondocks. We'll get to my mother's Friday night."

She turned around. "You girls about ready? I'd like to stop in Carrizozo for lunch. There's not much for the next hundred miles."

Suze nodded. She got up from the back steps, where she'd been playing with "Raymundo," a small flocked bear, a going-away present Ynez had given her the night before. When she wound him up, he waddled with a grinding of motors and gears, a sound almost like a long, trilled *r*. Ynez had stayed late, brushing Suze's hair—two hundred strokes—and giving her a luxurious shampoo with a lemon-juice rinse before plaiting it into a braid. "Easier on a long, dusty drive," she'd said.

Suze stood next to her father, then wrapped her arms around him and kissed his cheek, smooth with coconut suntan oil. "See you in September?"

"Absolutely, honey." He had moved all his things out to a hutment at the proving grounds, for the summer, at least, but promised to be in Berkeley when the baby was born. As far as

Dewey could tell, nothing more permanent had been decided.

Dewey fingered the chain of the ID bracelet around her left wrist. It had come in the mail two days before. She'd been disappointed when she found a jeweler's box under the brown paper wrapping. Not her kind of present. But it was from Rita, who didn't know her that well yet, didn't know she didn't go for girly fashion stuff. It was still a nice thought. She'd pulled it out, expecting to see DEWEY or DMK engraved on the silver disk, then laughed out loud, because it *was* her kind of present. The disk said:

$$V = \frac{1}{3}\pi r^2 h$$

The formula for calculating the volume of a cone.

A note tucked into the box said:

D—

Turns out there's a library in Tucson, so here's the answer to your question. Only a month late.

I'm not going to join the caravan north after all. Ran into some friends, and we're heading to a couple of rallies. Hollister's the 4th of July, so I might head up the coast and see if Frisco's everything people say. Maybe I'll give you a jingle, and we'll go for ice cream.

Drive safe.

—R

"C'mon, kiddo!" Terry Gordon called. "Shake a leg."

Dewey climbed into the backseat with Suze and laid the cedar box with Papa's things between them, on top of the second issue of *The Sprocket*. She put her feet up on Rutherford's cat carrier, which sat on the floor next to a red painted box Ynez and her grandmother had made. Suze had given them *Tenth Street* in exchange.

Terry Gordon gave her husband a brief hug and a peck on the lips.

"Be careful," he said.

"You, too." She paused, as if she were going to say something more, then got into the car.

They drove down the alley to Tenth Street, then turned for the last time onto Pennsylvania Avenue. Not left, toward White Sands and the rockets, but north, to Route 66 and California. The thick stand of cottonwoods in Alameda Park disappeared behind them as the street became the state highway. Ten miles later, the wall of mountains to the east angled down to low hills, and there was nothing beyond the car but the vast brown desert and the endless blue sky.

Dewey Kerrigan smiled, and cranked down the glass. Surrounded by her family, she leaned out the window and let the wind blow though her hair.

AUTHOR'S NOTE

The late 1940s is a fascinating but overlooked period in American history. When I was in school, our textbook skipped from World War II directly to the 1950s, as if nothing happened in between. But those "missing" years are like the eye of a storm—a time of deceptive calm that set the stage for the events that would define the rest of the twentieth century. They are the first years of the Atomic Age, the beginning of the Space Age, and the start of the political trends that would lead to the Cold War.

My research was wide and varied. I went to Alamogordo and White Sands. I found books on science, politics, and popular culture in public libraries; vintage magazines (and several spinthariscopes) on eBay; and newsreel clips on DVDs and You-Tube. Below are some of the sources I used. (Be aware that the Internet, like the Wall, is a work in progress, and some URLs may have changed.)

If you'd like to explore further, ask your teacher or local librarian for recommendations.

1940S

This Fabulous Century, Volume V: The Forties 1940–1950. Time-Life Books, 1975.

ATOMIC BOMB

Boyer, Paul. *By the Bomb's Early Light: American Thought and Culture at the Dawn of the Atomic Age*. University of North Carolina Press, 1994.

Hersey, John. *Hiroshima*. Knopf, 1946.

"Operation Crossroads" and "Bikini Test Baker" (on YouTube); videos of the Bikini atomic bomb test.

SPINTHARISCOPES

Vintage spinthariscopes (and Lone Ranger Atomic Bomb rings) are frequently for sale on eBay. United Nuclear (www. unitednuclear.com) sometimes carries a modern version.

V—2 ROCKET PROGRAM

The White Sands Missile Range has a great museum, about twenty miles from Las Cruces, New Mexico, with a restored V-2 on display. Their Web site has text and pictures about the history of the V-2 program at www.wsmr-history.org.

"First Pics Nazi Rocket Bomb" (YouTube).

"From Vengeance to the Edge of Space," *New Mexico Space Journal*, vol. 1, no. 1, June 2001. (A publication of the New Mexico Museum of Space History, Alamogordo.)

LIFE Magazine, May 27, 1946. "U.S. Tests Rockets in New Mexico," pp. 31–35.

Popular Science, July 1946. "Firing V-2s Into No Man's Air," pp. 77–79.

V-2 Rocket at White Sands Missile Range—DVD collection of V-2 films, available for sale at the WSMR museum, or at www.elpasogold.com.

WHITE SANDS

White Sands National Monument is located fifteen miles from Alamogordo, New Mexico, and has a gift shop and small museum. Their Web site is: www.nps.gov/whsa/

Houk, Rose, and Michael Collier. *White Sands National Monument.* Western National Parks Association, 1994.

IN CASE YOU WERE WONDERING

KROD-TV, El Paso's first TV station, went on the air December 14, 1952.

and

Yuri Gagarin, a Russian cosmonaut, was the first person to travel into space, on April 12, 1961.

ACKNOWLEDGMENTS

Writing a sequel is a very interesting process. I was getting reacquainted with Dewey and Suze at the same time that readers were meeting them for the first time. I am so grateful to the sales reps at Penguin, the Scott O'Dell Award committee, and to booksellers and librarians all over the country whose enthusiasm for *The Green Glass Sea* gave me the confidence to continue the story.

I spent several weeks in Alamogordo, trying to piece together what it had been like more than sixty years ago. The reference librarians at the public library steered me to the microfilmed rolls of the weekly *Alamogordo News*, which gave me a feel for the day-to-day life of the town. Everyone at the Tularosa Basin Historical Society went out of their way to help me find photos and oral histories, and Dolores Rodgers was heroic in her efforts to answer my very odd questions about irrigation ditches, drugstores, and landmarks that no longer exist.

Robert Callaway spent hours answering my questions about being a teenager there in 1946, and his stories about school and the salvage yard—and the race to get up to the rocket crash site before the army—gave me insights and details that made it all come alive for me. I gave him a speaking part in the book.

(Note: While historical, scientific, and Hollywood figures mentioned are real, I have otherwise fictionalized the population of *my* Alamogordo; the buildings, streets, and geographical features are as historically accurate as I could make them.) I had read about V-2s for a year before I had the chance to go to the White Sands Missile Range Museum and see one. The exhibits and displays there are amazing. Forty miles northeast is the White Sands National Monument, which is my favorite place on earth. I go there every chance I get. At sunset, it's magic.

Charles N. Brown is a walking encyclopedia of science-fiction history, and I spent several afternoons at his house, listening and scribbling notes. He was generous with his time and with his library, which is a treasure trove beyond compare.

The Wall came out of my experience as a writer at the Exploratorium, the hands-on museum founded by Frank Oppenheimer as a true collaboration of art and science. Working with Pat Murphy, Linda Shore, Ned Kahn, Paul Doherty, Ruth Brown, and Shawn Lani, I learned something new about the world every day, and rediscovered my own curiosity.

My writing sister, Delia Sherman, has the patience of a saint; I sent her chapters out of order, out of context, higgledy-piggledy, and she read them all, with comments and advice and support. Thanks also to Elizabeth Bear for her teapot and its cracked lid; to Emma Bull and Will Shetterly for food and companionship during my writing retreat at Endicott West, outside of Tucson; and to Madeleine Robins for games of darts and glasses of wine when the going got tough.

As always, my undying gratitude to Sharyn November, who is the best editor I have ever worked with. She knew the book I wanted to write, and with vision, skill, and persistence, pushed me until I did. Thank you.

ELLEN KLAGES is the author of the acclaimed *The Green Glass Sea*, which won the 2007 Scott O'Dell Award for Historical Fiction and was the #1 Winter 2006/2007 Book Sense Children's Pick. Her story "Basement Magic" won the Nebula Award for Best Novelette in 2005. Her short fiction has appeared widely, and her first collection, *Portable Childhoods*, was published by Tachyon in 2007. She is a graduate of the Clarion South Writers Workshop and also serves on the Motherboard of the James Tiptree, Jr. Award (www.tiptree.org).

Ellen lives in San Francisco, where her house is full of odd, old toys. Visit her Web site at www.ellenklages.com.